SIMON VALE

DON'T SLIP UP

Dear reader!

You have no idea how much it means to me that you're holding my first book right now.

Thank you!

If you have any questions about it, reach me at forsimonvale@gmail.com

FANTASIA
BOOK#2

MAGIC DOME BOOKS

Fantasia
Book #2: Don't Slip Up

ISBN: 978-80-7619-494-6

FANTASIA LITRPG SERIES:

SECOND SHOT
DON'T SLIP UP

Table of Contents:

PROLOGUE

A STEEL TRUSS was attached to the ceiling, and from it hung a rectangular frame about the size of a door. In the center of the frame, held in place by thin, synthetic cables, rested a mount with a mechanical arm bent into a V shape. Installed opposite the frame was a set of old VR equipment — a smart treadmill and harness system to keep the body in place.

A man walked into the room holding a long object in one hand — a spear. He walked up to the equipment and leaned his weapon against the frame. Metal sounded on metal. The man opened the frame, grabbed the spear and put it in the nearby holster, closed himself in and attached the free end of the mechanical arm to the spear shaft, then turned and stepped onto the smart treadmill. The carabiners clicked into place, securing the harness to his body, and the man hung there, checking the tension. His spear was at chest level. With his hands in sensory gloves, the man pulled on a thick mask with lenses over the eyes and a breathing hole cut out over the nose.

A voice command sounded and the system turned on. Dozens of lights flickered on and various bits of data popped up on the monitor. The man gave the server address and stood silently on the smart treadmill for a while. Then he said clearly: "I authorize running the program with real fatalities."

The block holding the spear began to move. The weapon turned sharply, aiming at the man's left leg, then tore diagonally across the frame, the steel tip pointed towards the man's right shoulder. The mechanical arm worked, checking the Z-axis of the spear. The man under the mask didn't flinch when the sharp spear tip came to a halt inches from the surface of his black suit. The monitor lit up with the words:

Initial check complete
Establishing connection to server

The smart treadmill under the man's feet sprang to life.

CHAPTER 1

I AWOKE RELATIVELY EARLY. Lying there, I opened my eyes, but didn't budge. Yana had started to complain about the fact that I toss and turn in the mornings and wake her up. In reality, even cannon fire couldn't get her out of bed before ten. That is, the alarm clock and work got her in an upright position, but she always kept one foot in dreamland until her second cup of coffee. Funny — now she had her other foot in dreamland as well. And no alarm clock.

I lay there and tried to listen to Yana's breathing. Yet another process that had no bearing on our body's functioning. Another simulation.

"Good morning."

"Why aren't you sleeping."

"You aren't tossing and turning, it's annoying."

"I thought you were annoyed when I did toss and turn."

"That was before. Now that I've told you to stop, it bothers me."

"Okay."

"What's okay?"

"Okay, it bothers you," I said, getting out of bed. "Much better than if it didn't. You bother me too!"

"Whaaat? Do go on!"

"So annoying!" I threw a pillow at her that I had discreetly pulled out of bed with me.

"You pathetic coward!" Yana cried, throwing everything within arms reach at me. "Dodging a fair fight!"

I continued to dodge until she was out of ammo, but in hand-to-hand combat, the win was inevitably mine. I, grinning, prepared to go on the offensive. Yana had a challenge in her eyes.

"Annoying!" I said gleefully.

At that moment, some person with absolutely no shame, conscience or tact, banged on the front door. I, of course, had no intention of opening it. But the knocker was insistent, realizing that sooner or later victory would be his — it's impossible to live a normal life when people are constantly knocking at your door.

Behind the door stood an ordinary-looking gentleman in a dark suit and hat, with a quiet and slightly inhibited demeanor. It was the police chief's assistant, Mr. Parks, and I have never met someone with a more deceptive appearance in my life. No one would suspect that his short, crooked legs held the capacity for such speed, that his arms or frail shoulders, covered only in a greasy cloth, would be so strong. But his features made the biggest impression of all. He had the face of a textbook fool. If he existed only in the world of cinema, Mr. Parks would be a comedy star, especially since his looks acted as a flawless natural disguise. I knew, however, that hiding under that mask was an extremely dangerous person.

"Good morning, Mr. Mursley. Please forgive me for the early intrusion. I'll wait until you get dressed."

I sighed, closed the door and turned around. Yana went upstairs.

"Sorry," I said. "It's Parks. Apparently it's something important."

"And how!" Yana quipped, trying to find the opening to her blouse with her head. "The secret police are constantly on guard, keeping law and order...aaah!"

She stumbled on a short step and tumbled downstairs. I rushed to meet her and caught her with her head just a few inches from the railing.

"Still have doubts about us needing a secret police?"

"Put me down and help me with this damn blouse!"

"Yes, mam."

I carefully untangled her long, grown-out hair from the buttons. I so wanted to just tell Parks to go to hell! But I couldn't, he'd demolish the door with a battering ram, if necessary.

"I have to admit," Yana sighed, "the police are useful. Now I can finally do some actually important work."

She put special emphasis on the words "actually important." My ears pricked up.

"What work?"

"Don't you have to meet Mr. Parks and the other spy kids?"

"Okay, you plucky little chicken, how about a bet?"

"I'm listening."

"If my work turns out to be more important than yours, you owe me something. I've been wanting to test your country music chops out in front of a crowd for a while. For example, at the celebration next Saturday."

"If your work turns out to be more important for whom?"

"For the city and its residents."

"And how will we determine whose work is more important?"

"We will make a decision after a thorough discussion. Both must agree with the conclusion. In the event of a tie, a neutral judge will be named."

Yana thought for a long moment.

"Okay, it's a bet," she said. "I also have a plan to test out some of your skills at Saturday's party. But I won't tell you which. Let it be a surprise."

The knocking on the door started up again.

* * *

The day was sweltering. The town heated up considerably in the sun, which is why the streets were not particularly crowded. Mr. Parks, stuffed into a three-piece suit, but somehow experiencing no visible discomfort, strolled slowly down the middle of the road.

"The day before yesterday, three university types traveled northeast to Lake Yogu," he said. "They intended to go birdwatching."

"Why?" I asked, trying to stay in the shadow of nearby houses.

"The goal of their expedition is completely unknown to me," Mr. Parks snapped after a long pause. "However, two of the three, by all appearances, died under some set of circumstances. Perhaps at the hands of an NPC from the village there."

"What did they do there to piss off an NPC so bad?"

"Hmm...maybe nothing. But maybe not."

Mr. Parks. stopped in front of a pole and examined it with interest. I was getting irritated.

"A village in the northeast...Linden?"

My companion looked at me.

"That's the one," he confirmed. "One interesting detail: the victims' bodies didn't vanish immediately. The NPCs humiliated them..."

"What were the names of the dead and the witness?" I interrupted.

Mr. Parks pursed his lips slightly.

"Thomas Gardner, Darcey Winskett and James Plymton."

I went through my mental list of everyone I knew and came to the conclusion that it was the first time I had heard these names. How is that possible in a town of less than two thousand people?

"James returned yesterday evening. On the verge of insanity, although physically he was completely healthy. We let him sleep, because the guy could barely string two words together."

"So why are we wasting time?! What if they're alive?! We need to go there!"

"I don't think they're alive, Mr. Mursley."

I suddenly realized where we were heading. To the jail. One of the old houses in the western part of the city, by the stream, served as a prison. From the outside, it looked like an ordinary house, but inside it was different: thick steel bars, heavy locks and guards.

"Why are you keeping him in prison?"

Mr. Parks winced.

"We still don't know for sure what happened

to the others."

"So he was charged?"

"No."

"Then you need to let him go."

"I'm going to assume you're joking, Mr. Mursley."

"Not at all."

"I'm still sticking to my original opinion," said the agent in a raspy voice. "The man will stay in jail, at least for a little while."

"I'm curious why you're so sure of this."

"Maybe it's the gourmet meals? There's also a good view of the river, although from behind bars. But I think there's another reason why James Plymton doesn't want to leave his cell," Mr. Parks smiled wickedly, and his countenance changed, momentarily betraying his true nature. "The jail is perhaps the only guarded building in the city."

It was cool inside the jail. Perhaps I wouldn't be averse to staying here a little while either. On the first floor was the front desk and drunk tank. Upstairs were the cells for those awaiting trial. According to the law of the city, those guilty of serious crimes were not executed or locked up, but expelled from the city without the right to return within a period determined by the severity of the crime committed.

Behind the desk sat a young guard named Zach. A few steps away and behind bars, there was a man. He sat on the bed, head lowered. His long hair fell across his knees. The man swayed slightly from side to side.

"Good morning, Mr. Mursley!" Zach was clearly happy to see me. "I'm trying to persuade Mr. Plymton to have breakfast. But he doesn't seem to be in the mood."

I walked over to the counter, leaning my elbow on it. Zack immediately bent down and added in an undertone:

"He gives me goosebumps, Mr. Mursley. He...well, ten minutes ago he was sitting quietly by himself, and then he jumped up and started screaming! I spilled my tea, it scared me so much. Just look at the state of my papers now! Why is he yelling, not speaking normally?! If you want my two cents, something weird is going on with him."

"Thank you, Zach. Give me the key, please.

Zach placed a simple double-toothed iron key on the table.

"I still don't suggest you go in there," he said.

"Why not?"

"He won't like it."

I took the key, turned and approached the cell. The man on the bed did not react in any way to my presence. Mr. Parks waited quietly to the side. With my left hand I lifted the lock, with my right I inserted the key into the keyhole and turned it. At that moment, the young man stopped swaying, but did not raise his head. A soft whine came from under the curtain of matted hair. I pulled the lock back to open it. The whimpering intensified. I involuntarily glanced over my shoulder. Zach subtly shook his head...

Nevertheless, I opened the door and stepped into the cell, and the man's whining immediately intensified tenfold. The sound seemed to tremble every grate and nail. The entire prison building was vibrating. Dust danced in the air in front of me, curling up into unthinkable loops, and I suddenly realized there was really very little time, and hastily raised my hands. The familiar weight of the cold sphere pressed against my left palm. The fingers of my right hand slid along the incorporeal icy surface, spinning the sphere counterclockwise...

The seated man suddenly raised his head and I saw his face, tense and pale. His mouth was closed, his lips compressed into a thin white line. The sound seemed to be emanating from his entire body, which shook with a small convulsive tremor like a giant resonator.

The cold light of the spell hit the man, enveloping him from all sides. For a moment, the frequency of the howling rose again and it felt as if our eardrums were about to burst. And then there was a clap, and I felt the force pushing me out of the cell disappear. The windows rattled for a few more moments, and then everything was silent.

James Plymton lay there unconscious. I went up to him and lightly patted him on the cheeks. The eyelids fluttered open. The young man's eyes were hazy and dim.

"James? Do you hear me?"

His lips moved, but the sound he made did not in any way resemble human speech.

"It's alright, buddy! You're back at home, in good old New New York."

I involuntarily smiled, realizing that I had just recited — almost verbatim — a quote from an old film. James, however, had no time for movie trivia. His gaze continued to wander aimlessly around the cell.

I looked back at the others. Zach stepped out from behind the counter, palms still over his ears. Mr. Parks stood in the same place with a completely casual expression on his face. Dust was settling on his hat.

"They took off their clothes and took charcoal..."

I quickly spun around.

"...and with the charcoal they drew a line where to cut. She gave me the knife and said I should be certain. I don't want to!" the young man suddenly cried, springing to his feet. "They didn't respond...they never respond, they never respond!"

"Who are they?" I whispered.

"Cut along the line down to the bone, the bone is braided with veins that lead to the main artery. It will lead you to the heart. An incision should be made in the striated tissue in the area where the pulmonary veins join..."

I was silent, listening to this incoherent

speech, and then a feeling of horror gradually washed over me. This was something new. Not from here, not from our world, where everything was supposed to be simpler, not more complicated. People don't go crazy in computer games...although where did I get that idea from?

I turned and walked out of the cell, allowing Mr. Parks to lock it behind me.

"Mr. Mursley." Zach walked quickly over to me. "I'd like to request...I'm not saying I'm refusing...I mean, I'm not..."

"Don't worry, Zach. I'll send the order for reinforcements to be sent over immediately."

"After that trick with the screaming..."

"Let's try to find you a mage, Zach. What level are you?"

"Seven."

I mulled things over for a moment. Then a sudden thought occurred to me, and I turned again to approach the cell. James Plymton stood in the same place and continued to mutter his barely audible monologue. I stopped so that he had a good view of me and turned on my nametag hologram. The young man did not react in any way to the words hanging in the air. I was already turning to leave when a similar inscription flashed over his head:

James Plymton
Level 13
Missing parameter 13944f

Tears ran down the young man's cheeks.

* * *

I left the jail in a sour mood. We still knew too little to draw any solid conclusions, but things didn't just look bad. They looked terrifying. And I also had a premonition. Despite what they say in pulp romance novels, you should always be careful when following your intuition. And yet, the gut feeling remained. And it was very, very bad. I glanced at Mr. Parks. From the face of my colleague, one would assume that we had just left the restaurant after a lunch break on an ordinary workday. I opened my own stats - what if I too now had missing parameters?

Bryan Mursley, level 19 (378 520 XP)

Strength: 1 (base level)
Dexterity: 1 (ranged damage — 1)
Intellect: 9 (build a bonfire — 1, cartography — 4, language — 1, fishing — 0, magical damage — 2)
Wisdom: 6 (meditation — 1, lore — 1, mana regeneration rate — 3, Divine Voice — 1)
Constitution: 3

Damage: +0.5 (light weapon), +1.5 (magic)
Armor: +2
Health: 30 hp

Speed: 5.5

Stamina: 100

Mana: 150 (regeneration rate — 1 point every 3.5 mins)

I noticed nothing out of the ordinary.

"Have you ever seen anything like it, Mr. Parks? I mean the third line of his hologram."

Mr. Parks shook his head. It seemed like some sort of glitch in the system. If the game's code was starting to get buggy, that could mean any number of things. But most likely, none of them were good.

There was one positive aspect to all this. Now I had no doubt that Yana would have to sing at the upcoming festival. But how could we celebrate now? I was not in a particularly festive mood.

"What now, to the chief?"

"No," Mr. Parks replied unexpectedly, and for a moment I saw a shadow of gloating smile on the spy's face. "The chief is occupied with more important business. If I am not mistaken, he is helping your...friend."

Chapter 2 [Sylvia]

MORANDO RKAELI, the head of intelligence and Bryan's boss, was waiting for me in his office. Oddly enough, it was located on the very outskirts of the city in a tiny shack that was once either a warehouse or a utility room.

The room was nondescript. A beam of light barely broke through a lone, dusty window. As for furniture, there were several cupboards, a desk and three chairs. Rather, two stools and one chair. The guests were apparently supposed to sit on the shorter stools in order to highlight the power disparity, however, the bareness of the room around them somewhat diminished this effect. But where did I get the idea that this was Rkaeli's only place of residence?

The intelligence officer was wearing a loose-fitting gray shirt, the right sleeve of which hung empty. Bryan said that he lost his arm during the battle for the city. DHCs had lost limbs before, but they always regenerated. For some reason, this was not the case with Rkaeli. Lucky for him, he was left-handed.

"Strange place for the office of the head of the secret service," I said, taking a seat.

"I don't like noise," was his laconic response. It was clear from his tone that he had no intention of going into detail.

"If you don't mind, Ms. Duleski, let's get straight to the point."

"I believe I described the situation in detail in my note."

"I wanted to hear you tell it."

I was silent for a while, wishing I could cross my legs. It's not an easy thing to do while sitting on a stool.

"Do you have coffee?"

"No?"

"How about tea?"

Rkaeli shook his head.

"What kind of people are you intelligence officers? Do you exclusively drink the blood of enemies of the homeland?"

The man waited in silence. I sighed.

"Listen, Morando, I have no intention of wasting any time on your investigations or explaining why you should listen to my story. It's plain and simple. Running Fantasia costs a huge amount of money annually, most of which is allocated by the State Department. But there is no long-term act or legislature that will secure this money for us, and a new face will soon appear in the White House. Now, the leading candidate is openly declaring that our world, and your luxurious office in particular, is literally ripping bread from the mouths of average American citizens.

"You think they could actually shut us down?" the spy asked after a pin drop silence.

"I'm certain of it."

"May I ask why?"

"Because the average American is offended by our existence. My article about the game opened interesting new horizons, but it soon became clear that no one would be allowed access to them. It's no longer possible to set up video feeds in Fantasia, as you know. In addition, a significant number of citizens believe that within our servers, a sinister artificial intelligence is growing, which will eventually enslave humanity."

"Alas, we can't do anything about that."

"We not only can, we must! We need strong diplomatic channels with the nations of Earth. We need funding sources. We need an independent, dedicated server and reliable infrastructure. This is a matter of our survival, Mr. Rkaeli.

The intelligence officer was quiet a long time. Then he shouted, "Pete!" A lanky young boy burst into the room.

"Be a lad, go pick up some coffee for Ms. Duleski."

Pete left without saying a word.

"Black, with sugar!" I yelled after him.

Rkaeli waited for a moment, then asked:

"What are you suggesting, Sylvia?"

The sly little asshole never offered anything in response. The journalist in me grit her teeth in frustration.

"In a few hours, my alter ego is flying to Geneva, where she'll meet with some people. It's unlikely she'll be able to drag any serious funders into the program. You know the procedure requires that you connect through equipment with the mortality function enabled. But finding a goodwill ambassador won't be difficult. At least from among the journalists. If they show up, we'll need to present our society in the best light possible, and for that I will need your help. We'll have to make sure that none of them...hmm...get hurt.

"Who does she plan to meet with? And who do you want to bring?"

I opened my bag and pulled out a list. Rkaeli held out his only hand.

"I'm counting on your help," I said, passing him the sheet.

Morando examined the list carefully. I yawned widely. Suddenly he said:

"Thank you, Sylvia."

I was so happy I didn't know how to respond.

A few minutes later, Pete returned with my coffee. In a big mug! And the sugar was excellent.

"Pete, you're my savior!"

"No need to thank me, ma'am. Chief, Dr. Harris from the university is there and insists that you speak with her."

Rkaeli thought for a few seconds, then said.

"Let her in."

I grimaced into my mug. I knew Camilla Harris. Smart lady, but she thinks too much of herself. She was wearing an elegant green dress with a floor-length skirt. God knows how she managed to keep it clean with the omnipresent mud and lack of normal modes of transportation. I forced myself to smile and nod affably, but Camilla paid no attention to me.

"Mr. Rkaeli," she said, striding determinedly towards the desk. "I am protesting against the imprisonment of James Plymton! What right do you have to keep a scientist behind bars?! And why am I only finding out about it now?! I'm willing to bail him out!"

"James Plymton," Morando interrupted her, "personally requested to be placed in custody. He doesn't feel safe, Camilla."

"And what about Thomas and Darcy?"

"The search party is preparing to leave now."

"Why didn't they leave earlier? He returned last night!"

"Camilla." The spy suddenly rose from his chair. "Please, sit down. We didn't leave earlier because the situation seems relatively serious. We needed to prepare."

"And now they're dead!"

"It's still hard to say."

"I want to accompany the search team."

"Out of the question."

"It was my expedition, Morando! I should have been there!"

"It's dangerous, Camilla."

"Have your guys protect me! Do they have those protective bubbles?"

"That would put the entire mission in jeopardy."

"Morando, I'm going to use an argument we both know you won't dare refuse!"

I watched the verbal duel with interest, sipping my coffee. Poor Rkaeli. He's had two women on his case all morning, each demanding attention. Even I sympathized with him. But who was James Plymton? And what debt could this one-armed man owe the university professor?

With Camilla's coercion, the spy gradually gave in. You had to give her credit: she was very persistent. In the end, Morando said that the final decision lay with the officer in charge of the search party.

"Who is it and where do I find them?" demanded Dr. Harris.

The chief of intelligence glanced at me. Camilla also turned around, raising a questioning eyebrow. And my stomach suddenly went cold.

* * *

We met at the eastern gate. The detachment was assembled and prepared to march. There were Bryan's friends with whom he had traveled even before the siege: Fraudo, a black kid with dreadlocks gathered into a bun; the girl next to him was Quinn; the other boy was her brother, whose name I didn't remember. All three were very young. As if to balance them out, a gray-haired old man stood next to them dressed in hiking gear with a sword at his waist. I knew from Bryan's stories that his name was Mr. Myers, but I had never seen him before: the old man lived outside the city and was apparently anti-social. Bryan himself ran among the people and horses, checking things, asking questions and cracking jokes. He looked cheerful — you would think he was elated — but it didn't fool me. I felt his concern. Seeing us arrive, he came to meet us.

"Bryan, if you don't mind, I'd like to join the party," Camilla said bluntly as he approached.

"Out of the question, Dr. Harris. It might be dangerous."

"So you'll have to protect me."

"If we have to protect you, it'll be ten times more dangerous for the rest of the detachment."

"I know that. But you don't have a choice. I know exactly the places that the expedition was supposed to visit. You won't find anything without me!" Bryan glanced at Rkaeli. The exhausted intelligence officer shrugged his shoulders, as if to say, 'Decide for yourself.'

"Camilla, why is it so important for you to go there?" My boyfriend asked quietly.

There you go! This was one of his new features. Steve was inconsiderate at times, like all men. But Bryan knew how to listen when needed. Had his journey really changed him that much? Then again, he had been forced to lead a battalion.

Camilla didn't respond for a long time.

"Thomas..." she said at last. "We...we were close..." Bryan nodded, accepting her argument.

"Camilla, we'll do everything we can to find him and bring him back. I promise."

Dr. Harris suddenly sobbed.

"I don't think you will find him," she whispered, staring at the ground beneath her feet. She suddenly raised her head sharply. "I need to know what happened!"

"You'll find out everything—"

"Please, Bryan! I'm a good horse rider and I won't interfere with your work."

I don't know how she did it, but within ten minutes Camilla was among our ranks, despite the discontent of almost all the leading men. The decisive factor was her confidence in her riding abilities: if something happened, she would jump into the saddle and flee to the city.

I was still bothered by the concern in Bryan's eyes. When he finished negotiating with Rkaeli, I asked him with my eyes to have a word. He walked over, smiling wryly.

"Have you come to celebrate your victory?"

"You were the one who came up with that stupid bet!"

"Well well! Just you wait, the day is still young."

"Bry?"

"Yes?"

"What happened with James Plymton and Thomas from the university?"

He hesitated.

"I don't know. Honestly, I still don't have a clue. Let's hope that it's all just...one big misunderstanding."

"You'll be careful?"

He finally understood what was expected of him, came closer and kissed me. I knew we were being watched and allowed myself to get carried away a little. But two of the three women there were going with him, and I wasn't one of them, so I felt the need to...mark my territory. And yet, it seems I did manage to cheer him up a little, or at least his cheerfulness no longer looked so strained. He turned and walked towards his men. And I suddenly felt a chill from the realization that I would fall asleep alone tonight, in an empty house. There was still something I had to tell him. Something important.

"Bryan!"

He turned around. I ran up to him, looked into his eyes.

"Don't do anything stupid. Don't slip up. You hear?"

He nodded.

CHAPTER 3

"TELL ME, DR. HARRIS. Why did you need to organize an expedition to go birdwatching?"

The brown grass in these places was surprisingly thick and quite high in places, so we rode at a walk, and then at a light trot.

"Do you want the long answer or the short answer?"

"Short answer first, if possible."

"We need to go birdwatching because everything in this world happens for a reason."

"What do you mean?"

"You're asking for the long answer."

"The short one had a good hook. You should be a salesperson."

"Bryan, do you remember your interactions with animals here? Can you remember anything strange about their behavior?"

"Strange? The bear, I remember, almost tore

our detachment to shreds. I don't know how typical this behavior is for bears in real life. Hmm..."

Suddenly, one instance did come to mind:

"I remember the wolves acted rather unusually. I climbed a tree and two wolves watched me. One of them did not react to the arrows, although I hit him in the eye. And then, when I did kill him, the second ran after the pack."

Dr. Harris nodded.

"That's correct. And a very valuable observation, by the way, it's a pity you didn't tell me earlier. But I suppose I didn't ask. Wolves aren't the only animals that behave strangely in the game. Interestingly, species diversity is very important here. Different animals have different oddities. Wolves do not feel pain, hares can sometimes gallop at speeds of up to hundreds of miles per hour. No animal on earth runs like that. Badgers hibernate, although winter never comes. And they sometimes fall asleep right on the road. Some animals have very primitive intelligence. The local mice cannot escape from the simplest labyrinths," she paused, looking thoughtfully at the horse's withers. "But there is one exception."

"Birds?"

"Yes. Birds in this world are fantastic beasts. A huge number of species, all with their own anatomies and lifestyles. Many have amazing cognitive abilities. To be honest, I don't think that anyone on earth has managed to create anything like that until now."

"Why birds, specifically?"

"I don't have a good answer. I can conjecture that the creator of this world might have had a special relationship with birds. However, this is just one question, and it is, perhaps, at the very end of the list. You see, Bryan, we have reason to believe this world is not over. He is in work in progress status. But this very work for some mysterious reason stopped, and progress does not occur. And since this world - like the world outside - tries to rely on the natural evolution of the system, on its entropy, then we face the problem of a possible cataclysm associated with the fact that there is no balance in the world, which, apparently, was conceived. It's hard to even imagine how this could end."

"Today is just full of good news," I said grimly. "But I still don't understand why you had to go there to watch birds? Aren't there enough of them around the city? The same crows are constantly stealing food from the guardrooms.

"There are a lot more in the woods around the black stones."

"Black stones?"

Camilla looked at me with surprise.

"There is a clearing between the lake and the forest." Mr. Meyers pulled his horse closer to ours. "It has a circle of black obelisks dug into the ground, made of smooth black stone or metal. The lack of knowledge our intelligence officers have about the geography within a few hours' drive from the city is a little alarming."

"I know, I know! I mean, I haven't been there, but I've heard of it, of course."

Mr. Meyers chuckled.

"And what's the deal with these stones, Dr. Harris?" I asked quickly.

"Who knows?"

"Fair enough…"

* * *

We soon came across a road. The horses began to trot faster, and small groves popped up around us. The soil began to turn red with sand. Among the trees, I could guess bluish glints of water. The lake. We rode alongside it now, and after a quarter of a mile we could see it: huge, stretching out as far as the eye could see to the north and east. The entire southern coast was an endless beach covered in the finest sand.

"Someone should open a hotel here," Fraudo said, whistling. "Make a whole lotta green."

Quinn looked at him with displeasure.

We walked alongside the beach, keeping to the road. The path was lined with young birch trees. The wind blew from the lake, bending the trunks and moving in waves along the canopy.

"This place should be full of birds," said Dr. Harris. "But now the wind is the only noise."

"Is it far to the village?"

"Ten minutes. And the black stones are a bit further and to the left."

"We'll stop by the village first."

The village appeared unexpectedly. Several thatched huts were lined up on the bank. Moored boats swayed along the wide dock. On the road in front of the houses, dark streaks were clearly visible on the sand. It looked like blood.

We dismounted. I wanted to leave Camilla and two others with the horses, but I knew from the professor's eyes that she would follow. I sighed.

"Jerry and Quinn, stay here, watch the road and the forest. The rest of us will walk up to those barrels. From there, Fraudo and Quentin will go left, Mr. Meyers and Mills will go right. Explore the area. We won't go up to the houses yet. Mr. Parks, you'll go with me to the town square. The rest wait here.

"Mr. Mursley..."

"Stay here, Camilla. Give us time to check for danger. If everything's okay, you can follow behind us."

It was definitely blood. A large splotch in the trampled sand and a wide trail, as if the body had been dragged to an alley between the houses. I looked around. There were no other signs of disorder: a fishing net was drying peacefully on a wooden bar, a rake and a shovel were leaning against the entrance to a side building, and rainwater had accumulated in the barrels. If the

Predators had been here, the place would have looked completely different.

"Let's go."

The alley between the houses turned out to be narrow, with many objects lining the walls: boat and fishing equipment, sawhorses, blankets and some kind of pots. One was broken, and a viscous whitish substance spilled over the ground, from which a sour smell emanated. The middle of the aisle was littered with debris. I walked closer, bent down and shuddered. A thick beam protruded from the ground by the wall. A broken blade of a cleaver or small sword was firmly stuck into the dark wood, and on it lay four gnarled human fingers with fingernails stuck deep into the tree.

Mr. Parks approached and examined my find with interest.

"Mr. Parks, I would ask you to go back to Dr. Harris and..." I stopped.

Camilla approached the aisle between the houses. I gritted my teeth, turned and stepped over the clutter, trying not to step on anything. To hell with it! If she wanted to see, let her see.

Ahead, between the walls of the huts, the beach was visible, and beyond was the blue expanse of the lake. The sun was beating down hard. Suddenly the wind picked up, driving away the heat. It swept through the alleyway, bearing with it a strong smell. Once I took a whiff, I suddenly realized what I would see lying on the sand in the sun, and more than anything I wanted to turn around and leave without ever looking back. To just walk away, never to see this beach or the calm water again. But leaving wasn't an option. With a pang, I suddenly felt the inevitability of my path. I know it sounds terribly pathetic, but I can't explain it in another way. In the past, video games were linear. Then came the open world games. What could be further away from a linear plotline than our collective Fantasia? And yet, at that moment I felt like the main character of a game in which the world only exists to the extent that the hero sees it with his own eyes.

On the beach lay the remains of a man. An open chest cavity with ribs protruding from the hole. Drawings carved into the skin — dashed lines and some sort of symbols. Some of the entrails were spread out around the corpse, forming an eerie picture, as if someone tried to reproduce a poster from the medical room. I had already guessed what I would see there, but did not expect such a grotesque presentation. And then I saw the face of the dead man and felt my stomach roll up to my throat. The skin on one side was very skillfully removed, revealing the structure of the facial muscles and ligaments, and the picture was so terrifyingly realistic that I had to turn away almost immediately.

The nightmarish anatomical theater lay a dozen steps away, while further away and to the right on the pier, her back to me, was a girl in a simple gray sleeveless dress. The wind played with her long hair, blowing through the tight curls. Her left hand, which lay palm up on the boards, was covered in blood up to the elbow! I froze, trying to steady my breathing, but the girl somehow sensed my presence and turned around. A hologram flashed over her head:

Miriam
Level 6
Missing parameter 13944f

She had a pretty, doll-like little face, but when she smiled, chills ran down my spine.

The girl rose slowly to her feet and turned. The front of her dress was all smeared with red. I raised my left hand and cast a shield. For some reason, the transparent hemisphere did not inspire the confidence that, I confess, I had hoped for. The girl walked towards me, continuing to smile affably. She paused as she passed the corpse.

"Do you like it?" she asked, drawing out her vowels in a strange way.

"Did you do this?" I asked in response, trying to remain calm.

She tilted her head slightly to one side.

"You're beautiful, glowing," the girl said slowly, gazing at the energy runoff of my protective shield. "But you're still not real. Do you want to be real? Like you once were?"

I shuddered.

"Why did you do this, Mariam?" I asked, already knowing that this conversation was not going at all like I had planned. "What happened here?"

"Little spark," the girl smiled again and took a step towards me. "Little spark lived in a little house, and then they kicked him out of his little house. And now he's cold."

Suddenly I felt the cold. It was as if it had been injected into my veins. I tried to raise my right arm, fighting the numbness that had arisen with all my strength. It was a feeling you sometimes experience in dreams: all your movements become sluggish, slow, and you can't inch forward, you can't move! The girl's face was suddenly much closer than I expected and I suddenly understood what her words meant. God, it was the same thought I woke up with every morning! We all did! The body to which my consciousness was tied was nothing more than a three-dimensional image. Never before had it seemed so alien to me. Not even when I first appeared under that wretched tree, when I felt almost nothing at all. I'm not real. I...I'm the little spark! I'm cold! But she...she could make me real!

The girl raised her hand to my face, her fingers emitting icy waves that penetrated directly into my brain. My vision blurred.

An invisible log slammed into her stomach, forcing her fragile body to fold in half, then a monstrous force grabbed her and threw her back, almost to the very pier on which she had just sat. Mr. Parks supported me under my elbow.

"Thank you, you're...right on time...Mr. Parks," I muttered, gasping for air and trying to stop my head from spinning.

God, what the hell was that? I swear, just a few moments ago I was ready to go under this girl's knife!

Aring of soldiers quickly closed in around the pier. My friends had arrived, walking around the settlement in a circle. They had weapons in their hands, but they did not need them: the girl was dead.

* * *

While my guys were examining the scene, I tried to come to my senses. Nearby stood Mr. Parks, who had already considered everything that was of interest to him, and was now openly bored.

"Mr. Mursley," he squeaked when everyone had gone a sufficient distance away.

There was something in his voice that made me turn to look at him.

"Yes, Mr. Parks?"

"I want to ask you to turn on your hologram for a second."

It was a request. For now. At the same time, he had waited until the others had moved away. A polite gesture?

"Of course, Mr. Parks."

I switched on my hologram, and looked through my stats myself.

Bryan Mursley, level 19 (378 520 XP)

Strength: 1 (base level)
Dexterity: 1 (ranged damage — 1)
Intellect: 9 (build a bonfire — 1, cartography — 4, language — 1, fishing — 0, magical damage — 2)
Wisdom: 6 (meditation — 1, lore — 1, mana regeneration rate — 3, Divine Voice — 1)
Constitution: 3

Damage: +0.5 (light weapon), +1.5 (magic)
Armor: +2
Health: 30 hp

Speed: 5.5
Stamina: 100
Mana: 150 (regeneration rate — 1 point every 3.5 mins)

My stats looked normal, nothing out of the ordinary. I switched it off. Mr. Parks stood looking at the lake, and I understood that I had passed the test.

"Sir." One of his agents approached him. "It seems we have a witness."

I followed the man. Colin was his name. I

remembered him from Mr. Kaomi's squad — a great guy.

"Did you find more bodies?"

"Four more."

We again went through the alley between the houses and turned right. At the door of one of the houses were two soldiers with weapons in their hands. We walked past them inside.

The house had two rooms. The narrow foyer was hung with fish wrapped in fly nets. The odor was so strong here, so we quickly hurried to the second room. It contained a bed, a small polished wood dining table, and several narrow cabinets. Nets hung everywhere, and in the corner stood a blackened metal stove. Surprisingly, the smell of fish was almost absent here.

I gave Colin a questioning look. The man nodded toward the bed. I looked closer and noticed a pair of bare feet sticking out from under it. The feet were dirty and definitely belonged to a living person — by the looks of it, about five or six years old. However, I hadn't seen children for a long time, so I didn't trust my own judgment. I went to the middle of the room.

"Hey, buddy, what's going on?"

No response. I figured out which side the owner of the feet was facing, walked around the bed and sat down a step away from the old sagging mattress covered with a woolen blanket.

The boy was lying on his side, knees tucked in, staring at me with piercing blue eyes. Now that

I was looking at him a hologram flashed over his head, but most of it was inside the bed and could not be read.

"Hello," I said.

The boy continued to stare at me in silence.

"My name is Bryan. We won't hurt you."

I noticed that he was hugging a toy close to his chest. It looked like a rabbit.

"Don't be scared. We chased the bad guys away," I hesitated, thinking that the girl we killed could have been his mother or sister before...whatever had happened to her.

The boy didn't move and said nothing. Camilla entered the room and stopped next to Colin and Mr. Parks. I looked at the boy and tried to come up with a strategy. I felt that it was necessary to proceed very carefully. I thought for a few moments, then opened my inventory and pulled out a sheet of paper. Taking it in my hands, I looked doubtfully at the dusty floor, but then decided I didn't care about the dirt and sat down. The paper was thick and stiff enough. I bent it several times and tore off the uneven edge, achieving the desired rectangular shape, and then quickly folded an ordinary airplane. The boy watched my movements carefully. I gave it a test throw and some unseen wind blew the tail of the airplane and launched it along the bed. The aircraft obediently glided towards the log wall. The boy lifted his head, following its flight path. Then he looked at me.

"Imagine how far it could go if you threw it from the window," I said.

* * *

The boy's name was Malcolm. He was a level two, and he had no mark. I questioned him carefully, and found out the following: the day before, a man had come to the village. He moved strangely (Malcolm even tried to depict the gait of an alien). He was very courteous with the inhabitants, had asked for water but did not drink, instead pouring it into his flask.

"Did you get a good look at him?"

"I saw him from the window," Malcolm replied. "He stood right there. He held a stick in his hands, had normal clothing, his face too. You know, like totally normal? I haven't seen one in a long time, but I remember how they look."

I nodded and turned towards the others.

"A player from the real world," Mr. Parks whispered.

The boy looked at him in surprise.

"What happened next?" I asked.

"Then he went to the black stones, and Uncle Burt volunteered to go with him. And after sunset, three more came. A woman and two men. They asked to spend the night, and the last hut just got empty, because Uncle Howard sailed to the other shore.

The boy fell silent, looking out the window.

His lower lip was quivering slightly.

"And then?" I asked quietly.

"Then Uncle Burt came back from the woods…"

The boy suddenly turned sharply away from the window, ran back to the bed and grabbed his bunny, which had been briefly replaced by the airplane. I asked a few more cautious questions, but the overall picture was clear. Poor Malcolm. He had seen and heard things that no child should see or hear. And the fact that he was just an NPC didn't matter. What I saw in his eyes was real.

* * *

We moved towards the black stones, carefully searching for any clues along the way. We took Malcolm with us. The boy was scared, and I could not leave him alone in the village with the corpses (which for some reason did not disappear). He sat on the horse in front of me and showed me the way.

Twenty minutes later, the road began to climb up, winding between the tall trees. The foothills began. The clearing with the stones appeared from behind the scrubby bushes. The anthracite faceted slabs contrasted sharply with the brightly colored grass. We dismounted and cautiously approached the stones, holding our horses by the bridle. Silence hung heavy, broken only by the barely audible rustle of herbs. The black obelisks absorbed all of the generous sunlight cast across them, remaining dark silhouettes. For some reason, the polished surface had no gleam whatsoever, and even standing just a step away, only their outlines could be seen. No grass grew in the center of the circle. The ground here was firm and level.

The officers scattered in different directions in search of any evidence. I stayed near the center of the circle, pondering what to do next. Malcolm tried to stay close to me.

A voice fell on me from all sides:

When spring came, a pair of coral jays weaved a nest in the branches of a cedar, and a month later, chicks hatched. Five or six furry lumps, whose feathers would soon take on the same hues as their parents ...

Raising my shield, I stepped towards Malcolm to protect him from any possible danger, and the voice thundered so loudly that I wanted to cover my ears. Malcolm gave me a surprised look. The agents turned their heads in search of a threat, but gradually they all froze, looking at me, and I could see the questioning look in their eyes. It took me a good minute to realize that I was the only one who could hear the voice.

CHAPTER 4

"THERE'S NO WAY you guys can't hear that!!"

They couldn't. It was clear from their expressions. The voice continued its ceaseless broadcast, delving in unbelievable detail into the lives of jays. At first, it reminded me of Animal Planet, but the more I listened, the more it seemed like the voice was reading some sort of strange work of literature with no subject or concrete characters, but rather an uninterrupted stream of unwieldy descriptions. The style was something that may have belonged two hundred years in the past.

Camilla came up to me and started asking something, but then the voice spoke again, and I signalled to her that I could not hear anything. There was something strange about the voice. But I could not find the words to correctly describe why it was peculiar. As if at certain moments the voice could be saying one thing or another, depending on how you listen to it. It was not clear why this feeling arose: overall, the speech was very smooth, without any stuttering or incomprehensible noises. The voice belonged to a man with good university English. His intonation was monotone, but I had no doubt it was a living person.

Camilla said something to me again. I once again couldn't hear her, so she shouted:

"Get out of the circle!"

At that moment, the voice finished a long ornate phrase and fell silent. I hastily followed Dr. Harris's advice and stepped out of the circle of black stones. After walking a few steps away, I stopped and listened. And I heard it! The voice sounded again, but this time much weaker, as if the speaker was sitting at a neighboring table in a restaurant. I took another step away from the stones and the voice became even quieter.

The discussion was short and intense, but constructive, until Mr. Meyers hypothesized that I had "overheated in the sun." We fought for a while, and then something dawned on me and opened my character sheet to make sure:

Bryan Mursley, level 19 (378 520 XP)

Strength: 1 (base level)
Dexterity: 1 (ranged damage — 1)
Intellect: 9 (build a bonfire — 1, cartography — 4, language — 1, fishing — 0, magical damage — 2)

Wisdom: 6 (meditation — 1, lore — 1, mana regeneration rate — 3, Divine Voice — 1)
Constitution: 3

Damage: +0.5 (light weapon), +1.5 (magic)
Armor: +2
Health: 30 hp

Speed: 5.5
Stamina: 100
Mana: 150 (regeneration rate — 1 point every 3.5 mins)

There it was! The Divine Voice skill in Wisdom. I remembered where I had gotten it from. I remembered falling after my mid-air battle with the Predator because I ran out of mana. I thought then that maybe I could replenish my stock if I put a point in Wisdom, and fortunately, I had that point, and DIvine Voice was the only skill that came to my mind. There was no description for it, and everyone I asked about it shrugged their shoulders. The purpose of the skill had remained unclear. Until now.

Camilla demanded that I repeat what the voice was saying. I stepped towards the stones again and tried to shadow the speech of the invisible reader. It turned out to be unexpectedly difficult, in part because of the ridiculous content:

We flew, surrounded on all sides by a

magnificent forest, with all its colors, smells and sounds. I wanted to breathe in the full harmony of this place, and we laughed and danced in the air, and around us, early spring was in bloom with its fragile islands of remaining ice and the scent of earth awakening from sleep...

I, stammering, repeated the tricky and tedious text while Camilla listened most attentively. Five minutes later I was exhausted and announced that I had had enough.

While we stood over by the stones, the guys searched the entire clearing, but found no clues. Malcolm couldn't help us either. We needed to decide what to do next. Would we really have to return to the city with nothing? We'd probably still have to comb the local forests. Hmm...

"Bryan?"

"Yes?"

"What do you plan to do now?"

"Do you have any good ideas, Camilla?"

"Not a single one. I hope you're not intending to leave right away?"

"Maybe."

"Don't! Listen, don't you see how important this is? I don't want to jump to conclusions, but I think that your discovery is one of the most important ones made in all my time in the game."

I looked at her, astonished.

"You got that from the story about the forest and birds?"

"Give me a little more information and I'll tell you what my understanding is."

Mr. Parks approached us and unexpectedly took Camilla's side:

"The man the child told us about was looking for these very stones. If we figure out what they are, maybe it will help us in our search."

Mr. Meyers and Quinn, who stood behind him, nodded in agreement. I sighed.

"Please tell me one of you has a character point to spend!"

* * *

Once it finished with birds and flight, the voice switched to "rays of the sun, piercing the quiet water surface, sparkling like a silver mirror." There was, it seemed, an entirely separate story about fucking sunbeams! Then the voice paused, and I had a gulp of water and swore, but Camilla was relentless.

After an hour of interpretation, I was going crazy. My throat was scratchy, my thoughts were confused and I, not heeding the professor's protests, stepped farther away from the circle and sat on the ground, massaging my temples. The others gradually followed suit.

The sun was slowly edging towards the horizon. Everyone was ravenous, so we set up camp quickly. We made trail soup and ate in silence. Then we changed lookouts so that they could also enjoy a hot meal. Eventually we all congregated around the campfire.

"So, Camilla, we're listening," I said when everyone had settled in and were hitting their pipes. "I hope you managed to make some valuable observations after all that hullabaloo."

I rubbed my still sore throat.

"There is still a critical lack of information," the professor retorted. "To start, I would like to ask you to give a more detailed description of the voice itself."

She certainly was painfully thorough. I tried to lay out my impressions of the voice, including the strange word choices that stood out to me. Hearing this, Camilla moved closer, listening attentively.

"I think," I said, finishing my description, "that if you buff that skill, there's a chance you'll hear a lot more."

This was the conclusion that had only just popped into my head. Camilla spent some time regaling us with her own notes and observations then, with a sigh, removed everything from her inventory. We watched her expectantly.

"I want to reiterate that everything I'm about to tell you is just speculation on my part."

Mr. Meyers rolled his eyes.

"The skill that allows Bryan to hear the voice," continued the professor after a short pause, "is called Divine Voice. I believe that this voice belongs to the creator of Fantasia. A man whose name is supposedly Abdullah Hakim Jarkhan-Ali. I don't know whether you're familiar with the name, but in any case I'll remind you that there's a statue of him in the city. Some of our fellow citizens have met a copy that looks like him." Camilla stared pointedly at me. "And they all reported that he was *unable to use his voice.*"

I swallowed. Could it be the voice of my erstwhile companion emanating from these rocks? And why had he remained silent? I had to admit, Camilla had managed to astound me. But it seemed the surprises were far from over.

"I must say that this is all rather trivial, since the description of the skill is in the name itself," the professor continued. "In my opinion, there is another detail that is far more interesting. I propose that the voice Mursley heard was in itself an act of creation."

* * *

We all needed a little time to wrap our heads around this information. Silence fell around the campfire, broken only by the rustling of the trees.

"I hate to say it, but...hmm...the idea isn't particularly interesting to me," I finally said. "However, based on what I heard while standing there..."

"I understand," Camilla smiled. "It sounds a little...unusual. But hear me out. One of the biggest puzzles about Fantasia is that one man clearly couldn't have managed to do all the work himself. I hope you understand me correctly: even if Jarkhan-Ali copied himself several thousand times and assigned each of those copies a domain to develop — one working on the physics of storm cloud formation, another coding raspberry bushes — just gathering all that information together would be an insurmountable task. And he wouldn't have even had the opportunity, because equipment at that time simply wouldn't have been able to pull that kind of power. He would have needed a way to optimize his work, and he found it.

Camilla took a small pause, looking at us like students who were supposed to guess what she was trying to say.

"Anyone who has ever gotten sucked into a good book knows how authentic an author's world can be. As you know, this effect is simply an illusion. A skillful author can carefully select his words so that a vivid picture is painted in the reader's head, and then wherever necessary, the brain fills in the rest. Imagination is a thing of infinite potential, you must agree. The benefit of this technique is that constructs of staggering complexity can sometimes be described using only a few trigger words. I dare say that Jarkhan-Ali used this very principle. He described the world by writing small texts and then harnessed the power of imagination from his or other copies to fill out his world.

"If this is the case," offered Mr. Meyers, "then I don't understand why the text sounds like it was written two centuries ago. The game is clearly a fantasy world. That means the text should sound more like *The Lord of the Rings*."

"It's unlikely the code of this world resembles any existing literary work," Camilla objected. "It's more like a technical document composed of many separate texts for describing different phenomena. The genre is chosen based on the preference of the listener. In other words, I think that Jarkhan-Ali was raised on classic literature, or simply enjoyed weird books. This style inspired his imagination. However, I'm not dismissing the idea that the style for other pieces may be completely different."

"I have a question." Quinn raised her hand just like a student during a lecture.

The professor nodded.

"You are suggesting that this process of creation...is happening right now?"

Camilla smiled.

"Precisely!" she said approvingly.

Quinn blushed slightly. Frodo elbowed her in the side.

"This is a very accurate question, added Camilla. "That is, the best kind of question. There is a lot of evidence in favor of the fact that the creation of the world is not taking place at this moment. I've already told Bryan about this. The world of the game, like the real world, is inert. It is governed by natural processes, like entropy. But there is evidence that it was different in the past. To answer your question, I think we are dealing with a recording. A sound recording of the process of creating the world.

We talked for some time, discussing what we had heard, arguing, trying to look for some other explanation. Meanwhile, the twilight deepened. It became clear that they would have to spend the night here so that they could continue the search tomorrow. I was concerned about Malcolm. What would we do with the boy? His relatives, God willing, would be reborn in a week, and we'd be able to send the guy home. Until then, would I have to lug him around with me, or what? As if Camilla wasn't enough on her own! Although admittedly she had been a useful addition to the detachment. We had learned some really good information thanks to her. The only problem was that all these wonderful hypotheses didn't give us any clue about what to do next. Where should we look for that real life player who visited the town before us? How did he do it? What was his agenda? These questions remained unanswered.

As I was lying on my old wolf skin, I thought that perhaps I still had a chance to win this morning's bet with Yana. This case may turn out to be more important than anything she and the boss could be discussing. But I wasn't at all certain that a problem of this magnitude was within my power to solve.

CHAPTER 5

THE NEXT MORNING I announced that the first order of business was returning to the village to bury the dead. I should have done this even earlier, but I was distracted by those stupid rocks.

I sent Quinn and Malcolm out to fish, and the rest went to the village, discussing what to do with the bodies. Mr. Meyers proposed to bury them in the sand, Fraudo said we should burn them. Camilla remembered that there were boats in which we could place the remains, entrusting them to the lake. "And set them on fire!" Fraudo added.

"They'll be surprised when they're resurrected," muttered Mr. Meyers. "Since the boats were there when they died."

Overall, I had to agree that his proposal was the most rational. There were shovels in the village and we got to work. We dug several somewhat shallow graves in a spot not too close to the water and made a stretcher out of thick fabric that we found in houses. Fraudo and I were working together when Mr. Parks approached us.

"Mr. Mursley, would you be so kind as to come with me?"

I put the stretcher on the ground and nodded to Fraudo to go take a smoke. We moved towards a small grove a hundred paces beyond the last house.

"Did you find something, Mr. Parks?"

He didn't respond.

In a small ravine at the very edge of the grove lay the body of a young woman. Completely naked. She lay on her stomach with her arms outstretched, her back and shoulders covered in intricate drawings.

I approached the body, grateful that her face was covered by her long hair, and immediately recognized the drawing. It was a map of Fantasia, drawn with confident strokes. I scanned and found our approximate location and noticed several tiny round wounds, as if left by a thin awl. There was blood caked around them. The wounds formed a circle. I examined the rest of the map carefully, then opened my own map and made a few notes.

"This is Darcy Winskett," said Mr. Parks without emotion. "From the University."

* * *

When we finished the burial, I sat down and wrote two letters. One was to the chief, the other — to Yana. I reluctantly addressed the letter to "Sylvia." She insisted I get used to it, and I had been trying, although to little success, I confess. "Yana" invariably slipped out during our conversations with others, and she would blush and become angry. But I couldn't help myself. For reasons I could only guess, it was much easier for her to get used to "Bryan."

After finishing the letters, I called everyone together and announced that the detachment was splitting up. Someone needed to send a report to the city, and I would send Camilla and the boy along with the messengers. But as long as no problems arose with Malcolm, Camilla flatly refused to leave the group.

"We still haven't found Tom," she said. "That means I'm sticking with you."

"Camilla, I thought you could get a group of your guys from the university together and tackle these damn stones. You'll likely dig up a lot more information than I will, because frankly speaking, my plan of action rests on very shaky foundations."

Dr. Harris raised her eyebrows inquiringly.

"We believe there are more black stones not too far from here, to the east. Maybe our man is heading there. We're going to try to intercept him."

"How do you know about the stones?"

I glanced at Mr. Parks and spoke briefly about the map tattooed on Darcy's back. Camilla listened to me carefully, but wasn't going to concede that easily.

"We'll deal with the stones, it's not a problem. All I have to do is write a letter, just like you." She showed me a piece of paper that had been folded several times.

"We're going a lot closer to the border, professor. We could easily run into Predators, and I'm not sure that we'll be able to protect you."

Camilla looked me in the eyes, unblinking.

"Don't worry about that, Mr. Mursley," she said coldly. "I guarantee you, I won't be a burden. Now let's end this silly argument. We don't have any time to waste."

Our group had to ride part of the way south together and we reached the crossroads in the prairie without any incident. Here, the messengers turned west. In a few hours, they would be home. I could not help but notice the joy on their faces, and I understood this joy perfectly. A fair fight was one thing — when you knew your opponent and what he was capable of. The incomprehensible bullshit we had stumbled upon was quite another.

Those who were leaving waved goodbye and trotted towards the city. We turned our horses to the west and rode the same route that I first rode with Councilor McKinnery's troops, now standing at the western gate of the DHC city.

* * *

The sun was high and blazing down with all its might. Both the horses and the humans were thirsty, and you can't store a lot of water in your inventory. Fortunately, there was a well a few miles away.

As we approached, we startled a herd of animals that scattered away from us into the prairie. They looked like large gophers, but were unexpectedly plump and clumsy. They drank the rest of the water from the old wooden troughs. The well itself was a good twenty feet deep and was paved with stones. Whoever had made it apparently lacked the imagination to attach a normal chain and pulley system, so the water had to be raised using a long pole with a rope and bucket attached to the end of it. At least there was a bucket.

The water had a slightly sweet flavor and I couldn't gulp it down fast enough. Then, catching my breath, I handed the bucket to Fraudo. And then we saw them again. The gophers had returned. They stood on their hind legs a few dozen paces from us. I noticed that they all had very swollen stomachs.

Fraudo wiped his mouth on his sleeve, smiled and handed the bucket to Camilla, who passed it along, since she still had water in her flask. Several gophers lowered onto all fours and ran a bit closer. We were all looking at them now. The gophers continued their approach. Mr. Meyers picked up a pebble from the ground and threw it at one of them. The gopher shied away, but immediately ran back.

"What's with them?" Camilla asked.

"I don't know," I said. "It's strange, as if they're frightened but are still coming closer. Maybe..."

I suddenly stopped short.

"Stop! Don't drink the water!"

Mills, who had just taken the bucket, looked at me, bewildered. And it was at that moment that the gophers rushed us. It was so quick and unexpected that none of us even had time to raise a shield. But the animals did not attack. They rushed to the drinking troughs and began to climb inside, trying to shove the horses out of the way, even biting them on the muzzle. Khan, Fraudo's horse, grabbed a gopher with his teeth and threw it aside. The animal squeaked resentfully, got up and trotted back to the trough. Gradually, the horses retreated under the furious onslaught of the animals as they dove into the water, and we hastened to pull them aside.

"What was it we drank?" Fraudo asked, perplexed.

"Everyone who drank that water!" I cried. "Two fingers down your throat immediately!"

Understanding the difference even a second can make, I was the first to set an example. When I had expelled most of the water I had drunk, I looked around. Only three people in the entire squadron hadn't taken a sip: Mr. Parks, the professor and Mills. The others looked pale and frightened after carrying out my order. I heard a high-pitched whistle and turned around.

The gophers were crawling out of the empty trough. They looked terrible! Their stomachs were monstrously swollen, preventing the animals from moving normally. They jerked sporadically, emitting whistling sounds, and fell to the ground, scrabbling with their claws, until they one-by-one fell silent.

We gazed upon this sight in horror, each of us who drank searching themselves for signs of this terrible sickness. However, aside from the discomfort of purging my stomach, I felt surprisingly normal.

"Maybe it's not the water?" said Fraudo horsely. "God, anything but the water!"

We quickly packed up and prepared to depart. Everyone wanted to get away from the unpleasant place. I was thirsty after vomiting, but Camilla and Mr. Parks had already drunk any remaining water they had. We drove about a quarter of a mile and stopped. Quinn, who had been the first to drink, reined in her horse.

"What's going on?" I shouted."

"I have a notification. Dehydration. I need water, now!"

"What?"

"Me too," Quentin said quietly.

A few seconds later, the notification popped up on my screen:

Low body fluids!

You are at risk of dehydration!

The only nearby water was in the well. Quinn turned her horse around and started back.

"Stop, Quinn!" I yelled. "You can't drink that water!"

But she didn't listen. Quentin spurred his horse and started after his sister. And then we were all galloping back to the damned well! I could feel my swollen tongue taking up more and more space in my mouth. I was dying of thirst!

When she reached the well, Quinn jumped off the saddle and rushed to the bucket, which the gophers hadn't yet managed to drink. Almost half of the party had returned and the girl began to drink without hesitation. Even off, the notification continued to flicker alarmingly somewhere on the edge of my vision. My tongue involuntarily darted over my lips. Quinn handed the bucket to Quentin and flashed him an unsettling grin. I left my legs carrying me towards them.

When I got to the bucket, for a moment, I forgot about everything else. It was a moment of fabulous, inexpressible bliss! Water! Nothing sweeter in the universe! I took a few greedy gulps and felt my body recover. The corpses of the swollen-bellied gophers lay all around.

"So," I said, giving the group a dull look. "Listen to me! First, pour water for the horses or they'll attack us. Second! Don't keep the water to yourself! I'll make a fire now, let's try to boil it. Anyone with herbs or non-offensive spells, come with me. After cleansing the stomach. And lastly, I ask everyone to turn on their holograms for a second.

They obeyed. And I saw it. On all but three of them. *Missing parameter f1762.*

Spells, herbs, boiled water — nothing helped, and the attacks became more frequent. I started to realize that soon my life would be reduced to two things: drinking and vomiting. Then, our kidneys would probably start to fail, if we had them. I decided that I wouldn't drink any more and sat off to the side. The rest sat with me and people instinctively moved away from one another. I held out for about ten minutes, then I got up and wobbled on jelly legs to the well. The bucket was in someone's else's hands, but I grabbed the wooden side and pulled it towards my mouth. But the other guy wouldn't let go. I struck him with Lightning, grabbed the container from his contorted fingers and began to drink. And as soon as I took a few sips, the cloudiness in front of my eyes dissipated, and I saw Quinn, who was kneeling in front of me. She was shaking from the electrical discharge.

A tidal wave of despair washed over me. Orders, pleas, magical spells — they were all useless! We were dying a terrible, nightmarish, impossible death.

I threw the bucket aside, turned away from the well, and walked off on unruly legs. I wanted to leave, I had to leave while I still could! Before I started killing my friends. I walked, barely making out the road in front of me. A notification flashed in front of my eyes. I closed it and kept walking. They say that when you're dying of thirst, all you can think of is water. This isn't true! At some point, the body's ability to feel degrades so entirely that imagining anything becomes completely impossible. You feel the life literally draining out of you. As I walked, I already knew I wouldn't have the strength to return to the well. Thank God! It even cheered me up a little, and I walked faster. And then I stumbled and fell, and realized that I wouldn't get up again. As I lay there, I couldn't tell if it was day or night. There was only the continuous, eternal thirst.

At the edge of my hearing, I heard footsteps, but didn't turn my head to see who it was. And then a thought flashed in my mind: *this person is full of blood. You can drink it.* And then my body ceased to obey me. Something else was in control — something hiding somewhere deep inside me.

I jumped up. A tall man in a traveling cloak stood two steps away. His plain features, straight nose and dark skin reminded someone, but I didn't care now. I jumped, my hand reaching out to claw at his throat. I missed. The man was on my left, raised his hands, and his palms were fire.

Long fingers flickered rapidly, weaving an intricate pattern from beams of light that he melded as if they were tangible matter.

The man stepped towards me and quickly touched my head. I lunged, but somehow he held me back, ran his fingers over my face, and in the next instant I collapsed to the ground. It felt as if I had just been hit by a freight train. But I felt like myself! Overcoming the pain, I got up and bowed before the man who had saved me from a terrible fate, but lost my balance and would have collapsed again if the Silent Man had not supported me. He smiled. The Silent Man made a polite gesture as if to say, 'Come now! Anyone would have done the same in my place!" The Silent Man patted me on the shoulder and was very glad to see me.

And then I remembered the others. Grasping the sleeve of his cloak with disobedient fingers, I dragged the astonished god with me to the well.

CHAPTER 6

WE MADE IT ON TIME. The others had held out pretty well thanks to the fact that the three uninfected people had established a steady water supply system. But the horses looked terrible, and the Silent Man took care of them first, then people who were afraid to move even a step away from the well, and finally — the well itself. When he finished, our smiling savior pulled out a full bucket and handed it to us. Everyone refused. Then the Silent Man put the bucket down and explained that we need to drink some water and relax, because fear of hydration is a terrible thing. I couldn't help but agree with his arguments, and we all drank water. Then I apologized to Quinn and offered to restore her health, but it turned out that the Silent Man had taken care of that too.

Now that it was all over, the incident with the water seemed like a bad dream, although I knew it wasn't. It was as if part of my conscious mind was trying to find a simple explanation for what had happened and was now grasping at straws.

As I argued with myself, Camilla carefully observed our guest. Wasting no time, he had made a large fire on the ground (a little away from the well and the unpleasant consequences of our stomach cleansing).

"I'm surprised you haven't asked a single question yet," I said to Camilla.

The professor pursed her lips thoughtfully.

"*When he comes, he will say only what he considers necessary,*" she said, watching the Silent Man pull out some items from the inventory. "If the classics teach us anything, it's that you need to treat gods with caution."

Noticing that we were looking his way, the Silent Man straightened up and beckoned invitingly. We obediently approached. The silent one solemnly invited us to sit. His face was serious, but there was a cunning glint in his eyes. He pulled a bunch of plants from the ground. I recognized them immediately: a long, stiff stem topped with a densely packed cylinder of velvety seeds. Cattail. Just like in reality, it grew here on the banks of rivers and lakes. Why had the Silent Man carried it with him all the way to the prairie? As I considered this, the Silent Man started distributing a cattail to each person, then sat down closer to the fire, and I saw that he was trying to conceal a smile.

Lifting his reed, our savior put it into the fire and began to fry it. We followed his example. The Silent Man made sure that everyone was roasting them correctly — without sticking it directly into the flame. And then the smell wafted towards me, and at first I could not believe my own nose. Quinn, realizing what was happening, pulled her reed out of the fire and took a bite. Her eyes widened in surprise, and in an instant she had nibbled her plant clean. Seeing her, I couldn't resist.

The velvet pile of seeds melted, transforming into a thin sweet crust, under which a hot marshmallow filling was hidden. It was the most tender and delicious marshmallow I have ever tasted. The treat greatly lifted everyone's spirits, gave them strength, and the Silent Man was already passing out seconds. No one refused.

Once everyone had eaten and rehydrated (no longer fearfully), a peaceful silence fell around the fire for some time. The day was drawing to a close and I was beginning to nod off. But the Silent Man didn't let us sleep, explaining that he had little time. He spoke in short, silent scenes, which he acted out mainly with his hands. His fingers seemed to be independently thinking creatures: they were transformed, like artists, played different roles, reproducing situations and words and whole sentences. The Silent Man was a veritable master of gestures and didn't need any particular language to make his meaning clear.

And here's what we learned.

At first, there was only the Author. And the Author wanted to create a world. A real world, not a sad imitation. It was a daunting task, but the Author knew how to take advantage of the information sources he had, and for that kind of person, nothing is impossible. However, it didn't take him long to find what he was looking for. The Author borrowed the opening words of the very first book that came to his head: his world would also begin with the Word.

For the world to be born from the Word, there needed to be someone who would utter it and someone who would hear. The Author made his first partial copy, and it became the Listener. The Listener always appeared in a dream and was devoid of a body. The Author only had to raise him. The Listener was destined to become the future world.

The Author began to work on the Word, but when he had compiled the first tome and tried to read it to the Listener, it turned out that the latter did not interpret his words as intended. The barrier between worlds turned out to be not so easy to overcome, and all his efforts fell short. The Author struggled long and hard with this problem, but in the end, he found clues in all the same sources he had originally turned to and realized that he would need an intermediary. He made another copy, and it became the Reader, voice and instrument of the

Author. And the world came into being, and everything in it was beautiful, until one day the Reader noticed strange blackouts in his memory. Some of his works...he did not remember how he had read them...He began to search for a reason and found out that the Author had betrayed him. He had erased the Reader and restarted. More than once. The Author experimented with the Reader in an attempt to improve upon the world, and often these experiments were almost like torture.

By the time the Silent Man reached this part in the story, we were all sitting in a daze. The narrator's fingers trembled slightly, and his face changed expressions with amazing speed, switching between characters in the story.

The Reader did not understand how the Author could treat him this way. And when he understood, he was horrified: the Author didn't even consider the idea that his actions could be thought of as unethical.

And the fact that the Reader did not immediately understand this, alas, meant only one thing — he himself was the same way. In the world of the Author, there was a name for this — psychopathy. Inability to empathize. However, having become a victim of his own psychoses, the Reader realized one important thing: empathy is not just something you are born with or without. It's a choice. And he also realized that their world was real, because only in the real world could you be born again.

The Silent Man suddenly raised his head and looked at us. "Your appearance in the world is no coincidence!" He announced. "You have lost a lot, but everyone has gained something to replace what was lost."

I knew what he was hinting at. As much as I hated this world, at least Yana was here with me. While in reality, she was not. And that meant that the proverbial second shot, for which I cursed Old Woman Fate, really did exist. I glanced at the others: everyone was in deep thought. And the Silent Man continued:

One day the Author told the Reader that they needed to make something for their world to be complete. The Reader asked what it was, and the Author replied: evil. The Reader said that he would not make evil, but the Author only laughed and said that he already had everything he needed: the information he had gathered during his experiments, which the Reader himself could not remember. He only needed to read some of this new information into the world and it would be complete. The Author gave the Reader the text, but the Reader, having seen it, stolidly refused, and the Author subjected him to tortures anew. But this time the Reader was ready. He was to be manipulated no longer. A new law had sounded in the world: only one copy of a person could participate in Fantasia, and once he was gone, he would never be able to return. And the world heard him. And then the Reader gave up the Voice, ceasing to be the Reader. The Author ceased to be the Author, because without the Reader he could no longer create, and it became impossible to connect a new copy of himself to the world. And the world itself lost the ability to ever become complete. There was no one to read fairy tales to the sleeping Listener.

The Silent Man's fingers ceased their fluttering and we sat for a while in silence, looking at him, while he stared into the coals of the fire. Then he turned and looked into my eyes. I swallowed.

You know the next part of the story better than anyone else. Your demand letter was useless in persuading the people on the outside. Only the Listener can change the conditions of the world, and without the Reader even his powers are severely limited. But the Listener is not blind. He sees in a dream what is happening inside him, and I believe that your story with Yana touched him in a sense. The world has changed.

Upon learning of this, the Author returned. No law of true death could stop him. He returned, realizing that not all was lost and he had a chance to complete what he started. Somehow, he's dragging all of his creatures here — the fruits of his experiments to make my nightmares come true, and it has something to do with the resonators — the places where I read the world. That hold the echo of my voice.

The Silent Man masterfully depicted an echo: putting his hand to his ear, he made several quick movements with it, as if rhythmic waves of sound were hitting the side of his palm. It's how they would portray it in a Disney cartoon. Then he suddenly straightened up, looking at us. His hands were no longer playing characters. He spoke with simple gestures, showing individual words. It was direct speech, not a story:

There are only ten resonators, they are scattered all over the world. But the main resonator is in the tower of the players' city to the east. That's where the Author will go, because there, he will be able to unleash all the evil he has in store for the world. And he has plenty in store. War will follow, and Fantasia will be covered in darkness.

"Why does the author need an empty world?" Camilla asked.

The author needs a world that he can build on his own terms. Who he will seed it with and if he will at all is a different question. The author conceived the world for himself alone. Then he had to let people in to cover the financial costs in real life, as well as test the equipment. But now everything is different, and therefore he must not be allowed to reach the resonator in the City of Players. It will mean doom for everyone!

A hologram suddenly flashed before my eyes:

The Reader has given you a quest: prevent the Author from unleashing evil on the world

Accept? : Yes / No
Amazingly, the program had never offered me a choice. This was new. We looked at each other.
"Don't even think about it!"
I caught a bitter look from Mr. Meyers.
"Why not?"
"Because it's not our business!" he burst out. "Why would you make a deal with him? You, it seems, are prepared to negotiate with one hemisphere of his brain while you fight against the other. And I'm just wondering, why the hell should we?"
I glanced at the Silent One. The Silent One smiled. And then he responded:

I cannot approach my own voice. This is the Law. But I can go and protect your city. I can feel that it has markings similar to those that were hanging over you a few minutes ago. Let's make it a fair deal: I will protect your loved ones and try to get you help. You go there and stop the Author.

I threw a glance at Mr. Meyers. He was red with rage.

"This isn't a fair deal. This is blackmail!"

The Silent Man bowed his head in an expression that showed he acknowledged this reproach.

"The main resonator is in the City of Players, and there are the Predators," Quinn said slowly.

The Silent Man nodded again.

This is true. But you will find a way, I am sure of that. Your story is woven into the history of this world from the very beginning, and breaking those ties is not so easy.

I saw sadness in his eyes. The Silent One was truly silent now, just waiting for an answer. Blackmail or not, a picture appeared before my eyes: Yana in the middle of the city, caught up in all this madness. I nodded slowly, accepting his terms, then restored the minimized notification and mentally clicked yes. The inscription flared up and disintegrated into golden sand, which streamed towards me like a serpentine ribbon and disappeared in the region of my solar plexus. Mr. Meyers turned away with a displeased look. The Silent One, smiling, nodded gratefully at me, then imitated a drum and opened the inventory.

* * *

Needless to say, his gifts were wonderful. This was the first time I'd seen any normal items in the damn game. The Silent One handed out one to each of us.

Quinn received a thin velvet ribbon to wear around her neck, giving her +4 in Acrobatics. She already had this skill, but it was now buffed to an impressive level. The girl's flexibility, strength and coordination improved immensely.

Quentin received a bracelet with +3 in Constitution. Three dozen HP was a good gift on its own, but the Silent One promised that the bracelet would present other useful properties in the future.

Fraudo got a ring. When he handed it over, the Silent One doubled over with silent laughter. The ring looked like something he had bought at a flea market for 3 cents. Faux ring for Faux-Frodo. The accepted the gift with a sour grin, but when he saw what the ring gave him, his displeasure vanished instantly. The artifact carried a special skill that made it possible to turn his shot into something similar to our magic ram. However, unlike our short-range ram, the arrow retained its lethal effect throughout its entire flight. To Fraudo's disappointment, the skill took fifteen minutes to recharge, but was still an excellent improvement: the not-Hobbit shot an arrow at a stunted tree growing a hundred paces from the well, and the unfortunate tree was uprooted — in its place, only a small crater remained.

For Camilla, the Silent One had also prepared an unusual gift. They were glasses. In Fantasia, everyone had the same perfect vision. I knew that there were several people living in the city who had made the transition just for this reason. Apparently, in real life the professor wore glasses, because now she looked at the Silent One with a strange expression on her face. But she accepted the gift. The Silent One explained that glasses increased Intelligence, but they also had another useful property: anyone who wore them could copy a spell from a book for themselves and have a 50% chance of saving the book. Councilor Tom Gallance would give everything he owned for such a skill. The Silent One also gifted Camilla several books.

Mr. Parks and Mr. Meyers refused the quest that had been offered to all members of the group. Mr. Parks explained his decision by the fact that consent, in fact, would mean entering the service of a certain political figure, which meant treason for us, and the fact that we accepted gifts from the afore-mentioned figure only exacerbated things. I stared at him incredulously. It was as if Mr. Parks had been somewhere else for the last few hours. I even tried to argue with him at length, but he was adamant. At the same time, he had no plans of leaving the detachment and fully agreed with the importance of the upcoming mission.

Mr. Meyers was also not going to leave the company, and refused the quest for his own reasons, which were apparently purely opportunistic.

When it was my turn, I must confess I couldn't help but feel excited. Fantasia was, of course, a game, but in fact there were insanely few valuable items and artifacts here, and most of them were concentrated in the City of Players. In the west, people tried to live their usual lives, buffing up their skills, most of which made it possible to more effectively cripple others, and were much less interested in other kinds of items. I was counting on a good increase in Intelligence or Wisdom, or better, both. Imagine my surprise when the Silent One handed me a ring, and I was surprised to read that it was a ring with Strength +4. I fought with spells. Why did I need strength? But the Silent One had shown that the strength would definitely come in handy for me. Wow!

Once all the gifts had been bestowed, the Silent One gathered us all in a semicircle. He looked upon us dully. He began to talk about our holograms. The missing parameters in the profiles of those infected. These things were a lot like viruses, leaving markings on people that could be passed on if one came in close contact with a carrier. They had been created by the voice of the Reader and therefore easily integrated into the world and its inhabitants. The Silent One said that he would teach everyone a spell with which they could remove a fresh marking, but warned that if they left it for too long (and not all of them created extreme thirst), then the spell would be of no help. You could fight the markers and the afflicted not only with weapons and spells, but also with calmness, courage and mercy. In a way, this is even more important, because many markings had long-term effects, and we had yet to understand ours.

We exchanged worried glances. Long term effects? What were other long-term effects? The Silent Man shrugged his shoulders and explained that he did not know for sure, and then began to show us a spell, which turned out to be very complicated in design. We repeated after him for a long time, until the program reported that the spell had been added to our libraries.

Before parting, the Silent One called me aside. After making sure that no one could see us, he took out another gift in the form of a small brooch. The artifact contained a shield spell that could be used even without Wisdom and Intelligence points. The Silent One explained that this gift was for Mr. Meyers. That he wouldn't want to accept it now out of pride, but that he would probably change his mind. The Silent One asked me to take it for safekeeping until the right moment presented itself to give the artifact to its rightful owner.

Chapter 7 [Sylvia]

SHE HAD A BORED LOOK on her face. The avatars of real players had pretty primitive emotions, but at least they tried, and she was trying very hard to make me notice. And I, of course, did notice.

"You look good," I said, and she immediately bristled.

There you go, give her a piece of our mind. I'll talk to you instead, since talking to myself is a terrible torment. It is almost impossible to communicate without being self-conscious, which is why each word can be taken any way you like, except at face value. I know it's hard to understand. Try to imagine that you are saying something to a person who already knows everything you want to say. Because it's you. And she always understands what you really mean, because she herself uses the same techniques.

"As you can see," I said, "I've done everything

I can. The city is ready to welcome ambassadors. There are people, there is a program, there is…"

"Forget it," she interrupted with a wave of her hand.

We were sitting at the table in the home I shared with Bryan. I would have preferred a cafe, but for some reason she insisted on a more private setting, so we were sitting in our living room. I think she would have given a lot for the opportunity to take a look at the second floor, but of course I wouldn't give it to her.

"What do you mean, 'Forget it?'"

"Something happened," she said. "Complications arose."

I went cold.

"What complications?"

"Teresa Hardy from the New York Times and a certain Alexandra Kotova, I don't remember what publication she's from, some Russian paper. Both died with the mortality mechanism enabled in the game. The doctors who were on duty next to the equipment tried to save both of them, but it didn't work. It turned out that deceiving the microprocessing system is much more complicated than it seems. The AI that controls the equipment knows how to get things done.

I choked.

"What the hell, Yana! Why did they enter the game before we prepared everything?"

"Please don't yell at me!" she snapped. "No one asked my permission…*Sylvia.*"

This again. The mocking way she said "Slyvia." Why? Because this was a name we both shared! As a child, we had a Sylvia doll, and each of us was Princess Sylvia, and then, of course, that one time in college...Hmm. And now one of us had really become Sylvia, the other felt that something had been taken from her.

"Wait," I said, raising my hands and sighing. "Let's start from the beginning. Teresa...We knew each other! God, how horrific! How did it happen?"

"In short, the story goes like this." Yana once again feigned condescending boredom. "The New York Times, it turns out, hired programmers to outsmart the mortality mechanism. The programmers assured us that no matter how smart Fantasia's AI was, it was still governed by the conditions we set, and that they could almost certainly deceive it. Most of the program was rejected by the AI and didn't connect, but several of the lines of code did pass, and they had a blocker built into them, which was supposed to prevent the death of the connecting person. One of these systems was used by Teresa. She appeared in the forest, according to their estimates, somewhere to the northwest of here. Not far from the city, and they were logging nearby. Everything was going well, until some creature jumped on Teresa from a tree. Teresa saw almost nothing: she was thrown to the ground, and then the mortality mechanism flipped on and, bypassing all the blockers, the beast pierced her artery. Causing immediate death."

I sat there listening and couldn't believe my ears. This whole story smacked of some dark mystery.

"It was a terrible scandal," said Yana. "And naturally, it didn't work in our favor. And most importantly, the number of willing ambassadorial candidates took a nosedive and is approaching null, except for a few weirdos."

"If the situation's that dire, we shouldn't be turning away the weirdos," I said.

She looked at me with a grin, and I immediately went berserk. What was she hinting at?!

"What the hell!" I threw back at her. "Aren't there war reporters? They could get killed just as easily on the battlefield!"

"When you get hit with a bullet, you know what's going on. But nothing is ever clear in the game," she retorted. "But in this case, the story gets even more tragic. The second journalist was killed in Moscow. In the editorial office of a large holding. Russian engineers also thought they could deceive the AI, but it didn't work out. But as you know, they never blame themselves.

I sat there trying to comprehend exactly what had happened. Then I looked back at her, searching for signs of deception. But the standard avatar sitting across from me was completely stone-faced.

'But she, too, is at the whim of the

microprocessors,' I thought, and my anger subsided a little. Now I understood why she insisted that we talk here.

"So what now?"

"Now the scandal surrounding Fantasia has gained a political flavor, and this, as you can understand, is very bad. Worst of all is that in the minds of people, the game is a direct threat to life. This greatly lowers our chances. The Russians claim that the game is a CIA project specially designed to harm them."

"Russians always say that."

"In this case, the opinion of many Americans is no better. Considering the fact that, in their opinion, the game was created by radical Islamists in order to destroy the Americans. If you remember the name of the game developer, you'll understand where they get their fuel."

Yana fell silent and I looked around helplessly. It was amazing that the fate of the whole world could be decided just like that! Her story had pulled the rug out from under my feet and only now did I realize how precarious our position was. And she knew! And had come here to tell me about it in her condescending, bored tone. And this was the same woman who had given everything to save this world and this person. I both understood and did not understand her, and this duality weighed terribly on my brain. Communicating with her was so hard! But absolutely necessary. And we both knew it.

"Listen, sister," I said, although both of us shuddered at this name, "Tell me you have some good news too!"

She looked over our living room for a while. Then she asked:

"How do you take a shower?"

I sighed slowly, then took a slow inhale.

"We fetch water from the well."

"And cook?"

I nodded towards the stove.

"Bryan lights it with a spell. It heats up pretty quickly, actually. And I'm sorry, it's just funny to watch a man on his hands and knees in front of the stove, casting Fireball."

She bit her lip, and the gesture gave her away. Even the dead-eyed camera of her VR helmet couldn't have missed it.

"How are you guys doing overall?" she asked, trying to sound as casual as possible.

Alas, I heard her bristle with every syllable. She knew it too, and immediately lashed out.

"Don't! Don't say it! I—"

"Yana, listen," I said. "You don't need to apologize."

"I wasn't apologizing."

"You were going to. You shouldn't! I know. I completely understand your interest. I'll tell you this much: this is a very strange place, and being here really tests you. And he..." I hesitated. "He became really different, I think...I don't know why it happened. He was in battle, but I still don't have a good idea of how it works here with all the spears and spells. But something changed him. He became more attentive, sharper. At the same time, he works in intelligence, which does who knows what. He doesn't even want to hear about the administrative side of things. Just imagine it! But still, of course, at times..."

"Stop," she asked suddenly.

I fell silent.

I couldn't see it, but judging by the tone of her voice, my conversation partner had grown pale. Apparently she had gotten more information than she had bargained for. Hell. There was nothing more to say. It was better if they just sticked to their old way of doing it — only discuss work. We sat in silence for a while. Then I got up, made myself a cup of tea and returned to my seat. Yana was hunched over on a stool. I felt sorry for her, of course. And for myself too, given the news she had brought.

"I had one idea," she suddenly said in a hoarse voice. "I talked with the guys, and they think that, in principle, it could be done. We don't know exactly how the game will react, but we could try."

I froze, my tea lifted halfway to my mouth, then set it down on the table.

"What idea?"

"It's impossible to establish live feeds inside of Fantasia because the layout inside the existing neural network is still not fully understood," said

Yana, unexpectedly flashing her professional jargon — or something like that. "But we can hone in on the codes of the Digital Human Copies within the game. Theoretically, nothing prevents us from intercepting the flow of visual information, which is coded in a way we understand, before hacking into their digital brains. The Creator didn't invent anything new, in this case. Theoretically, we could set up our own stream on one of these channels. Do you understand what I'm getting at?"

I didn't. So far, I didn't understand anything.

"This is a rather risky undertaking, because, in fact, the game is very careful about its own autonomy. But as long as we don't set up multiple channels, just the one — then, perhaps, there would be no serious consequences."

I raised my hands in protest.

"Stop! I don't understand. You want to broadcast the mind of someone from real life into the mind of one of our local residents?"

Yana nodded.

"If it's this hard to send an ambassador to Fantasia, you should think about sending ambassadors from Fantasia to our side," she suggested.

I was somewhat taken aback by this turn in the conversation.

"I...how do you imagine that would happen?"

"I've already figured out the plan. And it's pretty simple. Some of the inhabitants of Fantasia must find a level and safe area, at least thirty by thirty feet. Someone should have a black blindfold and earplugs with them. He puts them on and blocks most of the incoming flow of visual and auditory information from Fantasia. After that, we begin to transmit information from the real world into his head in a way that has already been rewritten to work with his coding. The channel works in both directions, and we even hope that it will even be possible to track the movements of the arms and legs.

"You mean to say," I said, hardly believing my ears, "you'd be able to connect a DHC to reality using...a VR device?"

"That's right," Yana affirmed. "If all goes well, the ambassador will have to be able to speak in the name of the new government. There will be a lot of people watching, and the responsibility, as you understand, is not a small one. It must be someone who understands life here much better than me, for example, or even you. Sorry. You say Ste — Bryan has changed for the better? He's more clever? Well, if he can't do it, maybe no one else can."

I looked at her in amazement. I didn't understand. Is this all an intricate plan to test what I had said about him?

"Brain's not in town," I said mechanically. "He left to investigate some case he's working on..."

"When he comes back, then—"

"Hold on. Why Bryan? There's Tom Gallance, a councilor to the city, who would be much better suited for the job. There are other councilors, people who have been playing for much longer than—"

"You don't understand," she interrupted me, and I fell silent, astonished, and once again lost. "I want it to be Brain. That's my condition, and you'll have to agree, because the plan won't work without me."

She pulled herself together on her chair.

"But why?" I managed to get out.

For the first time, I couldn't understand her motivation. Our paths had begun to diverge. I had been following the plotline so carefully, but suddenly it ran off the rails. She leaned across the table to me and said angrily:

"Because I sacrificed all I had for him. And now I want to understand what he's willing to sacrifice to save your precious little world, alright?! Because I want to know that my sacrifice was worth something! And then I found him in bed with some…" she still refused to say this word. "He was somehow able to forget about it. And I don't want him to forget, understand?"

I sat leaning back in my chair, completely floored by this confession. And she, without waiting for my reaction, logged out. Her avatar melted into thin air. The house was empty. As was my head. Only one thought wandered somewhere in the distance: I have to find Bryan.

CHAPTER 8

THE MORNING WAS GRAY and hazy. Moisture settled on all surfaces, soaked the fabric, squelched in our shoes. We drove East, and soon the outlines of the forest appeared through the fog. In this very spot six months ago, a hundred scouts had tried to stop the advance of the Predator army towards the City of DHCs. They weren't successful, and the enemy lost a lot of people on the breakthrough. Enemies burned the log barricades with spells, making their way through the fire. The forest was on fire, although I could no longer see it: half-dead from fatigue, I galloped to the city, thinking only of how to escape from the enemy on my heels. There it was, a landmark of military glory.

Not so long ago, everything here had been painted black with ash, but time had passed, and the forest was gradually recovering: grass had started to push its way through the earth again, the animals had returned, and in many places, the foliage was snaking its way through the dead trees. And yet, enough charred trunks remained to remind of those events.

We rode along a precipice to the left of the road. We had once organized an ambush at the top of it. As we rode, I recalled the details of the story of the Silent Man, trying to understand how it was that we still managed, as Mr. Meyers put it, to get caught up in the fight between the hemispheres of this man's brain. Who were we to him? The inhabitants of his world? A tool to achieve his goals? In fact, why had we so easily accepted all the explanations he had offered? However, I knew why. I remembered that the Silent Man was talking about the second shot that the new world had given each of us (including the Silent Man). Maybe this was true when it came to me. But the Silent Man, I remember, had appealed to all of us, and no one had refused. But how could this be? Fraudo was riding on the left, and I asked him if the game had ever given him a choice like that. The not-Hobbit shrugged hesitantly.

"I don't know," he said after a pause. "When we were in that mess up six months ago, I kept wondering how I had gotten myself tangled up in all that bullshit. But now...you know, Warchan, I'm trying to remember what was so important about my past life. And nothing comes to mind! I was the most ordinary kid, worked in a diner three blocks from my house, smoked weed, hung out with the boys...overall, nothing special. Here, of course, everything is different, and sure, at times life's a lot harder than it was back at home. But I ask myself, would I wanna go back? And then I realize the question doesn't make any sense, because even if I went back, I'm not the same kid anymore, you know? And nothing would ever be able to put me back in my old shoes again."

I looked at my old friend with astonishment for saying such things. Yes, perhaps he really has changed since the first night we met in the forest to the south. I turned and looked at Camilla, who was riding from the other side. She was wearing the glasses, which suited her. But the artifact was strange, to be sure. You can easily keep a ring or bracelet on forever without taking them off, but what about glasses? Camilla looked at me and, anticipating my question, said:

"That's right, Bryan. Apparently, the transition granted each of us some opportunity to change our destiny. Me too. But I would not like to dwell on this now."

I nodded.

"Understood. You know Professor, I wouldn't be surprised if the game presented opportunities to those who fled here in search of those very opportunities...But I myself am living proof that everything is different. After all, I was not looking for another life, and no computer program could have known that everything would turn out in this way."

"Perhaps not. It's just…"

"Yes?"

"None of that's important now, Bryan. We're here. And we do what we're told. We're working on our second shot. Maybe your Silent Friend wasn't planning on putting us through the ropes, but that's what he did.

She waved her hand, then spurred her horse on and rode past me. Mr. Parks rode up to fill her place.

"And you, Mr. Parks? Also ended up in the game by accident?"

The spy turned his head to me. The expression on his face was as if he did not understand the question, but I knew him well enough: he not only understood, but also heard and remembered every word that had been said before. I thought he wouldn't answer. I was wrong.

"In my situation, Mr. Mursley, it's clearly a second shot. I would even say it was strikingly clear. However, I am not a fatalist and am not inclined to believe in some mysterious unseen hand."

"And what was this second chance, if it's not a secret?"

I certainly didn't expect an answer to this question, but Mr. Parks surprised me again:

"In the old reality, I'm sitting in a jail cell," he said simply. "And in all likelihood, I'll never get out again. Until they cart me out in a box. Are you satisfied?"

I certainly was satisfied...Wow! How did it turn out that the right hand of the chief of intelligence of our city was a criminal? I wonder what he's in prison for? I looked at Mr. Parks and saw in his eyes that he perfectly heard my unspoken question, but this time there would be no answer. I can't say that the information shocked me in any way. However, I was curious.

A quarter of an hour later, we reached the familiar rocky ledge, behind which I sat as I watched Stork's army approach on that memorable day. The forest was burned here more than anywhere else, because it was in this spot that we had barricaded the path with fallen trees and the Predators started to burn their way through. A stone canine tooth, reminiscent of a milestone, was in place, and I noticed birds circling above it. Large black birds. Lazily flapping their wings, they wound unhurried circles over the protruding stone, as if imbuing the place with some kind of mysterious symbolism.

We rounded the cliff and stopped. There was something in the road ahead that we couldn't see because of the creatures surrounding it. It seemed that representatives of all the forest residents had gathered here: a couple of wild boars, an elk, several wolves, hares and some sort of rodents, as well as a creature that looked like a mid-sized bear, possibly a wolverine. And among those gathered there were several creatures I wasn't familiar with - stocky two-legged beasts with long, pointed ears protruding out to the side like Master Yoda's. The creatures were covered in short, dark fur, with large eyes and wide toad mouths. Gremlins? There were many birds in the trees on either side of the road.

As soon as we rounded the bend, the crowd of creatures, as if on command, turned their muzzles and froze, staring at us. The horde of forest dwellers didn't number anywhere close to the army of monsters that had walked this road not so long ago, and yet I felt a chill running through my skin. This whole silent scene was terribly strange — animals don't act like that! I had a feeling that we had interrupted some sort of secret ritual and the practitioners now stood frozen, understanding the awkwardness of the moment. The moment dragged on and on, and suddenly I caught a movement, not among those standing on the road, but further down in the shade of the trees. Someone was there. Someone human.

The man waved his hand, and time started again. The forest dwellers silently rushed towards us. The distance separating us was no more than a hundred feet, and there were so many animals. I thought with horror that there were enough of them to simply demolish our small detachment, but the faint-hearted thought flashed and left, and meanwhile, my hands got to work. A fireball ripped from my palm and shot towards the attackers. But before it reached its target, the boar, rushing in the front, was struck by Frodo's arrow that struck with the force of a ram. The effect was as if a truck rushing at full speed had crashed into the unfortunate pig. The crumpled boar flew back, leaving a clearing in the ranks of the animals running behind him, and then my fireball hit the ground, breaking into hundreds of fiery drops that splashed right and left. Our logs were full of damage messages. The wave of attackers hesitated and halted, and I felt the thrill of the battle awaken inside me.

We used the short interlude to dismount. If we were facing an ordinary enemy, we could try to fight them from our saddles, but now I was afraid that if the creatures managed to get close enough, the horses might get scared and buck, and the diameter of the magic shield was too small to cover both the rider and his horse. The decision turned out to be not only correct, but also very timely, because in the next moment the birds entered the fray. I'd seen Hitchcock — I knew these little dinosaurs with wings could pose a very serious threat. I just didn't expect it. None of us did. And, I must admit, if it were not for the shields, we would have been in a bad spot. The spell worked in such a way that it was possible to penetrate the translucent sphere, but only at a very slow speed. Feathered shells stuck in the barrier, fluttering and emitting heart-wrenching shrieks. Then, the larger animals arrived and the real battle broke out.

Huddled together in a dense group and covered with our magic domes, we fired, stabbed and burned, trying our best not to hurt each other and our own horses. As soon as one of the shields burst, the birds pierced through and rained down upon us. A second later, a new sphere flashed, which immediately began to be covered with new screaming carcasses. Fighting in cramped quarters was uncomfortable, and Quinn, seizing the moment, twisted herself out of the line of fire and slid to the side. I shouted for her to get back under the protective dome immediately, but the girl just grinned. And then...I have never seen a person move with such speed and grace in my life. The short spear, which had only recently become her constant companion, struck with the speed of my lightning, and at the same time she managed to dodge the many attacks that rained down on her from all sides.

I was running out of mana, and there was no time to gulp down a potion, so I was already ready to grab the bow, although I realized that it was not much use in close combat, I couldn't afford to lower my shield, and shooting required the use of both hands...And then my gaze fell on a short thick branch lying on the ground. Without thinking twice, I grabbed it and swung it down onto the face of the wolf that was rushing through the barrier. I did not expect a big effect, wanting to scare the beast away rather than wound it, and was very surprised when the wolf collapsed to the ground as if knocked down. I looked in surprise at the branch in my hand, but then I remembered the power boost that the Silent Man's ring gave me.

Meanwhile, the creatures' attacks were growing weaker. Fortunately, many of the attackers, having received even minor damage, immediately lost motivation and retreated into the forest. As soon as I had a free moment, I glanced over to where I had previously noticed a figure among the trees. The man stood in the same place, watching the battle, but not interfering. Was that who I thought it was? If so, then we had the unique chance to end this journey before it even began.

I nudged Fraudo in the side and pointed to the mysterious observer. The not-Hobbit understood my meaning immediately and, after shooting another arrow towards a stubborn gremlin, who was trying to stab Camilla with a long stone knife, rushed towards the horses. I follow him.

"Cover us!" I cried, already mounting my saddle.

However, the man was not going to wait us to approach him. Seeing that his henchmen's attack had failed, he turned and rushed headlong into the forest. He ran quickly and dexterously and could well have broken away from the chase — but not on my watch. Had I not climbed through all these damn forests while we were preparing to ambush the Predators?! I knew every path here, and I wasn't about to let this damn druid go unpunished.

However, we soon had to dismount. The fugitive had retreated to the north and the terrain here was mountainous, covered with deep ruts and signs of landslides around the edges. We continued our pursuit, trying not to lose his red dot on the map. It was not easy, as the man moved very swiftly. Before, I would have definitely fallen behind due to my lagging stamina, but now, with three additional strength points, I had no difficulty keeping pace.

We caught up with him in ten minutes. The path took us to a small clearing surrounded by fluffy blue spruces that grew so close to each other that they looked like a hedge. The man stood in the center of the clearing with his back to us, but even from this angle, I realized that this was not Jarkhan-Ali. It was not a standard avatar, and the person did not move like a player from the real world.

"Stop!" I cried.

The man had no intention of running away. He turned slowly towards us. A ragged beard, dirty hair hanging down like icicles, tattered clothes — he looked less like a powerful magician who ruled over forest creatures than a beggar. And only the look in his dull black eyes hinted at the fact that he had just tried to send us to our Final Quest. He looked emaciated and incapable of resisting any further, but suddenly a spasm went through his body, a grimace distorted his thin-lipped mouth, and he raised his hands, twisting his joints in a strange, unnatural way. But the spell was not cast as it was interrupted by Fraudo's arrow, equipped with a rolling ram. The man was caught like a feather and thrown straight into the wall of bluish needles. He slid to the ground and remained motionless, as spruce needles rained down on him.

We approached carefully. The fugitive was unconscious, but still breathing. Close up, he looked terribly small, somehow shrunken. His eyes suddenly opened wide, black pupils trembling finely. The man wheezed and coughed, covering his filthy caftan with drops of blood, and after a moment I was surprised to see that he was laughing. A new spasm made his back arch, and then a single word came through all his coughing and wheezing: "Help!"

"Hold him!" I ordered Fraudo and closed my eyes, recalling the spell that the Silent Man had taught us.

The spell was difficult, but the main problem was that it required a huge amount of mana, and I was practically empty. Grabbing a bottle of blue liquid from my inventory, I ripped off the wax stopper with my teeth and tipped the potion into my mouth without even tasting it. Then I took a few deep breaths to even out my breathing and began to recite the incantation. Obeying the order, Fraudo came in from the other side and knelt down, holding the man by the shoulders, although he did not think to escape, but simply lay there, shaking his head senselessly from side to side. However, as soon as the first glimpses of light flashed between my fingers, any sense of calmness left him as if a switch had been flipped.

The man roared, grabbed Fraudo by his arms and suddenly threw him aside with great force, as if he were not a withered bum, but a professional MMA fighter. Fraudo, not expecting such agility, rolled across the earth. The druid looked at me with a hazy gaze, and his own palms also flashed — not with white light, like mine, but with a pale green. And the next second, an incomprehensible force hit me in the chest, knocking the wind out of me, crushing bones and twisting the veins into a knot. I was lifted off the ground and thrown back. The impact on the ground knocked out the rest of the air from my lungs, and I lay there, opening my mouth, like a fish cast ashore. But it was impossible to lie down, and, having gathered all my will into a fist, I forced myself to get up.

A few steps away from me, our enemy rose from the ground. He lifted his body without using his hands, as if he was being pulled by an invisible thread at the top of his head. Tracks of greenish light wrapped around his body, forming a ghostly vortex. I raised my left hand and folded my fingers into the shield, noticing out of the corner of my eye that Fraudo was also back on the battlefield. My right palm barely felt the usual surge of energy when a desperate cry came from behind me.

"No-o-o!"

I spun around. It was our guys rushing down the path, and at the head — Dr. Harris.

"To-o-m!"

I turned back to the druid and noticed that his feet weren't touching the ground — the green funnel, like a small but very powerful tornado, kept him aloft. Tom's dirty hair fluttered, his pointed face two black holes for eyes slowly turned towards the running woman. The green funnel flashed brighter. I rushed to intercept Camilla, but didn't have time — a bolt of ghostly energy escaped from the surface of the funnel and hit her in the chest. With a short cry, the professor collapsed to the ground. The druid, having drained his energy, sank to the ground, and then another spasm rocked through his body. When the attack subsided, Tom looked up, and I saw that the haze was gone from his eyes. Instead, there was only unspeakable suffering. He dropped to his knees, holding out his arms to the open woman. This was our chance. I darted forward, fingers intertwining to perform the spell. But I was too late. We all were.

Tom snatched a short dagger from his belt and, without the slightest hesitation, drove it into his throat. His body fell to one side with a thud. The pool of dark blood grew rapidly. Spruce needles floated across the surface.

* * *

Camilla was alive. Even though she had been infected with the marking. Just like me and Fraudo. Fortunately for us, this one wasn't as bad as the *thirst*. To be honest, we had no idea how it worked. But I had to wait it out for a long time. Only I could cast the Silent Man's spell, but I also had to replenish my mana several times in order to remove the marking from everyone. Then we buried Tom, and as a result sat in the clearing almost until dusk. Everyone was in a depressed mood. Camilla did not say a word in response to our timid attempts to express our condolences to her. So we ate in silence and began to prepare for the next leg of our journey. No one wanted to spend the night next to Tom's grave.

Packing up camp dragged on a lot longer than usual because of the horses. Apparently, there really was something wrong with this place, because our horses became restless, let out long whinnies, chomped at the bit and looked sideways at their owners in disbelief. After a while, we nevertheless left this ill-fated place and, returning to the road, continued to move east. Everyone was already in low spirits, and then it started raining again. We rode, wrapped in raincoats and pausing every minute to soothe the horses.

Soon we reached the Okwe — a small rivulet that finds its source in the mountains and flows into Ikwen in the south. Six months ago, General

Obelix brought down the only bridge that led across the river in an attempt to delay the advance of the Predators westward. It was unsuccessful — our enemy built a pontoon bridge in half a day and drove us into the forest. This bridge still held up even now, although it was in shoddy condition. However, we didn't plan to cross the river yet. To the south of here, in the place where the Okwe ran into a larger river, in the middle of the wetlands stood another circle of black stones, and our path lay in that direction. After some discussion, we decided to spend the night here and move on tomorrow.

I woke up early the next morning feeling a little strange. My head was pounding as if I'd been on a bender the previous evening. And for some reason my whole body itched. I must have been bitten by the local ants. However, perhaps my body was simply reminding me of the need for regular hygiene, so I went to the river to wash.

The water in the Okwe river was cold. I rinsed my face and felt an unusual sensation when touching my own skin. Apparently, my face was sunburnt. I rubbed my eyes and bent over the stream, trying to assess how bad things were. An eerie mask gazed at me from the surface of the water, and I staggered back in fear. Jumping ashore, I pulled off my clothes with trembling hands, whimpering with horror. My clothes were cracked and torn, clinging to the hard, horny, brick-colored scales that stood out against the skin. They covered my entire body, and on my head my fingers clearly felt the piercing sharp projections of horns.

Here were the consequences that the Silent Man had spoken about. It was like a nightmare come true. I was turning into a monster.

CHAPTER 9

THIS WAS — AND I SAY THIS without hyperbole — the worst morning of my life. And it seemed I wasn't alone. Everyone who drank that damn well water showed signs of change.

I'd seen a lot of things in this game. I'd survived being uprooted from my comfortable life and transported into this imaginary shithole, I had been a slave, I'd fought against enemies in a real (although not very long) war, was beaten, humiliated and crushed, and yet nothing had inspired as much despair as I felt at this moment. Even the little that I managed to get back — how could I save it now? I knew what I was becoming. These red-skinned demons were often found among the Predators — huge horned creatures with predatory faces. How would I be able to show this face to Yana?! No matter what lovers and philosophers may say, no relationship could withstand such a test. Who would be able to stand living next to a monster? And I had never heard of cases where this had been reversed. Predators have always been Predators. And I was now one of them. The natural enemy of man, a creature, the sight of which causes people to faint — or run and grab a sword.

We used up all our mana, trying to cleanse ourselves with the Silent Man's spell, but we knew our efforts were in vain. Our bodies had changed, and so we now had to wander around this world until some merciful hand ended our miserable existence.

The horse's reactions were the final nail in the coffin. Now we knew why they had been so restless the day before. They felt that something was wrong with their owners. When I had approached Starlet, the horse had gone berserk. Her reigns prevented her from escaping, but her hysterical whinny and attempts to buck me spoke was evidence enough. She wasn't going to let the monster her master was turning into anywhere near her, and this suddenly made me feel so awful that I sat down on the ground and burst into tears like a three-year-old. It was an absurd scene: a scaly demon sitting on the bank of the river, bawling in despair, and next to it a horse with a white star on its forehead straining to get away.

I don't know how long I sat there. I don't know how the others felt. To be perfectly honest, I didn't give a damn. I knew that my life was over and I didn't have any idea what would happen next. And then the answer came. At least I still had something left to live for. Revenge. The only thing that still made sense. I must find and destroy the one who created all this! And it was not just Jarkhan-fucking-Ali. If the Reader had been around, I would have pounced on him without hesitation! It was he who read this damn world and these fucking rules! That hoity-toity Oxford-accent asshole! But I had been stupid enough to believe him — I thought he was on our side! But now it was clear that there were no more sides. There was me, the monster, and there was them, the creatures that did this to me. And they would pay!

I got up heavily from the ground and looked around. The other members of the detachment were scattered along the river bank. Someone was crying, like me. Another spewed curses. Those who were fortunate enough to remain human huddled together in a bunch, looking at us in horror. I assembled the detachment.

"Listen, everyone," I said and stopped short when I heard that the changes affected not only my appearance, but also the tone of my voice, which had become lower.

"Bryan!" Camilla said quietly. "Don't give up hope! I'm sure there's..."

"No," I said, looking her in the eyes.

Oh, how quickly and obediently she fell silent! Without a doubt, my new appearance inspired fear. And the others' appearances were no less effective. Frodo was clearly turning into an orc. His dark skin had already begun to change color. Fangs appeared in the mouth, causing him to lisp. What a surprise — the ring-bearing Hobbit had become an Uruk-hai. Quinn's slender figure had grown even thinner, and it seemed that she had grown half a foot taller overnight. These creatures were familiar to me too — long, emaciated, coal-black bodies with reed-like hands and legs. The same thing had happened to Mr. Meyers. Quentin, in contrast, had slumped in on himself and shrank. He was already sporting a second chin.

"There's no way," I continued. "If there were, there would be precedents. And they're aren't."

Everyone was silent, eyes downcast.

"I'm calling the mission off," I continued, and my words fell around me with the weight of boulders. "It doesn't make sense anymore. We cannot approach the city, because the city will never accept us in this form."

"But..." Camilla began, but then fell silent under my gaze.

"I'm disbanding the detachment. Each of you is free to decide your own destiny. However, I want to inform you that I will continue to keep moving forward. Not to protect this world from being threatened. I'm going to make the creature that did this to us pay for his actions. You can come with me, if you want. But keep in mind—" I paused, looking at their faces " — that from now on our goal is not protecting the weak, not noble self-sacrifice and not heroism in the name of a just cause. I am going to take revenge, and I will show no mercy to those who stand in my way! I'm not fighting for hope or justice. I'm going to kill and most likely be killed. You decide if you're ready for that!"

I got up and, not hearing anyone's reply, went to the water. An echoing emptiness spread through my mind, and any thought I had was so painful that I tried my best to keep this emptiness undisturbed. I didn't look back at my men, but heard their quiet conversations behind my back. Maybe they were better at dealing with the neverending tension than I was. Well, fantastic! I was happy for them. As for myself, I knew one thing for sure: the game was over, and the reality was more than just harsh. It was unbearable.

I sat by the water for about ten minutes, looking at the current and not thinking about anything, and then I noticed that I no longer heard voices behind me and turned around. They were all standing just a few steps away, and I realized that they had made a decision. Well, I must admit that their choice warmed my soul a little, even if this warmth was no more than a smoldering cigarette butt at the North Pole. But at least I wouldn't be alone. After a short discussion, we set the horses free. Mills, Mr. Parks and the professor unsaddled them, because the horses would not let anyone else come close, and once they were free, they immediately rushed along the road to the west. We reluctantly walked south on foot.

Soon, the ground began to squelch underfoot. The soil became muddy, and our footprints were instantly filled with murky water, wafting a rotten smell into the air. Everyone found a branch to use as a walking stick, but our progress slowed significantly. Big, open patches of water among the grasses were becoming more and more frequent, and from time to time, our sticks sank so deep into the water that it became clear that we wouldn't be able to cross so easily.

I walked ahead, carefully checking the depth with my walking stick before every step, but even this did not save me. At one point, a small mound that had seemed quite sturdy groaned and went under, taking my leg with it. I tried to lean on my stick to keep my balance, but the damn thing suddenly sank in deeper too, and I fell forward. The mud enveloped me with a loud slurping sound, and I immediately felt myself starting to be sucked in. I started floundering and screaming, but that only made things worse. In the end, I was dragged out to a relatively firm plot of land. All my clothes were now a single, mud-crusted unit, but somehow I didn't feel the cold. Perhaps it was the scales covering more and more of my skin with each passing hour. I grinned to myself — how timely my transformation into a scaly monster had been! This was my new natural habitat. I furiously slashed my nails (which were gradually turning into claws) across my new skin and, unable to restrain myself, exclaimed:

"Fucking scales! What the fuck is this?!"

The question was rhetorical, but Camilla answered unexpectedly.

"Races. I think that's what this is about."

"What?!"

"I think this is how he wanted to create new races."

"Why not just let the players choose their own race like they do in normal games?!"

"Because race isn't something you can choose," Camilla said. Whatever you're born as, you die as. But more importantly, race is not just physical. Jarkhan-Ali understood that elves differ from humans not only in the shape of their ears, but also, for example, in their dislike for gnomes..."

I looked at her, thinking she was joking, but the professor was completely serious.

"What the hell are you talking about?!"

Dr. Harris looked at me, and I could tell that she regretted starting this conversation. The words stuck in my throat. She wasn't to blame for what happened to us.

"I'm sorry, Camilla," I said, lowering my head. "Please, continue, I'm actually interested in what you think about this."

The others voiced agreement. The professor cheered up a little.

"This is just a guess, but I think Jarkhan-Ali

was trying to create some contextual difference for the races. Skin color, nose or ear shape — all these differences are not particularly significant, and they would be easy to ignore. Especially considering that the people playing the game are adults. Roughly speaking, even if we see a monster in front of us, we understand that there is an ordinary person inside."

I involuntarily gritted my teeth. It made a frightening sound and I quickly covered my mouth with my hand.

"Traumatic experiences, on the other hand, are a different matter. They can change people, and in a pretty significant way. I think he was trying to do just that. Roughly speaking, if you take a person who will be tortured by gnomes, and then give him sharp ears and a thin skeleton, then you end up with an elf not only outside, but also inside."

"Monstrous!" Fraudo concluded indignantly.

Camilla nodded.

"So it is. But gods cannot be creatures with human morality."

"Christ wasn't evil!"

"Christ didn't create the world," retorted the professor with a slight grin. "But his daddy was pretty harsh!"

"Not true! In the Bible, it says…"

"Son, have you actually read the Bible? The Old Testament? Christ was a Jewish preacher, if anything. And the oldest chapters of the Bible describe horrors that many dictators never dreamed of."

Fraudo's eyes widened. I sighed.

After about an hour of wandering through the swamp, we came across a river. More precisely, a branch of the river. The Okwe split into many small streams, and one of them was blocking our way. The stream was small, but its banks were a completely impenetrable bog, and we had to stop. The sun was already setting, but its warmth was still sufficient, and my dry clothes were stiff and hard to move in. Soon, however, I would not need clothes — my scaly skin was perfect for walking around naked, especially since the cold didn't seem to bother me. But I was one of the lucky ones. Quentin was the worst off. His new guise was heavy and clumsy. If he fell into the swamp, I'm not sure we would have had the strength to pull the hippopotamus out.

For some time we wandered back and forth along the stream that blocked our path, trying to figure out what to do next. An attempt to make a fire failed quickly, as there was no dry firewood to be found. The dark wall of the forest loomed far to the west, a river babbled in the east, and the swamp pushed in on us from all sides. And we were all being swarmed by mosquitoes. During the day, their numbers had been low, but apparently the news of the arrival of warm-blooded animals had spread like wildfire through the mosquito communities, and more and more regiments of bloodsuckers flocked to their prey. Mosquitoes! Who in their right mind would dream up a world with mosquitoes? If only there was a breeze. Suddenly my thought caught on the word "breeze" and the next second I burst out laughing.

Everyone stared at me with amazement and a little fear. Indeed, the gnashing sounds emanating from my mouth did not resemble human laughter. Winking at the dumbfounded comrades, I threw my stick to the ground, closed my eyes for a moment, and then spread my arms and pushed myself off the ground.

I had completely forgotten about levitation! In fact, I hardly ever used it in my daily life, because the fluctuations in gravity upset my stomach terribly. But still, a levitating magician almost drowning in a swamp really is funny. I looked down and saw the elongated faces (and muzzles) of my friends. Shouting to them that I wasn't leaving them, but just wanted to look around, I happily climbed a couple hundred feet, finally feeling the long-awaited breeze on my face.

This was perhaps the first real joy I had felt since our metamorphosis. Until now, flying for me has always been associated with stress — first of all, because it's really difficult, and secondly, because I used it mainly during combat missions. But now, flying was just freedom, and I was loving it.

I couldn't see too far in the twilight, but still I made out the swamp continuing on the other side of the stream. Somewhere beyond, Ikwen slowly bore its waters downstream. However, it was not the river that attracted my attention, as I wouldn't have been able to see it due to the distance and deepening darkness. Something else had caught my eye.

A mile from the stream there was a small hill on which I saw tiny black dots. I was pretty sure I was seeing another fucking resonator, but I pulled out my telescope and aimed it at the target to be sure. There was no doubt. The hill was crowned with a circle of crooked black stones. But it wasn't the stones that set my whole body aflame. It was the tiny light that could be seen between the stones. Someone had lit a fire at the top.

* * *

I didn't waste any time thinking. Even if there was a road by land, it would take my friends at least an hour to get up to the hill. And through the swamp, most likely, even longer. But if HE really was there, I could destroy him without any help. After all, he was just a real player with a level hardly much higher than the third. In addition, my rage now gave me such strength that it seemed I could set the whole damn hill on fire.

At first I was going to go and warn my friends, but then I decided this was useless. Time was precious — the enemy could hide, and then I'd have to look for him in the dark. Besides, I was afraid that they might talk me out of it. Glancing at the bunch of people waiting for me below, I pulled out a couple of vials of mana from my inventory, drank one, and then moved gravity so that it pushed me from the south, and rushed like an arrow towards the hill. The wind whistled in my ears, but I still didn't feel the cold. Perhaps there were advantages in my new appearance, although I would prefer to be freezing and in my normal body. However, it did not matter in the slightest. Nothing really mattered at all, except for that gradually growing spark! And with every foot, I felt the purpose of my journey edging closer. Then I saw him: a tiny figure standing by the fire, and from that moment the rest of the world ceased to exist.

I reached the hill in a minute. Now I clearly saw a man standing by the fire, and any last doubt I had vanished. It was the standard real-life player avatar in a long cloak. I did not notice any weapons on him, although he could have them in his inventory, but so be it! I'd be happy if this bastard tried to resist. The only thing that mattered was making sure he didn't have time to escape to the real world — this is what I was most afraid of! If that happened, we'd have to stand guard here for God knows how long.

At first, my plan was to attack him from the air, but I surprised myself by slowing down, turning around and going to land. I had to look him in the eye before unleashing my entire arsenal of weapons of destruction on him.

I had a relatively smooth landing (experience had taught me) a good twenty feet (a bad experience had taught me) from him and stepped towards the black stones, hearing the growing muttering of the Voice.

"Well, look who it is! At last!" cried Jarkhan-Ali, and a joyful smile lit up his face.

* * *

I looked at him. The Creator of this whole fucking reality.

Do you know what a standard male avatar looks like in most video games? Slim with dark, shoulder-length hair. The diamond-shaped eyes, combined with the straight line of the cheekbones, make him look a bit like an anime character. There were some mechanisms available for customizing players' avatars, but Jarkhan-Ali did not use them. Now, however, I noticed some resemblance to the Silent Man. Perhaps the standard avatar was copied from him, albeit with some adjustments.

"Jarkhan...Ali?" I asked.

He, smiling, nodded.

I could have asked him something, probably could have squeezed from him another version of the story told by the Silent Man, but I wasn't going to. Enough! I've heard enough! Instead, I stepped forward, raising my arms and preparing to hit him with two bolts of lightning. And he just stood there and kept grinning, the goddamn son of a bitch! I could almost see that grin contort into a grimace of pain as the muscles contracted with electricity, but nothing of the sort happened. Lightning struck the shield raised with lightning speed, powerlessly dancing over it like white snakes.

"I like your style!" Jarkhan-Ali shouted gleefully. "No pointless verbal preludes, eh?! Right to business! Ha! No wonder he Heard you!"

I didn't hear him. I was thinking, looking at my mana pool.

Mana: 128 / 150

I hit him again, with equal success. I tried Fireball, but the flame dripped helplessly over his rainbow sphere. The burning drops set fire to the grass around the border of the shield, but that was it.

How did this asshole have this kind of shield? Although, on the other hand, why not? If he had enough mana, he could hold a shield. But no shield could withstand such an attack! I should know! I used Shield all the time! I felt faint. What was I doing?! Who knows what powers this creature possessed?

Mana: 65 / 150

Desperately, I dropped my hands. Jarkhan-

Ali stood there, completely calm.

I suddenly realized that my options were now limited to two: run or...go for broke, that is, throw yourself under the shield, hit with a ram or lightning, pull out the sword, finish him off. But although I was plenty angry at the time, I didn't lose my head, and instead spread my arms and crouched down, preparing to take off. I suddenly realized that I was afraid of him! The moment I made my decision, my fear seemed to materialize from somewhere inside me. And, as it turned out, that feeling wasn't unfounded.

Jarkhan-Ali raised his hands, and the earth beneath me sprang to life, becoming liquid. I fell into it ankle-deep, and the shock that should have sent me into the sky died out in the quagmire. At the same time, the spell worked, I was in a field with zero gravity. My stomach immediately rolled up to my throat, and I suppressed the spasm with difficulty. Then I realized that I could turn on gravity, and did so immediately. I jerked upward, and the viscous stuff below me hissed, closing tightly around my ankles. Now I looked like a rocket tied to a rope, unable to take off. My mana quickly exhausted itself and I collapsed to the ground. Black tentacles instantly gripped me from all sides, hindering any movement.

Jarkhan-Ali walked towards me, still smiling like a doll.

"Why didn't you introduce yourself, Mr. Mursley? That's a bit impolite of you!"

The next moment, an electric shock ran through my body, bringing with it such pain that I let out a cry, which broke into a screech.

You took 1 HP damage

God, so much pain for just one hit point?! I had no doubt that if he decided to kill me with this spell, I would lose my mind long before my health ran out!

Jarkhan-Ali came close to my body. By this point, the black ooze had completely paralyzed my limbs.

"You came," he said, his mouth once again stretching into an eerie smile. "And now you're mine, Warchan."

He hit me again with his sadistic spell, and I felt my teeth shattering and crumbling in my mouth.

You took 1 HP damage

Jarkhan-Ali bent down, and the black goo leaned towards him, as if presenting the prey it caught to its master.

"You will help me fix this world, my friend," the Author said calmly, looking into my eyes.

"F...fu...fuck off." I immediately regretted saying it, almost breaking into tears with the realization that there may be retribution for my insolence. But he didn't hit me this time. He just stood there, looking at me, completely calm.

"You will not only help me, but do it voluntarily," he said quietly. Do you know exactly what I'm going to do with you? Did he tell you?"

"Oh yes," I croaked. "He said you were a goddamn nutcase!"

"Try to separate good and evil from a person," said Jarkhan-Ali, "and what remains will automatically polarize. Physics, my boy, physics is everywhere. Roger Penrose would shit himself if he knew..."

"What the hell are you talking about?"

"Yes," he drawled. "It's clear to me that you know nothing."

"I'd rather die than help you!"

"Naturally. Anyone would choose to die in your place. It's a feature of the programming, so to speak. But why die! I see my mark has visited you, and you already think your life is over. It's a gift! You can sculpt yourself into whatever you want!"

"Yeah, I'll sculpt it out of play-dough, asshole, then shove it up your—"

You took 1 HP damage

The third bolt of the pain spell seemed to twist every nerve in my body into knots. For a few moments I lost consciousness from the pain, and when I regained consciousness, I howled and jerked. The black shit held me tight, but I continued to fight until my stamina ran out and I hung in my black bonds like a limp rag.

"You know, Bryan, it's no accident that you came to me. Instruments always yearn to be in the hands of their master, understand? But you're not the only instrument here — Yana is too."

I looked up at the sky. Stars shone high over Fantasia. I tried to turn off reality, withdraw into myself, hide, but he knew how to pull me back.

"You changed the world together. The world is not just created by the Word, but also by Love, understand? There are also books about that, and it's not metaphorical at all. It's really quite surprising how accurately and in what detail the manuals on creating the world are able to describe the problems that arise along the way. And all because people have been creating their own worlds for thousands of years — that's what experience is! A rudimentary property of our likeness to God. Do you know the mistake most holy books make?"

Jarkhan-Ali made a gesture and the black tentacles lifted me upright. Now we stood face to face.

"The creation story is presented as a singular, one-time thing — there is only one Real World. However, the very existence of humans, each of which is a little bit of a god and a creator themselves, refutes this. Creation is a conveyor belt, and each reality has to fight for its existence. Out of billions, hundreds of millions are capable of creation, hundreds of thousands will achieve success, thousands will change the history of their world, hundreds will create worlds capable of manifestation, and only a few will actually manifest them. And after that, they will become real-life gods and eternal hostages of their own offspring, who sooner or later gain freedom."

Jarkhan-Ali went silent for a while, and then said:

"Do you remember when I said the instrument yearns for the hand of the person who can use it? You came to me first, but you arrived only slightly before your other half."

He stepped to the side. The fire was still burning behind him, but he extinguished it with a wave of his hand. The coals hissed resentfully, as if a bucket of water had been splashed over them, and darkness fell on the hill.

The night was clear and cool, like a late summer night in August. From this height, I saw a wide ribbon of the river stretching from west to east. To our left, the Okwe split into many different arms, surrounded by a quagmire that glittered brightly in the moonlight.

The author raised his hands and drew an oval in the air in front of me. traced an oval in the air in front of me. The space inside the figure suddenly refracted, the space swelled, turning into a lens, and the image was suddenly magnified, so close...

There was an island in the middle of the river to the southwest. I saw it clearly and distinctly through the lens.

"Listen," I said hoarsely. "I'll do it."

"You will?" Jarkhan-Ali turned towards me, smiling sweetly.

"I will." I tried to nod. "Under the condition that you don't involve her."

"Hmm ... You know, you still managed to surprise me. I thought you would only start bargaining when you saw the boats."

"I said I'd do it, for God's sake! Let's fix the world...or whatever we need to do."

"Excellent!" He clapped me on the shoulder. "See how quickly we came to an agreement? Yes. So he didn't tell you after all. Pity. Maybe reasonable, considering how impressionable you are. You see, my friend, this is not how the instrument works. In essence, little depends on your voluntary consent. Magic arises at the moment when you have such a goal that will lead you forward, make you a weapon in the hands of fate. Hmm...that sounds so awful, but I have to explain it to you somehow."

Jarkhan-Ali walked up to the fire, thoughtfully toeing the cooled coals with his boot.

"You had the same goal once, and you achieved it, remember? Well, the best way to give a person motivation is to break him. And here come the boats..."

With a sinking heart, I watched through the lens as one after the other, three long, narrow boats sailed out from behind the island. There were people in them, but their faces were still too small to see. And yet the terrible, nightmarish confidence in the veracity of his words did not leave me. I really had come to him myself! Why me?!

"Please," I said through dry lips. "I understood what you said...find another way of breaking me...please..."

"Another way? We could find another way," Jarkhan-Ali said cheerfully. "But why? Understand, Bryan, that since the very beginning, your life here has been leading up to this very moment! Really, you shouldn't worry so much. You are doing this so that the world can be born! You will be its godfather."

The boats were approaching. In the boat slightly ahead of the others, there were three people. They were in heavy hiking raincoats. Two rowers and the third, the lookout, at the bow. Desperately wriggling, I tried to look over the lens to make sure the damn thing wasn't trying to trick me. Jarkhan-Ali noticed my movement and obligingly pushed the lens down. I peered into the darkness. At this distance, the island was about the size of a shoebox, but I could clearly see the black dots of the boats.

"Please — another way!"

"Buck up, Bryan. I'll tell you exactly how you'll feel! At first, you will be surprised, but then, nothing special. This is how our brain protects us. The duration of this protection depends—"

"I beg you! Fuck! You! Let me go, shithead!"

Jarkhan-Ali suddenly raised his hand and made a long ornate gesture, at the same time swinging the lens back into place. The water in front of one of the boats began to swirl into a funnel. The rowers desperately swung their oars, but it was too late. The boat rushed forward, caught up in the accelerating current. I saw how all three, realizing that nothing could be done, made the only right decision and jumped overboard, trying to get as far away as possible from the foaming whirlpool.

"Asshole! Fucking scum bag! Stop it! Do you hear me, you bastard?! Just hit me with more bolts! Help!!!

And help arrived.

CHAPTER 10

AN ARROW HIT THE BARRIER surrounding Jarkhan-Ali. Had it been a simple arrow, it probably would have met the same fate as my spells. But it was not. There was a clap, and the shield of my invulnerable enemy finally burst, and the arrow continued towards its target. To my great regret, the barrier had slowed it down a little, and this gave the Author time to dodge it with lightning speed, like a snake. The arrow aimed at his throat instead hit his shoulder.

But more shells flew after the first arrow and I felt a cry of relief escape from my throat. Alas, it was premature. Jarkhan-Ali jumped aside and cast a new shield in a fraction of a second. All the projectiles and Mr. Parks' magical attack either whizzed by or discharged across his new dome.

Jarkhan-Ali straightened up and burst out laughing.

"You're just on time, ladies and gentlemen! Let's make the show even more spectacular!"

I noticed that his right hand was hanging limp and I remembered that he was in the VR apparatus with the mortality function engaged. Apparently this thing really hurt his shoulder! Really? Even after this, he wouldn't log out?

But Jarkhan-Ali was in no hurry to flee the battlefield. He suddenly spoke in a language I didn't understand. Behind him, the black stones started to pulsate, turning an even deeper shade of black. I heard chomping sounds, and the screams of my friends. Something was climbing out of the swamps! I struggled to turn, but the black tentacles held my head. One of them crawled over my face, trying to clamp my mouth shut. I twisted with all my strength, and suddenly my right hand escaped from the grip. The spell may have weakened when Jarkhan-Ali was distracted. I grabbed the tentacle crawling down my cheek and jerked, and then folded my fingers, intending to cast Fireball from some unthinkable position, but suddenly I remembered that I had no mana! Opening my inventory, I grabbed the bottle of blue liquid with a shaking hand, tossed it into my mouth, and then pulled out my short sword.

Jarkhan-Ali, as if in a trance, was repeating a series of gestures over and over. Contorting my arm, I tried to slice through the damn tentacles with my sword, but the blade got stuck in the fucking shit, and after jerking it several times, the hilt came free. The next attempt was at the ring that held my left hand, but it was slimy and I couldn't get a grip on it. Meanwhile, the blue indicator had grown slightly. Barely waiting for my mana to restore enough, I twisted my hand a second time and tried to cast Fireball. Not a damn thing happened, because I simply couldn't move my hand in this position. I also couldn't keep my eyes on the target, which was the most important part of almost any targeted spell. I took a deep breath, closed my eyes and began a gesture, my fingers flying, and as soon as my palm felt the usual burning sensation, I turned it behind my back, trying to picture the target and the aim as best I could.

The sludge hissed loudly and loosened its grip. I freed myself with several strong jerks and jumped up. My sword caught my eye, sticking out of the black mass writhing in the fire. I grabbed the handle and pulled it out. Then I raised my head and saw Jarkhan-Ali, still focused on his spellwork.

I stepped towards him but at the top of the hill, one of the creatures this bastard had summoned suddenly appeared: short, overgrown with moss, with burning yellow eyes and claws half a foot long. The beast rushed towards me in long leaps.

I barely had time to raise my shield, and the monster got stuck in the dome, leaving his unexpectedly long front legs swinging. Seizing the moment, I unclenched my fingers and the shield went out. The thing collapsed to the ground, and I stepped forward and slammed into its gnarled skull. The head of the creature burst like a rotten watermelon, spurting a foul-smelling mucus all over me.

You killed swamper
Critical hit 16 HP
You gained 266 XP

Jarkhan-Ali looked at me with approval, then turned and waved his hand. Without a magnifying lens, I couldn't see exactly what was happening on the river, but I saw the gray smudge of the whirlpool. It had sunk another boat!

I threw myself directly at the iridescent dome of his shield, slashing at it. I collected all my strength and in the next instant, took a nosedive into the ground, losing my balance and only by some miracle not chopping my own leg off with my blade. I jumped up, glancing around wildly. The hill was empty.

I looked towards the river. Something was happening there, but I couldn't make out. The lens cast by Jarkhan-Ali had disappeared. I opened my inventory and pulled out my old telescope. I had gotten the glass re-polished in the DHC city, making the image much cleaner than it had been during the war. I saw boards floating across the surface of the water. I moved the scope back and forth and suddenly found it: a boat. The last of the three. There were five or six people in it, and it was evident that the ship was heavily overloaded. Yana was among them.

She was standing, bent over someone lying at the bottom of the boat. Her hood was lowered and I recognized her by her hair. Suddenly a voice rang out, and I almost dropped the telescope in surprise.

It sounded from the hill to the northwest. Covered in dirt and gore, bloodied and frightful. My best friends in the world.

"What happened?" asked Fraudo, keeping his bow at the ready. "Where is he?"

"He disappeared," I said. "Maybe he logged out, but maybe not. I need to fly!"

"Where?!"

I did not reply and crouched down.

"Warchan, stop!"

Ignoring their cries, I kicked off with my feet, hoping that I had enough mana. It should have been enough! Perhaps, I thought, I'd be able to tow the boat to the southern coast. I was gazing at the river as I took off and didn't see Jarkhan-Ali reappear on the hill a few steps away from my friends. He dodged Fraudo's arrow, deflected Mr. Parks' spell, and rammed the twins, throwing both of them over the edge of the hilltop. The Author spoke in his incomprehensible language and the black stones came to life again.

My flight slowed, as if the air I was moving

through had become denser. I had to wade through it. I increased the thrust as much as I could, but the resistance increased as well, and for the second time tonight I felt completely trapped. An invisible force was pulling me to the ground faster and faster. And then I yelled, cursing the fucking Author with the blackest words I knew. I demanded that the damn stones release me immediately, and suddenly the invisible ropes disappeared. I flew out like a cork from a bottle of champagne, but at that moment, my last drop of mana ran out and I fell to the ground with a scream, almost hitting my back on one of those cursed stones. The blow was so strong that I blacked out for a moment, and when I regained consciousness and was able to get up, I saw Jarkhan-Ali and my friends.

The last ones still on their feet were Mr. Meyers and Mills. The old man had been saved by the shield the Silent Man gave him, but it did not save him from a second ram, which sent Mr. Meyers over the hilltop with the twins. But Mills was much less fortunate. He was an experienced and fearless warrior, but Jarkhan-Ali did not give him the slightest chance — the Author's hand expelled a flame that instantly engulfed the fighter from all sides. There was a blood-curdling scream, and the air smelled of burning flesh.

I tried to jump up, but immediately collapsed back with a groan: my left leg was sticking out at an unnatural angle. Fractured. An extremely rare and unpleasant situation that wouldn't get better until the bone was set.

The fire fizzled out, but Mill's figure was nowhere to be found. In its place stood a pile of fine, grey ash, destined to blow all over this accursed swamp.

Jarkhan-Ali walked towards me, a light dancing in his eyes. I couldn't believe it. Had we...lost?

I opened my inventory, but I had run out of mana. My blade was gone and there was no time to raise my bow. I had no other means of fighting my enemy.

"Just a warm up," the Author said nonchalantly. "Grab your telescope if you don't want to miss the finale. I'm tired and not going to cast another lens."

"Please! I—"

"Enough, Warchan!" he cut me off. "You had a chance, but you didn't use it."

I ran through arguments, options, deals and threats in my head...although I knew that nothing would not help. All my reserves were exhausted.

"Do it," I croaked, "and I'll find a way to turn the rest of your miserable life into hell..."

He merely grinned in reply, then turned and raised his hand.

I closed my eyes and didn't open them again immediately. There, on the water, the worst thing I could possibly imagine was about to take place. There was no way I could watch, but I couldn't look away either. I didn't even try to pull out the telescope. My hands were shaking too much to see anything through it now. And anyway, I could see the boat without any assistance — the current was driving it towards the bank. How strange! After all, it was here that the largest of its tributaries flowed into the Ikwen. Shouldn't it be pushing the boat southward instead?

Jarkhan-Ali sharply lowered his hand, and a glimmer of light appeared on the surface of the water and began to grow rapidly. I closed my eyes, praying to any god I could think of. Opened. The overloaded boat rushed towards the whirlpool. I screamed, thrashed, feeling that something terrible was happening to my mind, something irreversible. The boat was not being pulled into the whirlpool. Barely visible figures of people began to jump into the water. All but one in the middle. I closed my eyes. A ringing void filled my head. Opened. The white funnel was still visible on the surface of the water. The boat was gone.

He was right. When you're broken, all you feel at first is blissful nothingness. All you feel is surprise at the complete numbness. You try to push yourself to feel the emotions that seem appropriate to the situation. But any emotions, thoughts or actions crumble and are empty on the inside like Chinese fortune cookies.

When he turned and bent over me, intending to set my leg, I felt a slight twinge of pain — and that was it! My life in this world had just ended, and I was afraid of a pain in my leg! It was absolutely astonishing! I suddenly heard my own hoarse laugh, which surprised me even more. But I couldn't stop — a fit of laughter overcame my entire being and did not stop, even when Jarkhan-Ali sharply twisted my leg. I screamed, but continued to giggle, shaken by stronger and stronger attacks. Then he set in motion his torture lightning, and it gave him the result he desired. The pain was incredible, but the strange giggle-fit died down, and I was almost grateful to my tormentor.

"That's it, Bryan. Only one small task remains — finishing off the rest of your friends. The swamp should have taken care of them, but who..."

He suddenly cut himself off mid-sentence and straightened up. Dark figures stepped onto the hilltop from different directions, their raised shields flickering.

"It can't be..." Jarkhan-Ali gasped.

The figures approached slowly, never taking their eyes off the Author. For a moment, I thought that my squad had miraculously managed to regroup, but then I realized that the Predators I saw before me were unfamiliar. Each had a weapon in its hand. And not just simple weapons — enhanced swords, spears and flanged maces from the city treasury. Chain mail. Each one had a magical shield and battle training that was apparent even to the naked eye. This was the Predator elite.

Jarkhan-Ali grimaced with annoyance. The Predator Commander, a bald, thin vampire with shimmeringly pale skin, gave the signal and the warriors rushed forward. The Author met them with a ram, knocking two to the ground and Blinked two dozen feet to one side. The expression of displeasure never left his face.

The ground around Jarkhan-Ali began to move in waves, spitting out creeping stems of entangling roots. Several yellow magical arrows (I hadn't seen these before!) tested the strength of his shield. The Author's palms flared and the magical bonds turned to ash, but the Predators didn't let him gain any ground. Splitting into pairs, they attacked the enemy from different directions, moving quickly and in perfect harmony, slashing at the shield without allowing the weapon to get bogged down.

Overcoming the pain in my leg, I got up and suddenly I noticed an object lying on the ground. It was a small book bound in gray leather lying just a few steps away from me. I grabbed the book, opened my inventory, stuffed the find into the nearest free slot and pulled out my bow. Perhaps, seeing the weapon in my hands, the Predators would attack, but I should at least try to shoot the bastard. And then I'd go after her. I'd find her.

Wherever she was.

But the Author didn't put up a fight. Apparently, his powers were not unlimited, and his arm was still giving him issues. He Blinked again, a little farther from his opponent, and then without crouching down, shot off into the dark sky. Several Predators rushed to pursue him without hesitation.

The pale commander turned and looked at me intently. For a second, I thought about sticking an arrow between his eyes, but they may torture me before they kill me, and I'd had enough torture for one day.

"Bring the rest. And the prisoners too," the pale man ordered, and then he walked towards me with a decisive step. Stopping a couple of steps away, he grinned wryly, showing sharp triangular teeth.

"You can lower your bow," he said. "We do not kill brothers in battle."

Chapter 11

WHEN I REALIZED what, in fact, had just happened, I fell into a slight stupor. He mistook me for a Predator. Come to think of it, this was no surprise, considering my new appearance. But if I was a Predator, then I had to behave like a Predator. The longer I could pretend, the longer I would stay alive.

"Greetings, free warrior," said the pale one. "My name is Adalius the Cunning, Reaper Clan. Who are you?"

Never before had I thought with such speed, tangibly feeling the time pass, waiting for the moment when the vampire would become suspicious.

"I am Urfyn. I greet you, Adalius the Cunning, and thank you for your help."

Adalius fell silent, looking at me. I knew that he was waiting for certain words, and I feverishly searched for what they may be.

"I owe you a debt," I said, following a vague whim. "Which I will repay in full at the first given opportunity."

God, what idiocy had just slipped from his mouth? Adalius stared at me for a while, then slowly tilted his head to signal that he had heard.

"Strange, Urfyn, I don't know you. Been in Fantasia long?"

"I appeared shortly before the march to the west."

"You were there?"

"Nuh-uh," I said, trying with all my strength to sound calm. "I don't need that kind of war."

Adalius smiled unpleasantly.

"And what kind of war do you need, Urfyn?"

I had gone wrong somewhere. The conversation was going off the rails. And suddenly, some invisible wall burst in my brain. Yana was dead! And she would never return to this world. The door opened and immediately slammed shut, because if it had not closed, I would most likely be lying on the ground, completely non-functional. Nothing was okay. Nothing would ever be okay again!

"My war is my own business, Adalius. And none of yours."

In a moment, I realized that what had just unwittingly spilled into my soul from behind the door may have saved the situation. My voice was cold and calm, and Adalius suddenly gave me a much more sincere smile.

The warriors returned, bringing with them...Fraudo, Mr. Meyers, the twins, Mr. Parks and Camilla. They had all survived the fight with Jarkhan-Ali! I understood that this was a miracle, but I must admit: the joy and relief that I experienced at that moment were just an echo of genuine emotions!

Mr. Parks and Camilla had looped lassos hung around the necks, the ends of which were held by the hefty arms of the guards. The task immediately became more complicated by several orders of magnitude. So what should I do now? The door inside opened again for a moment, but that was more than enough.

"Adalius, tell your people to remove the ropes from the necks of my slaves."

The vampire arched his brows slightly.

"Your slaves should have fallen before their master. So they are no longer yours. They are runaway slaves, that is, nobody's. Or have you forgotten the law?"

"My slaves simply failed to do what none of us were able to. Including you. They're my XP stock. And if you don't want another battle right now, tell your people to remove the fucking ropes, or I'll use them to personally strangle each of them.

The orc gripping Camilla's leash growled loudly and stepped forward. In his other hand, he held a heavy poleaxe. I took a step towards him and struck, imbuing it with all the power bestowed to me by the Silent Man's gift. The orc's fang cracked with a loud crunch, and the orc himself staggered back and fell to the ground, yanking the rope. Camilla screamed, grabbing the noose around her neck, but I didn't even glance in her direction. I looked into the eyes of Adalius. He calmly held my gaze. Then he said:

"You'll have to pay for that, Urfyn. And the price is not small." He paused for a moment. "But you haven't proved that you can pay. And maybe we can come to an agreement. Remove the ropes!"

The order was carried out quickly and without objection. The crippled orc stood up, holding his aching jaw. His eyes were filled with fear, mingled with respect.

* * *

A new fire was blazing at the top of the hill. While the Predators were setting up camp, I managed to exchange a few words with my guys:

"Change your names!" I whispered. "Right now! To ones that won't arouse suspicion in the city!"

I'd already changed my own nickname to "Urfyn."

"And we need a clan name."

"What's theirs?"

"Reapers," I said. "We need something scary, not too boring."

"Flayers," suggested Mr. Meyers.

"Hellbeasts," Fraudo chimed in.

"Bloody Axes," Quentin piped up.

"What kind of axes?" barked Mr. Meyers. "Do you see an axe in any one of our hands? Use your head!"

"Northern Star," said Quinn.

"That's not really menacing enough," I said.

"But it's pretty!" said Fraudo. "I'm for it."

"Me too — that is, of course, if slaves have the right to vote."

I looked at Camilla. Red rope marks were clearly visible around her neck.

"I'm sorry, Dr. Harris. You—"

"Not a word, Bryan. Your quick thinking saved us all. Besides, I have not forgotten about your and Mr. Rkaeli's attempts to dissuade me from going. It was — and remains — my choice."

I was silent for a moment.

"I'm afraid we all have to play roles for a while. And the fate of the entire group will depend on how well each one of us plays our part. But don't be mistaken: this is a very powerful group. We cannot beat them in open combat. Now tell me your names and repeat them to yourself until you learn! I am Urfyn. From the North Star clan."

"Baalu," said Fraudo.

"Legerix," said Quinn.

"Mr. Smith," said Mr. Meyers. "And I'll never remember Legerix in my life. I'll just call you Ku."

"Sparky," said Mr. Parks.

"Quentin."

"Quant."

"It'll do."

"I'll be Millie," Camilla said quietly. "In honor of the late John Mills."

"Mills is dead?!" cried Fraudo.

* * *

"Tell me a little, Urfyn, about this pleasant fellow who I've had the good fortune to meet in the midst of these wonderful swamps," said Adalius.

His voice sounded calm, but I felt that the vampire was pretty peeved.

"Are you sure you want to know the answer, Adalius? Knowledge, as you know, can be a dangerous thing..."

The vampire's eyes narrowed dangerously.

"Urfyn," he hissed. "Your silver tongue is one of the reasons why you can still open your mouth. I lost two people, and in return so far I have received only your arrogance. And I'm starting to lose patience."

"As you wish," I raised my hands. "But don't say I didn't warn you."

I'd decided in advance that I would give him part of the truth, and told about the Divine Voice, the non-vanishing corpses and the animals driven mad. The part about the Silent Man, the creation of the world and our quest, I decided to hold back for now. I wanted to first see how the vampire would react to the first part of the story.

Adalius didn't react in any way. He just listened.

"Then we stumbled upon this chump," I said. "He's a player from the real world, but not just anyone. The black stones somehow obeyed him, fed him strength."

"And does your story provide any explanation as to who it could be?

Apparently, the nickname "Cunning" wasn't given for nothing. The question was surprisingly accurate.

"None."

He looked at me without blinking and I could have sworn he didn't believe a word I said.

"Did you speak to him?"

"Yes." I hesitated a moment and decided to add suspense to the story. "And in the course of the conversation, it did become clear who he was."

"Who?"

"One of the developers of Fantasia. He called himself the Author."

Now I had obviously managed to win back some leverage. Adalius thought hard. Then asked a few questions regarding the further content of our conversation, and I fed him some of the information that Camilla had told us before our meeting with the local pantheon. Somehow the vampire sensed when I began to lie too much. Perhaps he had points invested in Aletheia's skill in Wisdom.

"And what do you plan to do now?"

"I've seen the shit this creature unleashed upon the world," I said quietly. "I suppose anyone who could hit this crazy asshole would be doing the world a good service. But, as it turned out, hitting him is not that easy."

"Where do you plan to search for him?"

"He said that the main resonator is in the City of Players to the east."

Adalius chuckled.

"And what, you're going there?"

I shrugged vaguely.

"And where exactly in the city is this…resonator located, do you know?"

"I do," I said. "Allegedly, it's in the central tower of the castle. I just don't know exactly where, the upper or lower floor. Or maybe in the middle. But he said that the resonator there is the most…"

"You already said that," the vampire cut in impatiently.

He was thinking intensely about something, glancing sideways at me. This went on for a while, then Adalius loudly and unexpectedly clapped his hands together.

"Your story was relatively interesting. It was pretty much entirely fabricated, of course, but amusing on the whole. As for the city of players, if things are as you say, then it's even better. I will only be glad if this…Jarkhan-Ali decides to hide there. So you think the black stones give him strength? And how do they do it?"

I shrugged my shoulders, aware that my

words would likely be the thing to betray me.

"My men heard him speaking in some unknown language," the vampire hinted.

I nodded.

"I also heard that. And the stones reacted."

"What language is it?"

"I have no idea," I said, this time without fear of a lie detector test.

"And you hear the Voice now?"

"No," I said. "Over here, I'm far enough away from the stones. If we go a little closer, maybe I'll hear them."

Adalius nodded.

"Alright, Urfyn. Now we'll have dinner, get to know your men. Let the slaves serve the food and take away. It's been a long time since we've had human skins in our service, so you'll have to share. And tomorrow you and I will work on a plan to pay off your debt."

The Predators' dinner was loud and rowdy. A couple of lamb's legs were fried over the fire, and they did it in such a way that the meat was burnt on the outside, but inside remained raw inside. Adalius men didn't care, the main thing was that there was beer to drink with the food. And there was plenty of beer to spare.

Mr. Parks and Camilla served food and drinks, while the jubilant soldiers treated them very rudely. But while Mr. Parks, with his dull countenance, received mostly harmless ridicule, then not a single Predator let Camilla pass by. She was showered with vulgar compliments, others tried pinch or slap on the ass. I believe that if it were not for one of the orc's broken fangs, all of this could have come to a very quick and sad end. The professor bore it all stoically, but was paler than usual.

The Predators made a strange impression on me. For the first time, I saw creatures that really didn't look like anyone I had known before. They were simple and sincere in their own way, very serious in everything that concerned the clan, and very lackadaisical in everything else. They were unworried by any structure and unburdened by any care in the world. Their life had always been only here and now, but, thanks to this, they knew each other very well and, in case of danger, turned into a powerful single organism - a clan. From somewhere in the depths of their genetic memory, this herd instinct had appeared and turned them into something primitive. However, "primitive" in this case did not mean rudimentary at all.

A drank a lot of beer, but tried to moderate. The detachment was supposed to be combat-ready the next day. The dinner, which we hoped would last until the morning, lasted only about an hour, and now the Predators were preparing to turn in for the evening. We were not told where to make beds, but Adalius's men, as it were, casually positioned themselves close enough and on all sides. In addition, sentries were on duty at the foot of the hill. Escape was impossible.

I lay down and turned my head to one side and began to ponder a thought that had come up during a conversation with Adalius and that I'd been unable to shake since then. When Quinn asked the Silent Man how we could get into the City of Predators, he said that a way would be found. And would be found very soon. At the same time, he looked rather dull, as I recall. Did he know what was going to happen to us? But if he knew, then how could he have sent us on our way?! If he knew that I and Yana were tools that would fall into the hands of that psycho, then...Could it be that this copy of the author had pulled one over on me like the last idiot, and Yana was the one who had to pay...

The door in my head cracked open again, but this time didn't slam shut, like earlier. A feeling of such melancholy slipped through the crack that I almost howled.

"Urfyn, are you asleep?"

Camilla lay a step away from me, eyes closed.

"No."

"I need to tell you something important."

I didn't care. I didn't care one bit, there was nothing important left in life. Just this endless sea of sorrow and meaninglessness. I was lying with my head to the river, looking at the sky, and suddenly, among the multitude of flickering points, I noticed one, larger one. Star. The North Star. Our clan.

"What are you thinking, Millie?"

"Farsi," Camilla said. "It was Farsi."

"What was?" I said, not understanding, turning on my wolf pelt.

"The language Jarkhan-Ali was speaking. It was Farsi," the professor repeated patiently. "The main language spoken in Iran. Persian."

I remembered what I had found, opened my inventory and pulled out the notebook. Opening it at random, I brought the yellowish pages closer, trying to see what was there in the darkness. The page was covered in fine script, the hooks and curls of the Arabic alphabet. I turned a few pages and came across drawings made with a confident hand. In some places there were pieces of a map, spell schemes and some formulas.

I turned to Camilla again, holding out the book."

"Professor, I believe that Jarkhan-Ali dropped this during the fight. The notes seem to be in the same language. Perhaps there's something interesting to be found."

Chapter 12

THE NEXT DAY, Adalius called for me and explained exactly how he wanted to be repaid for saving my life. I, of course, expected something like this, but I was still surprised at how quickly he had formulated his plan. It was about "punishing" one of the Predator clans who "broke the law" and hid in the mountains north of here. When I asked what law they had violated, the vampire replied: theft. I asked what the punishment would be?

"I have to kill them," Adalius said simply.

"Do they know about this?"

"Naturally. They're going to fight until the very end."

"How many are there?"

"Nearly twenty. But low-levels. The average among them is fourteen."

"And they're waiting for us?"

"Yes, of course," the vampire shrugged his shoulders. "Runaways are always waiting for someone to come after them."

"And my debt will be repaid after that?"

"Let's say this — it'll be a start."

"No."

Adalius stared at me coldly.

"Maybe my debt is greater than all this crap you want to sign me up for. But I don't intend on paying you back for the rest of my life. Please give me the full cost of your invaluable service. I am not your slave, Adalius."

The vampire thought for a while.

"If the mission is completed with minimal losses and a good profit, I'll consider your debt repaid."

"And if the losses are the result of incompetent leadership?"

Adalius grinned, showing two rows of tapered teeth.

"Let's take our time, Urfyn," he said. "It's better to act according to the circumstances at hand."

* * *

I stood on the western bank of the Okwe, holding a noose in my hands. The other end was tied to the bow of a fragile wooden boat that the Predators had dug out of nowhere.

"Come on!" cried Adalius.

I kicked off and took off. The rope was taut, the boat jerked and swayed violently, almost scooping up water with its lowered bow.

"Be careful, damn you!" shouted the dwarf Gorm, who was lying spread out across the bottom of the boat.

The dwarf Predators were fat and squat, and poor Quentin had become one of them. The hulking dwarves received a huge strength and could crush bricks with their fingers. The bony, skinny men were elves. Needless to say, there was no unearthly beauty in their appearance: the elves looked like victims of years of anorexia with flabby skin and swollen joints. The squad also included demons, vampires and, of course, orcs.

I remembered how disgusting Gorm had been to Camilla last night, and I wanted to drown him along with the boat.

It turned out to be unexpectedly difficult to pull. Watching how the levitating Predators handled this task, I thought I could do just as well. However, as soon as I took a course to the northeast, as the noose suddenly hit my shoulder hard, I was spun in the air, and the rope slid along my forearm, breaking free from my hand. I scrambled and caught it at the last moment. The predators on the shore laughed. Gorm swore. The loop was large enough, and I, turning on zero gravity, passed through it first one, and then the other hand, harnessing it like a horse. The horns made the task very difficult. From time to time the rope pulled me towards the boat, and with zero gravity I flew towards it faster and faster, because each push added speed to me. Gorm paused, staring in dismay at the red carcass rushing towards him. However, I turned on gravity in time, braked smoothly a dozen feet from the boat and flew in the opposite direction. Another jerk and the boat finally slid in the right direction.

*　*　*

For me, and, perhaps, for many others, the river was the border separating the world of the Digital Human Copies from the world of Predators. The western world from the eastern world. After General McKinnery's men had brought down the bridge, all communication between the shores ceased. I remember that right after the war, many insisted on a retaliatory campaign to capture the city of players, but the adviser Gallance had said: "Enough! We've seen enough bloodshed." "The predators won't be able to recover," he argued, "because the population of Fantasia is no longer growing. We live in a new world, where the lives of each DHC have a different price." According to his estimates, there were only about four hundred Predators in the world (and not all of them followed Stork). Very few of them did. And they deserved another chance.

And yet none of the former captives had put down roots in the DHC city, although attempts were made. The mutual enmity after the war was too strong. Then, by decision of the city council, the Predators were released, along with a message for the city. The reply never came.

* * *

"Did you take place in the march?"

The fat dwarf slowly turned his head in my direction, causing dozens of small folds to appear on his neck.

"Yep."

"Why?"

Gorm thought for a long time, then said:

"Everyone else went."

"Why did everyone else go?"

"Why? Because there are a bunch of ungrateful weaklings living in the west, that's why."

"Why are they ungrateful?"

Gorm looked at me suspiciously.

"You know, Ufryn, sometimes you're weird. As if you were born yesterday, or've been sleeping for the last few years. Where were you during the war? In the southern forests?"

I nodded.

"Well? You been to the villages? Most NPCs run without looking back or grab their weapons when they see us. The same with the DHCs. On the other hand, there are the players. They're usually the most cold-hearted, they don't understand that we just want to survive. People like us are killed at the first opportunity. Look at us! We're monsters! And these creatures in the western city..."

Gorm spat contemptuously, clapping his leg and cursing.

"They have a modern society! They live on carpets, coffee and credit! But we're not good enough for that! Fucking hypocrites! But then Stork came. And he explained that's not how it is."

"And how is it?"

"He said that people don't understand who we are or what role we play. And that role is protection. Without us, their whole fucking society would have collapsed in an instant. He said that if we eliminate the threat of real players, then people in the west will have nothing to fear. We will be honored as heroes!"

"And you took the City of Players?"

"And how."

"Were you at that battle?"

"There was no battle, buddy." Gorm smiled indulgently, and I realized he remembered those events with pleasure. "There was a massacre. And also, the fastest sacking in the world! Those pansies weren't expecting an attack, we rushed their king, and the king...hehe...well there's a new one now! When we won, Stork sent messengers to the city of DCH to tell them that they no longer needed to fear the real players."

Gorm frowned and fell silent.

"And?" I asked.

"They killed our ambassadors," the dwarf said grimly. "And Stork was given a letter that from now on the Predators — as they call us — are forbidden to cross to the western side of Okwe. And anyone who dares to show his crooked face on their territory is subject to immediate destruction. This is how they repaid us for our service! Wouldn't you have marched if someone had thrown something like that in your face?!"

"I probably would have," I said evasively. "How did they find out about the ambassadors? Their bodies would have disappeared."

"Their things. They returned their things to us. Without any of the valuables, of course! Damned animals!"

His eyes narrowed.

"It's people like you," he suddenly declared, "that made us lose the war! I don't believe that you didn't know anything! You knew everything! You just decided to save your own skin!"

"Gorm, I appeared in the game just a few days before your trip. On the southwest edge of the map!"

The dwarf snorted disdainfully.

"You're awfully clever for a newb!" He said. "You have levitation, and you also have strength. How did you buff yourself so much in just six months?"

"The NPCs in the village behind the bridge. After the war, almost no one touched it. Except for me and my clan members."

"Uh huh, of course. You climbed the ranks offing level five fishermen."

"Some of them are much higher level."

But Gorm continued to look at me doubtfully.

Almost half of the entire Predator squad treated me in much the same way. And yet Adalius dragged us with him, from which I concluded that things were going to get heated. Or maybe we were meant to play the role of cannon fodder. Even if this wasn't the case, I should assume that it was and make decisions on that basis.

We walked between the river and the foothills to the north. There was even a little road here, and our motley crew trampled it down in it in just a couple of hours. I thought the detachment would try to move quietly, but nothing of the sort: the Predators sang obscene songs, scolded loudly and incessantly used foul language on any occasion. As the sun was passing the zenith, I saw the remains of wooden structures on the left and realized that we were back at the destroyed bridge. Adalius announced a full stop.

In the east there was once a grove, but part of it had been used by the Predators to build a temporary crossing, and then the road wound upwards towards a pass through the mountains. It was there that Obelix had initially planned to set up the ambush, but we didn't have time. Stork had moved swiftly.

I had no doubt that the story of the dead

Predator ambassadors was bullshit. I knew Tom Gallance well enough to know that the council would not support such a decision. Perhaps the ambassadors really had died, but I suspected that the culprits would be found among the confidants of Stork himself. While I was thinking about it, the Predators set up camp. Bonfires were blazing. Then Krinj arrived and called me to the vampire. I went to the leader's fire and sat down across from him.

"Tell me, Adalius. Who now rules in the City of Players?"

"The Council of Clans."

"And the king?"

The vampire glanced at me.

"What king?"

"Well, whoever has the most levels. Before I got into the game, it was, if I remember correctly, a real player. Either Redrick the third or fourth. Then Stork became king. And after the march?"

"No one knows what happened to Stork," Adalius said slowly. "Maybe he was killed. Who the new king is, no one knows."

"How is that?"

"It just is. The king doesn't go around shouting that he's the king. The castle is locked."

"Why locked?"

"Because only the king can unlock the castle."

"And the arsenal and treasury?"

"In the castle."

"Wait, the resonator is also in the castle! What's going to happen? It's really impossible to enter?"

"It's possible. But first you need to find the king, or—" Adalius chuckled carnivorously, " — to become king himself. Personally, I think we've had a few different kings over the past six months. But none of them have declared themselves."

"Why?"

Adalius looked sidelong at me.

"You're too curious, Urfyn. My guys say the same thing. Everyone's dying to know!"

"You heard my story? Why then are you surprised?"

"I heard part of your story. And there's something missing. Namely — your interest in all this. You saw something and now you're going to save the world from some incomprehensible bullshit. But I saw with my own eyes what this mission entails. And I do not believe that you are doing this solely out of the kindness of your heart. So maybe you can already tell me what's really going on?"

"Nothing that would interest you, Adalius. I know what you're thinking: that I'm trying to access the magic of the black stones."

I fell silent, gazing into the fire. The quiet, sleepless night, and the persistent pain leaking out from the slightly open door in my head had done their job. I was exhausted and did not want to lie or play these games.

"I don't care a bit about the black stones!" I said. "I want to get this bastard, I want to personally tear through his veins. He killed someone...who was dear to me."

Adalius looked intently at me.

"We've all lost something to this world," he said philosophically.

I immediately wanted to break his nose. So that he understood real pain, through all his philosophizing. And he looked at me, eyebrows raised mockingly. As if my willingness to kick him in the face had aroused his genuine interest: would I make up my mind or not?"

I got up and walked away from the fire.

With every minute, the mountains grew ever closer to the river, gradually cutting off the path to the north, but Adalius confidently turned East, and we moved up the winding rock channel, the stream flowing below us. The predators no longer sang or swore; they walked silently, listening to the splash of the water.

After an hour's ascent, Adalius ordered us to halt, and then called Sinew to him. Sinew was an elf, but he looked even scarier than me. He was short, with a black, dessicated body, in which there was something insect-like. His swollen joints were unusually mobile; Sinew could bend them in different directions than usual, and this sight made me sick. He consulted with the vampire for a long time, then Sinew spread his arms and took off. Quickly gaining altitude, he flew somewhere to the northeast, where fluffy white clouds hung low over the mountains.

We waited, nibbling on strips of jerky, which seemed to have the same color, taste, and nutritional value as the sole of my boot. Steam was coming out of my mouth, but I did not feel any particular cold. But others clearly felt it. Especially Camilla and Mr. Parks. I opened my inventory, pulled out an old wolf skin and gave it to the professor, paying no heed to the mocking looks of the Predators. She uttered gratitude with blue lips, turned around, and stepped aside.

A quarter of an hour later, Sinew returned. He conferred with Adalius and Krinj for a while, then the vampire called a general meeting.

"The enemy is half an hour's walk from here," said Adalius. "The road there is difficult. In some places, we'll have to walk single-file. Other spots are unreachable without a rope, which, of course, no one will be able to throw down to us. Two posts, two people each. Then there is a platform between the wall and the abyss, a narrow passage between the rocks leads to it. If you're keeping guard, you should be able to hold people off for a long time. That's why we'll have two detachments, one of which will fly up to the site on the side of the cliff and make a little noise. The second unit will move on foot.

"What about patrols?" asked Fraudo.

"The second detachment will be on patrol. This is the plan."

"How long will we have to hold out and how many opponents will there be?" I asked, knowing which job my team would be appointed.

Adalius stared at me, his expression unreadable.

"There are four or five people on the site at one same time. There are several more in the cave carved into the rock. There will be four flyers with you. None of your other men fly, right?"

"No."

"So four. We'll fight on the ground, otherwise we may miscalculate our mana and end up falling into the crevasse. The first landing will just be an intermediary one. There's not much room, so land slowly. The order will be as follows: I go first, behind me is Bo, followed by Urfyn, then Sinew takes up the rear. This is important!" The vampire raised his voice. "Sound travels in the mountains. So don't drop anything, fart — in general, don't make a sound! If they discover we're coming, they'll just shoot us on the way. The second squad is commanded by Krinj. His order is my order. Wrap the bottom of the grappling hooks in rags, or they'll hear they'll ring out and be heard for miles. They'll send a signal to the camp by shouting, but you know what to do."

I looked at my friends. Their faces showed that they had no idea what to do. I myself did not feel any excitement or particular fear. And...perhaps I was even anticipating the fight. At least there, my attention would be entirely focused on something else.

Evening was approaching. Trying to levitate through the mountains after dark would be suicide, so Adalius hurried us along. Soon, we reached the place where the detachments were to split up — a small area on a narrow ridge of a rocky outcropping jutting out from the cliff face and following alongside it to the right.

I walked up to my friends and tried to cheer them up. It turned out badly. The reapers were standing very close, and I had to carefully censor every word.

"You," I jabbed a finger at Camilla, "Stay out of the battle! You're low level, so they'll only have to shoot you once, and then what, I'll have to take out the chamber pot myself? I don't think so."

Krinj, the head of the second detachment, heard my words and turned towards me.

"She'll do exactly as I tell her."

Krinj was a demon like me. With, dark reddish-brown skin covered with small bony outgrowths and many horns running down his back, making him look like an ugly overgrown hedgehog.

"So if something happens to her, I'll come to you personally."

Krinj hissed. I ignored him and turned to my own team.

"The same goes for you!" My finger jabbed towards Mr. Parks.

Mr. Parks has demonstrated incredible acting skills during our journey. I knew he was level eighteen. Many predators were stronger and could have made him switch on his hologram. If this had happened, the jig would most likely have been up. No one would keep high-level slave by his side — the risk was too great. But the thing was, not a single Predator had ever bothered to check the level of a gnarled man with the face of a complete idiot. No one even looked at him. Sometimes it seemed that Mr. Parks could have left the squad and no one would have noticed.

In mentioning Mr. Parks, I hoped he would understand my meaning and cover Camilla during the battle. Then I remembered something and discreetly pulled out the brooch that the Silent Man had left me for Mr. Meyers.

"Take it," I said, handing the brooch to the old swordsman.

"Why the hell do I need this trinket?" he asked quietly.

"Pointless trinkets are sometimes more useful than you think," I said quietly.

"It's time," said Adalius. "It will be dark soon!"

The four retreated to the edge of the flat platform. The sun was right in front of us, hanging low and heavy, painting the clouds in incredible hues of orange, yellow and pink.

Adalius spread his arms to the sides, pushed

off, and slowly drifted westward. A few seconds later, Bo — an orc with unusual white hair, which he gathered in a ponytail — followed behind, careful not to intercept his flight path. Sinew shoved me in the shoulder, and I remembered that it was my turn. I cast levitation and stepped into the abyss, turning the gravity in the direction of the orc figure clearly visible against the sky.

The rocky outcropping below me fell sharply and in front of me, the river shone in sunset colors. The orc took to the right, skirting the mountain. We followed him at a low speed — according to my estimates, something around thirty or forty miles per hour. I suspected that my visibility would decrease significantly if my view was blocked by Mount Bo, so I sped up, closing the distance. Now we flew very close to the mountain. To my right, the stone and moss merged into one solid gray-green wall.

After about five minutes, I saw the site and was horrified. The rocky ledge where we were supposed to wait for the start of the attack turned out to be a narrow perch. And all four of us were supposed to land there! I saw the silhouette of Adalius standing on the edge, waving his arms to us. Bo reduced his speed to a minimum, rolled over in the air and flew towards the platform, feet forward. I paused in the air, waiting for him to land. The white-haired orc was landing well, but his speed was still a little higher than necessary, and as soon as he touched the ground with his feet, momentum carried him forward and he smacked against the wall. I decided to act differently. Turning my body and feet to the wall, I landed a little higher. As soon as my legs rested against the mountain and, without removing gravity, straightened up and involuntarily grinned. I stood on the mountain, although my body was in a horizontal position, the earth was in front, the sky was behind. Under my feet is a solid rock, and above my head is a distant river and a setting sun. Stepping carefully, I walked down the wall to the waiting Predators. Adalius, appreciating my innovation, gave me the thumbs up. When I reached the platform, I pressed myself against the ledge and turned off levitation. My stomach bucked in protest, and I lay on the rocky ledge for a few seconds, coming to my senses."

When I got up, Sinew was already walking towards us, repeating my trick. And a minute later we were standing in a cramped bunch, nestled against the rock.

"Here's what I wonder," I asked, surprising even myself. "If they're hiding out in that damn cave, where are they getting food and water? They don't need to go down to replenish their stocks?"

Adalius chuckled.

"There are spells that summon food. They require quite a lot of mana, but hypothetically, a strong sorcerer could feed several people."

"And they have that kind of magic?"

The vampire shrugged his shoulders.

We hung out on the cliffside for a quarter of an hour. The sun began to dip below the horizon and darkness fell quickly. Adalius handed out several bottles of mana to each of them to replenish the energy they had spent.

"Wait," he said, throwing them to us, then stepping to the edge and soared upward with a small light.

He was going to check on the second detachment, I realized. Ten minutes later, he returned and immediately began gulping down mana potions, one after another.

"Five minutes," he said between gulps.

"How are our guys holding up?" I asked.

The vampire didn't dignify me with an answer.

The sun set and twilight fell. The mountain behind my back grew darker, and I thought with some anxiety about the upcoming flight. Measuring distances was different in the mountains than it was in the plains. In addition, the vampire had warned us that we would need to fly fast, because we'd probably all need mana during the battle. But who cares! Whatever will be will be. I pulled out a sword from my inventory and tried to hang the scabbard behind my back, so as not to interfere in flight, but the straps were constantly clinging to my horns. Sinew came to the rescue, and together we, at the very least, adjusted the weapon so that I could reach it. Adalius gave us a critical look and said:

"Alright, guys. We fly in the same order we came in. But we should try to land at the same time and away from the cliff. Our task is to hold out until the others approach. Be careful with your magic, especially battering rams — no friendly fire."

The Predators nodded silently, and I nodded as well. And then we launched from the rock ledge and headed east. The dark masses of mountains now towered on both sides, and I did my best not to lose sight of Bo's white hair as he flew in front. Below was unbroken gloom and darkness. Stars began to flicker into sight above me, and I noticed the North Star on the left, from which our clan derived its name. Soon Bo began to slow down, and I saw Adalius, gesturing to us to get closer. I slowed down smoothly next to them as best I could, and Bo unceremoniously grabbed my horn and pulled me closer. Sinew joined us a few moments later.

Adalius silently indicated our target. To the right rose a sheer cliff, so flat and level that it looked as if it had been smoothed out manually. A little higher and to the east, there was a little opening in the rock face, barely noticeable in the semi-darkness. This was the site. From the place where we were hanging, nothing suspicious was noticeable on the edge, however, even if there was someone there, I most likely wouldn't have seen anything. The vampire opened his inventory, pulled out a few more bottles of mana and handed it to us, instructing us to drink them now. I popped the cold, minty liquid into my mouth, glanced at the empty vial, and unclenched my fingers. The bottle sank soundlessly into the darkness below. It was time to begin.

Four dark shadows rushed towards the rock ledge. It had looked small from above, but it really wasn't that small — no less than seventy feet across, snugly sheltered by rocks on three sides and a dark cavern in one of the walls. As we approached, I noticed the silhouettes of the sentinels not far from the edge, near a set of barrels in which fires were burning, and a moment later an alarm signal cut through the evening haze.

Preparing to land, I freed my left arm and cast Shield. Mindful of Adalius' warning, I chose a landing point a little away from the cliff, but as my feet were approaching the rock, I suddenly noticed a dark figure rushing towards me with a torch. With a jerk of his right hand, I changed direction and awkwardly landed sideways. Inertia carried me further, and I rolled on the ground right under the feet of one of the defenders. My shield was extinguished. Fortunately, my opponent wasn't anticipating my small somersault, stumbled over my rolling body, and fell flat, the considerable mass of his body stretched out flat on the ground.

I jumped up and looked around. Chaos had broken out all around. The clatter of iron, desperate screams and the hum of shields. It was impossible to distinguish friend from foe with all the dark figures rushing around.

My first opponent, who had stumbled over me, was an elf. He swooped in, swinging a long, narrow blade like a rapier, and if it hadn't been for the shield, which I prudently raised again, I would have been toast. However, the rapier became safely wedged in the dome. I stepped forward and, extinguishing the shield, took a slash at him. The elf screamed. I slammed him with a bolt of electricity, causing his arms and legs to arch in opposite directions, and then, taking advantage of his confusion, jabbed my sword in his throat. The elf choked on the black blood gushing from the wound and sank to the ground, vanishing before my eyes.

The thrill of battle ran through my veins with a double dose of adrenaline. I felt fast and strong, confident and calm, I felt...A strong blow to the head cut these feelings short. My horn snapped with a loud crash, light flashed before my eyes, but I did not lose consciousness. Bending down, I leapt to the side, trying to gain distance. I fell, grinding my horns against the stone, then turned around and saw a huge shaggy Predator, armed with a club. The creature was somewhat similar to Chewbacca, only with much wider shoulders. His huge iron club seemed like a reed in his hands. The beefed-up Wookiee stepped towards me, raising his weapon. I automatically cast Shield, but with the very first blow, the protective hemisphere burst, sending a shock running along the nerves and a short, but intense burst of pain. What kind of power did he possess if he could break through my shield with a single blow?! There was no time to think about it. I didn't have time to cast anything else, and I barely managed to dodge the next blow. The club slammed into the rock a few inches from my head with such a huge crash that I went deaf for a few seconds. The Wookiee grinned viciously and kicked me in the thigh. I swore and folded the fingers of my left hand into a ram. Wookiee tried to dodge, but was hindered by the fact that his club was still stuck in the stone. The kinetic wave moved through the fur on the Predator's chest, and then with a drawn-out cry he was carried away into the darkness. I rolled onto my stomach, pulled my legs under me, and stood up.

Bo and Sinew were fighting near the cliff edge. Either they were pushed there by their opponents, or they had unsuccessfully landed too close to the edge, but their situation was dire: another minute and the advancing enemy would simply throw them into the abyss. I hurried to the rescue, and just in time: Sinew had lost his shield and fell under the mighty blow of a tall demon at the very edge. Bo tried to hit the creature from the side, but the demon deftly turned, taking the blow on its horn-covered back, then retaliating with a wide, swinging blow from below, throwing him back a couple of steps, then raised his sword over the ugly elf to finish what we had begun. The horned creature froze with raised hands, somehow reminding me of the stone statue of Obelix standing in the park at the western gates of the DHC city. I didn't want to use the ram as I was afraid of hitting Sinew and my mana was catastrophically low, so I just crashed into the enemy from behind, praying that the force of the blow would not carry us both over the edge. The demon tripped on the lying elf lying on the ground in front of him and fell with a huge crash onto the stones. The front half of his torso hung over the abyss. For a moment, the huge body balanced on the edge, and then with a screeching noise, began to slide down. The screeching noise was coming from Sinew. The demon's legs had somehow become entangled in the straps across the elf's chest and now the enemy was dragging him with him into the abyss. I fell down next to him, trying to unhook the crooked spur that was wrapped through a leather loop, but then the beast came to his senses and desperately rolled monstrous legs, kicking me right in the face. Sparks flew in front of my eyes, but I didn't let go, and after a moment I felt a jerk that almost pulled my finger bones out of the sockets. The demon was falling, and only the edge of his leg, still wrapped in the leather strap, was visible above the cliff. I held the elf by the harness on the other side, using all my strength to anchor us with my legs.

The leather harness snapped, whipping me in the arm. The demon roared dully, and I, losing my balance, collapsed on my back. For the third time in this short fight. A figure loomed directly above me, illuminated by the shimmering outline of a shield. It was Adalius. In the next instant, the dome went out, and the vampire used a spell that I had seen Jarkhan-Ali use: an incinerating jet of fire, as if from a flamethrower. I hastily jumped up and in the light of the dying enemy I saw numerous figures rushing towards us from the side of the cave. The vampire snarled and treated them with chain lightning. Apparently, his mana pool was significantly higher than mine. I raised my shield and out of the corner of my eye I saw that the elf had returned and did the same.

"Charge!" the vampire growled. "Counter-attack!"

I immediately understood and appreciated his decision. We couldn't let the enemy push us to the cliff. It would be best if we could fly away, but we didn't have enough mana, and in the mountains at night this would mean almost guaranteed death. The only correct move now was to take the initiative away from the opponent.

With a roar, we rushed at the enemies coming towards us and they involuntarily slowed down. Shields slammed into shields, sending out sparks of magical light. A ridiculous shriek erupted from my throat, bringing with it a furious strength. I suddenly realized that my revenge began right now, and even if it wasn't Jarkhan-Ali in front of me, this wasn't so important. The rage itself and the fact that I had something to take it out of was all that mattered. I extinguished my shield and threw myself at the enemy, chopping, crushing, taking blows and not feeling pain, feeling only hatred, every swing of my sword bearing death.

But there were many opponents, and even though our onslaught was a surprise for them, there were only four of us. We began to retreat towards the cliff, covering ourselves with magic and snapping. The veil of rage fell from my eyes, and fear came to replace it. Bo fell on his injured leg, hissing and swearing. Sinew wiped away the blood that covered his face. Adalius' terrible grin never left his face, even as he was pushed back by a huge orc shouting orders. The clan leader.

And then a battle cry rang out on the landing, bouncing endlessly off the rocks, and the enemy Predators turned their heads, trying to figure out what had happened, when Gorm crashed through their ranks like a locomotive at full speed. And then, instead of a battle, bedlam began, and very soon I realized that if we did not push back from the edge of the cliff, then our allies would involuntarily throw us over, along with the enemies. A passage opened in the ranks of the enemy as they were forced to regroup.

Warning! Low health:
12 / 50

Gritting my teeth, I dashed away from the cliff edge. I was out of mana and I couldn't hide behind a shield. A couple of good hits and I'm dead. But everyone was busy fighting, and it seemed like I would have time to slip through when the Predator-elf, knocked down by someone, suddenly rose from the ground. He was carrying an ax, a rare weapon in Fantasia because axes were not part of the starter kit. The elf looked at me and only at me. I had just my sword. The elf stepped forward, raising his weapon, but at that moment an arrow hit his neck. I turned my head and saw Fraudo.

I'd been surrounded by orcs lately. Previously, I could have easily confused one with the other (with rare exceptions), but now I instantly recognized my old friend, although in the dark I saw only his silhouette. Orcs were all very different. And demons, by the way, too. The new skin had strangely enriched my perception, making me realize that many things slip out of sight until you look at the details. This wasn't any big revelation, but I'd rarely had the chance to experience the phenomenon in real life.

Fraudo nodded almost imperceptibly, and then his silhouette was covered by that of Krinj with a sword. On his left arm was a huge rectangular shield. I noticed that the top of the shield was decorated with several bloody blades, which the demon used as an additional weapon when necessary. Performing a perfect pirouette,

Quinn flashed by.

The enemies fell, one after another. Pressed to the edge of the cliff, they desperately resisted, but were outnumbered, and in a few moments it was all over.

Part of the Predators of Adalius immediately turned around and rushed to the cave, while others examined the site. The vampire came up to me. Held out a few health vials. I accepted. Adalius walked away without a word, while Fraudo and Mr. Meyers approached.

"You okay?" asked Fraudo.

"Nice shot. Thanks."

"No problem. We're all good on our side."

I tried to rip the cork from the vial, but my hands were shaking. This often happened after a battle, but now a shiver ran through my entire body. My teeth clacked unpleasantly in his mouth. Berserk mode cost the body dearly, and I was brutally hungry and exhausted. I felt like I had a fever. Suddenly, Adalius was next to us again.

"Let's go," he said and set off towards the cave.

I followed him, tearing the corks off the health potions and chattering my teeth on the glass as I walked.

The cave was shallow — only a few dozen paces from end to end. The back wall curved slightly to the right, forming a small room with scanty furnishings, mostly supply crates and hides. There was a fire pit in the floor that had obviously not been used for a long time, I suppose due to the lack of a chimney.

Several people were kneeling at the far wall of the cave. Rather, a few Predators. Prisoners. Adalius' men, weapons at the ready, were guarding them.

The vampire turned to me and said:

"You proved yourself well in battle, Urfyn. Your debt is not only repaid — you earned a share of the booty. The far right one is yours. His strength is yours."

It took me a while to understand what he meant. But then I realized that Adalius was offering me one of the prisoners to kill for my share of the XP. To kill someone like me. And unarmed, nonetheless.

I looked up to see an elderly dwarf with a gray beard and a very long catfish-like mustache. His hands were tied behind his back, but he did not try to free himself. His whole appearance emphasized that this was not a warrior. I knew I couldn't refuse. In this case, my whole tall tale with the slaves would go out the window, and it would be the end. I could give my share of the upgrade to one of my subordinates. But did I have the right to shift the responsibility to them? In the end, I was the one who started this mission. I couldn't wriggle out of this one. This test was too simple and straightforward to cheat. And suddenly I realized that the murdering this creature wouldn't be nearly as intolerable as I thought.

Once the thrill of battle had disappeared, the longing had returned, the damned door had opened again. I wanted to think about nothing again, the way I had during battle. That was my oblivion and tranquility. And now my insides were once again covered in a crust of icy indifference again.

I took a step towards the prisoners, and the guards parted. The bloody sword was still in my hand. Absolute silence reigned behind me, but I felt a stream of unspoken words hitting my back. I didn't care.

The dwarf raised his head, grinned.

"You don't know who Adalius is yet, boy," he croaked. "But you'll find out soon. When you're in my place."

I let him finish the sentence, raised my sword and thrust it into his chest. The game mechanic was designed in such a way that a melee weapon thrust into an enemy's body inflicts a certain amount of damage every few seconds.

He wheezed and twitched, straining his shoulders and staring in horror at the blade in his body, while I stood and reveled in the feeling of any emotion other than grief. For a brief moment, I forgot her again. Notifications flashed in front of me:

TH took 8 HP damage
TH took 4 HP damage
TH took & 7 HP damage

TH took & 7 HP damage
TH took & 4 HP damage
TH died

You gained 411 876 XP
You reached level 20!

CHAPTER 13 [SYLVIA]

I WAITED FOR HER to return so that she'd explain herself in a normal way. In vain. I really wanted to go to a bar and have a drink, but instead I grit my teeth and went to bed. Tomorrow I'd need to do this fool's bidding. But the fool was me! Perhaps this was the main lesson in copying a human personality: you can see what you're capable of with your own eyes, and it always comes as a shock! Because you can't ever imagine that you would think or do or say such things!

I waited for her the next morning, but she never showed up. Then I went looking for Rkaeli. However, the chief of intelligence was not in the office — he had left on some urgent matter. I wanted to go to the counselor right away, but remembered that today was Reception Day, and decided to have lunch first. After lunch I walked around, wondering what words to use for this huge maelstrom of trouble we were caught up in. It was as deep as the sea. If politics had come into play, it meant that we could expect to be shut off at any time. Fantasia had excellent lawyers, but when it comes to matters of national security, that's unlikely to be enough. We urgently needed a connection with reality, and for this we needed to find Bryan, and I was going to demand council to postpone all other business and assemble a detachment to search for him. I was surprised to realize that I was trying to postpone the moment of explanation. As if problems of this magnitude could go away on their own! Without delay, I went to Tom Gallance.

There were a lot of people in the councilor's house, including Rkaeli. The reason for the gathering became clear very quickly: Bryan's messengers had arrived bearing sensational news. After making sure that everything was fine with the detachment, I retreated to a corner, hoping to wait out the influx of guests and learn the details later. I wasn't looking forward to performing at the festival.

I was surprised to see a child among the guests. A barefooted boy in tattered pants and a jacket stood next to the adviser and looked around with interest. At some point, his gaze landed on me, and I shuddered, because in his eyes shone a spark of recognition. The next second, the kid beelined to me. Then I finally realized that the boy was an AI. NPCs, as they're called here. I wonder why he is here?

The boy approached and suddenly uttered in a thin voice:

"Aunty Sylvia?"

I stared at him in amazement. He must have seen my hologram. Although Bryan taught me to always turn it off.

I didn't have time to answer — a clamboring stampede of feet was heard from outside and a detachment of guards in full uniform entered the room. Advisor Kaomi, a small dark-haired fellow with a very calm face, hastened to meet them.

"Find them!" shouted Tom Gallance, and only then noticed me standing off to the side.

The boy tugged brusquely at my skirt. I looked down and saw that he was handing me a letter.

"From Uncle Bryan," he said. "You are Aunty Sylvia, right?"

I took the paper and unfolded it. My eyes darted across the page. While I was reading, Tom came up to us.

"Sylvia!"

"I'm happy to see you, Tom. Do you always work in this kind of environment?"

"Do you mean to say, in this kind of chaos?" the adviser clarified. "More or less. I'm used to it. I see you've already met Malcolm."

"Not yet," I said, looking at the boy. "Although he seems to know me.

"He came with Bryan's messengers," Tom

said and patted the boy on the head, which seemed to surprise him a lot.

"Actually, I was hoping to speak with you and Mr Rkaeli, Councilor"

"Can it wait?" Tom grimaced. "We're dealing with some problems of our own, here."

"No, Tom," I said. "I'm afraid I'll just add to your growing pile of new problems. But that's how it works. When it rains, it pours. You already know that."

* * *

Hi!

I'm sending this letter along with an unusual messenger. His name is Malcolm. This is all terribly confusing, I know, but something happened to his relatives and I couldn't leave him alone in an empty village. His family should return within a week, but for now, please look after him! He's actually a great kid.

Our mission just got a little more complicated. Ask Rkaeli for details. He should tell you, given that you're working on important problems. But, you know, I've been thinking — to hell with this bet! I propose we perform a duet at the next city festival. In the meantime, I'll do my best not to slip up or do anything stupid.

Love you!

B

PS: Take care of Malcolm, he's a really nice boy.

I swore once again when I reached the line about "working on important problems," and at the end I frowned. The offer to "perform as a duet" was the worst part. Should I just read that as "I'll do anything you ask, as long as I return home from this mission?"

Malcolm sat at the table and dangled his legs, eating bread and drinking milk. An NPC child. A neural network playing the role of a village boy. The child looked like a child. He moved determinedly, examined everything, and now he was sitting there devouring food, having no idea why he needed to. However, the same could be said about me. It's amazing that we need to feed our fake bodies with fake food. Perhaps, if anyone really needed it, it was him. He was a child of this strange world.

The child took a bite of the bread and tried to ask a question with his mouth full.

"Swallow first," I suggested.

"Is Bryan your husband?" the boy repeated, fixing me with a piercing gaze.

I almost choked on the water I was drinking to hydrate for the journey. The question would have been completely ordinary if it were being asked by an ordinary child. I looked closely at Malcolm for the first time. A thin boy, with dirty nails and ears. He awaited my reply, completely forgetting about his food.

"Bryan," I said. "Bryan, Bryan, dandelion. How old are you?"

I wanted to compare the number he give with what I saw, but Malcolm unexpectedly replied:

"I dunno. What's a dandelion?"

"What do you mean, how don't you know? They didn't tell you?"

"They dunno either," Malcolm said, reaching for his cup.

I was confused and suddenly realized with surprise that it was hard for me to think of him as anything other than a person. The program that controlled him mimicked humanity with amazing accuracy, so much so that I was constantly deceived. It was as if I was speaking to the most ordinary human child. He finished his milk, licked his lips and said:

"Thanks, Aunty Sylvia!"

I chuckled.

And then, finally, Yana deigned to log in. A golden light flashed in the room, clinging to the figure materializing out of thin air.

Yana looked around the room with a sour expression and suddenly bumped into Malcolm, sitting in the same place where she herself had been sitting a few hours ago, and stared at the miracle, agape.

"What the hell is that?"

I laughed.

"That's Malcolm," I said. "Malcolm, this is my sister. Her name is Yana."

Yana stared at the child, as if she had never seen such a creature before in her life. Maybe she was wondering if this was Bryan and mine? Hilarious.

"And where...?"

She didn't finish the question.

"Bryan is still not here," I said. "His detachment stumbled upon something that is sort of like Fantasia's power generator. And they're having other difficulties. I'm afraid there's no way to get him back to town right now."

Yana froze in the middle of the room looking back and forth between Malcolm and I.

"In that case..." she said and stopped short under his blue gaze.

She looked tired. It's a shame I couldn't see the real her under the avatar, but I suspect I would have seen traces of a sleepless night.

"Fine," she grunted. "We'll discuss this issue later. Until then, get ready. I hope you found a suitable place? We'll test the connection."

* * *

The place we chose was very close to the city. Rkaeli's people had done a great job here: the ground was level, no hills, no wormholes.

Me, Malcolm and two guards assigned to us by the chief of intelligence stopped at the edge of the site (where I had asked them not to go). After telling me that she'd see me "on the other side," Yana logged out. Perhaps she was afraid to leave the city.

The guards split up: one went to the far end of the site, skirting it around the perimeter, the second stayed with me and immediately lit a cigarette. Malcolm was staring at the smoke blowing from his nostrils.

I pulled the wax out of my inventory and fashioned it into two neat plugs. I had a thick scarf to cover my eyes. But first I wanted to wait for the signal. I couldn't just stand there, deaf and blind, out in the open.

"Malcolm, do you want to help me?"

"What do I need to do?"

"I'm now going to walk around the area blindfolded and with my ears plugged. It's a ritual. Magic."

Why had she said that?

"A magical ritual?" The boy was intrigued.

"Sorcery. In short, it's important to not disturb me. But, if I leave this site here, I may stumble. And I don't want this. So if I get very close to the edge, you can come and turn me around carefully. Just be careful — I won't see anything and I might accidentally hit you. Can you handle that?"

The boy nodded vigorously.

"And what will you conjure?" he asked. "Rain? My mother always drops millet for the rain..."

"No, I'm going to...It's hard to explain. I will talk to people who are very, very far from here."

Malcolm's eyes widened until they filled half

of his face.

"And you thought we were just being silly?" I smiled. "Well, can you help? Do you remember what to do?"

Malcolm repeated the instructions. Pretty accurate. I nodded and glanced at the guard puffing indifferently on his pipe. His name was Norm. Level nine, by the way. Incredibly apathetic. Here we were, organizing God knows what, and he was sitting there, puffing on his pipe and counting crows.

I sat down, legs crossed, and waited.

At first it was like a faint interference, a rustle at the edge of my hearing. I got up and walked to the middle of the platform, closed my eyes and tied the scarf around my eyes and ears, just to be sure. My head crackled. And then a voice cut through.

"Testing, one-two-three-four-five. Testing! Sylvia, if you hear me, raise your right hand."

I raised my hand.

"She's there," said the voice in my head. "Raise it by 0.4. Sylvia, if it's too loud, raise your left hand."

I heard someone else talking directly in my head. The two voices argued briefly, not at all embarrassed by the fact that the meeting was taking place in my skull.

"Don't say anything," the first voice advised. "We're still debugging the incoming channel."

More negotiations followed, then a voice commanded:

"Better sit on the ground. We'll launch visuals, now, but it's a little different than what you're used to and it may be a shock. Breathe deeply."

I sat down on the ground and tried to breathe more evenly, but quite frankly, it was difficult. I felt the blood pulsating in my temples, compressed by the fabric of the scarf. The voice began counting down and when it reached zero, a picture slowly, slowly began to appear in front of my eyes: a greenish wall.

It was one of the most bizarre sensations I've experienced in my life. I felt that my eyes were closed, but at the same time, I could see! The picture was imperfect — too dark and not sharp enough. In addition, interference bands periodically ran across it. The voices in my head continued to talk, from time to time instructing me to raise one hand or another. Eventually the picture got better and the technicians set about setting up what they called the "output channel." I was required to twist my head, bend and unbend my arms and legs, and repeat all of these steps many times. My face was drenched in sweat under the scarf, but my tormentors were relentless.

"Okay," said the voice. "Now I'll turn on the bot, and you'll try to shake your head. Go ahead."

I slowly turned my head to the left. The image panned right and I felt a sharp pang of vertigo.

"Hold on, we'll smooth it out now. Damn, we'll have to blur from our side...Say something."

"I think I'm gonna puke!"

"Excellent!" the voice said gleefully. "I hear you loud and clear! Welcome, Sylvia. Welcome back to the real world!"

* * *

After another half hour of torment, I was able to get up and walk to the mirror specially installed in the hangar. I recognized my next body immediately. A two-legged Boston dynamics robot, like the ones that dance in those videos on YouTube. God! I couldn't believe it! I was a fucking robot!!!

It hit me hard. This was me! First I was a virtual being in a computer game, and now I was the Terminator! How did I get here?! Why was all this happening to me? Is this what I wanted with my life? The lenses of two hastily welded video cameras glittered on top of my head. Roman (my technician) explained that they were there to make my vision binocular, without which I would not be able to navigate normally in space. Ha! What did Roman know about orientation in space?!

I raised my hand and a length of plastic tubing with a black wiring tube raised in tandem. A three-fingered claw appeared in front of my eyes. I unclenched my fingers and the claw opened. I laughed (slightly hysterically) at this claw. I felt like I was going insane. I'd have to visit my mother like this.

"Careful with the arms! The dimensions are different and you won't feel if you hit something!"

The dimensions were indeed different. Due to the fact that my "eyes" were *on* my head, and not *in* my head, my height seemed gargantuan. The hands were not located where my real hands were, but below (all because of my eyes). On top of that, there was a tiny delay in the bot's response to my movements. Perhaps this had its own positive side: if the immersion were more realistic, I think that I would really have lost it. The whole time I just felt like I was driving some sort of vehicle.

Roman instructed me to make a circle around the hangar, moving as slowly as possible. It was a miracle that I managed to accomplish this after several attempts. Roman explained that the machine itself controls its own balance when walking, because without feedback I would hardly have been able to accomplish that. But at the same time, the robot had to take commands from my body and execute them. Both programs had to operate at the same time, synchronizing with each other. And since both were based on neural networks, the more I walk, the better the algorithm would learn and adjust. Indeed, after a few laps, it had already become easier.

"Sylvia, I'm turning on your speakers and mic. Say something."

After a moment, I heard the hum of motors accompanying my every movement. Ha!

"I need your clothes, your boots, and your

motorcycle."

"I doubt my clothes and boots would fit you," Roman chuckled. "As for the bike—I'll think about it."

When I had completed another circle, a door opened at the far end of the hangar and several people entered. Yana was among them. So my recent wish had come true — to see my sister in the flesh. The traces of a sleepless night were vividly imprinted in the dark circles around her eyes, and the thick layer of makeup didn't do much to mask them.

She was accompanied by two technicians. One, a young boy with glasses, turned out to be a Boston dynamics engineer named Roger Stone. He came up to me and began unceremoniously digging into my plastic body. The second, a middle-aged man with sharp facial features, was named Roman Lipovetsky.

"Roman? Wasn't I just talking to you?"

Roman nodded and smiled.

"You look different than I pictured," I said.

"Whereas you look exactly as I pictured!"

I smiled. Roman laughed merrily and clapped his hands together.

"What's that?" I said, not understanding.

"You have a semiotic display. Your emotions are transmitted in the form of emoticons. You are smiling right now, aren't you?"

I was surprised.

"Wow, you guys have accomplished a lot."

"Not so much, actually. Only the smile emoticon works. But a real American can't go into politics without a charming smile. And you have one!"

While we were exchanging pleasantries, Yana stood a little to the side. I turned to her.

"Hi! Nice to visit you, for a change."

She nodded, but didn't reply.

"Want to go outside?" asked Roman.

I turned towards him. He grinned broadly.

* * *

Going outside hit me a lot harder than anything I had experienced up to this point. My world! My homeworld! I missed normal life so badly, God, if only you knew! I knew what I was doing when I went to Fantasia, I'm not a fool. But reality, of course, quickly convinced me that I had no idea what I signed up for. It was cruel. It was cruel to bring me here. I only now realized this, and when I understood, I was terribly angry with Yana.

It was the most ordinary courtyard in the middle of an industrial site. Around it was a box of identical hangars, and then a factory building, pipes and a glass antechamber. I raised my head up as far as the construction allowed (just a little), and stared emotionally at the lifeless gray sky. Only in my real world could the sky be so amazingly ordinary! Lord, how I wanted to go there! Into my body, an ordinary living body, which, of course, would grow old, unlike its digital counterpart (although who knows?), but was still so familiar. I looked at the boxes of hangars around as through the eyes of a Bushman first introduced to the vastness of modern civilization. How huge and majestic!

Yana came up and stood in front of me, her arms folded across her chest.

"So? How is it?" she asked.

I expected mockery, but saw only fatigue.

"Tolerable," I said. "But like you, I would prefer if Bryan was here instead."

"Yes, but you have to make do with what you have. We're out of time. You have to write your speech tonight. Tomorrow you'll give it before the UN General Assembly."

"Are you joking?"

"No. This is our chance and there won't be another."

"But...tomorrow?!"

"Yes."

"Shit. I...will you help me write it?"

She threw me a tired look, and suddenly something happened. I felt someone grab my hand, squeeze my fingers. Instinctively reaching out to her ear to pull out the plug, I heard a three-fingered claw hitting somewhere in the neck area with a rip. The image swayed.

Malcolm's voice cried:

"Wake up, Aunty Sylvia! Wake up! Danger!"

I tore off the scarf from my head, and a

monstrous mixture of two worlds appeared before my eyes. I saw nothing and understood nothing. Yana's voice broke through Malcolm's screams and the utterly distinct sounds of...a battle?

"Disconnect! Quickly! We'll fry her brain!"

Something clicked in my head and the real world disappeared.

Chapter 14

AFTER LEVELING UP and looking through my new characteristics, I was surprised to find that there were new skills available in Constitution. Had the program changed, or did my new body open up new possibilities?

The list was impressive:

Magical Resistance
Armor
Regeneration
Whiptail
Chameleon Skin
View five more skills...

Could it really be that all Predators got such goodies? Although I did remember fighting a demon with a whip-tail during the siege on the city! I remember it got stuck in my shield...

Each of the five skills seemed useful and appealing in its own way, but I only had one point and I needed to make a choice. I chose the armor. I know, not a very interesting choice, but an important one! I could no longer wear my good old protective jacket from the DHC city arsenals — the horns on my back and shoulders would not allow it.

True, I was somewhat afraid that the armor would just increase the number and density of my horns, but it turned out much better than expected. The scales covering his skin became thicker and stronger, but the horns remained the same. So this was the big 2-0:

Urfyn, Level 20 (790 662 XP)

Strength: 5 (base level)
Dexterity: 1 (ranged damage — 1)
Intellect: 9 (build a bonfire — 1, cartography — 4, language — 1, fishing — 0, magical damage — 2)
Wisdom: 6 (meditation — 1, lore — 1, mana regeneration rate — 3, Divine Voice — 1)
Constitution: 4 (Armor — 1) +2.5 (melee weapon)
Armor: +1

Damage: +0.5 (light weapon), +1.5 (magic)
Armor: +2
Health: 40 hp

Speed: 5.5

Stamina: 225

Mana: 150 (regeneration rate — 1 point every 3.5 mins)

I sat on the edge of a cliff, trying to figure out what to do next with my life. Adalius announced that the party would remain here for several days, as there was a chance that several enemy scouts the vampire hoped to intercept would return to the mountain base. None of this bothered me much. I didn't care about anything anymore, and I was dangerously close to losing my fear of death — or will to live. Thoughts of revenge also did not warm my soul too much. Everything again plunged into the abyss of meaninglessness.

I heard footsteps, but didn't turn my head. Adalius paused next to me, standing on the very edge of the cliff. He wore a wide-brimmed hat that protected the vampire's pale skin from the sun. It made him look like some sort of village preacher.

"What do you plan to do next, Urfyn?"

"Nothing has changed, Adalius. I must go to the east."

"To the City of Players."

"To the City of Players," I confirmed.

"I don't think you'll make it through the front gate. But if they let you in, they definitely won't let you out. At least until they get the whole truth out of you about your mission."

"I'll find a way."

"And there is a way. You can go into the city with me. I have sway there."

I looked up at him. The vampire calmly contemplated the magnificent view from the landing.

"And what do you want in exchange?"

"In exchange you'll tell me what the deal is with those black stones."

"I've already told you everything I know."

"Not everything.'

I shrugged. The information he wanted had become too personal for me, and I was not going to confess to just anyone. None of my guys knew what had really happened in the swamps.

"I won't rush you, Urfyn. We'll stay here for another day, then move towards the city. You fought well, it's good to have allies like you. But the benefits should always be mutual. You understand?

"Perfectly."

Adalius turned and walked away. Well, I had something to think about. His offer was worthwhile. But I was worried about his lie-recognition mechanism. If this was truly a skill, then any story I tell that didn't not include the story of my transformation wouldn't sound true. And I couldn't reveal the truth — that would be a death sentence. That means we couldn't have a deal.

"Master," a voice whispered from over my shoulder.

I nodded to the seat next to me. Camilla knelt in a half-step, bowing her head.

"I have information," she said. "Valuable information. Now I'm certain that Jarkhan uses the language to control the stones. It is possible that Farsi is the language his relatives speak. I don't know it that well, but I could make out a few things. This is a manual with commands. Most of them concern forces unknown to me, but I managed to decipher some of them. I made notes: the meaning and a transcription of the voice commands. In theory, when Jarkhan-Ali says what is indicated in square brackets next to the stones, what is written opposite should happen."

She handed me the book, and I quickly hid it in my inventory. Camilla glanced around furtively and continued:

"Two things. First, the commands for different stones are different. Apparently, different layers of this reality were read in different places. The pages indicate which stones are meant. Second: pay special attention to the command," Camilla uttered a word in Farsi, something like "yek-shu-rah."

"It means 'patching the hole.' I have reason to believe that this command can deactivate the black stones."

"What do you mean, deactivate?"

"I'm not exactly sure. But I think there's a chance that they close, disappear or transform into ordinary boulders."

"You said that the commands are different for different stones, right? Is this command common to everyone?"

"Yes. Honestly, the likelihood that you will pronounce the words correctly is small. But it's worth a try."

"Try what, exactly?"

Camilla leaned down and said in a whisper:

"There's another circle a few hours away from here. I made a bookmark."

I thought for a while. Then I said:

"Thank you, Millie. I'll think about it."

"What more is there to think about, Urfyn? We can leave whenever we want, can't we?"

"Adalius made me an offer. Information about the stones in exchange for passage into the City of Players..."

Camilla looked at me in bewilderment.

"And what, I'm supposed to be a slave until the end of the mission?" she asked quietly. "I can't say I find it to be a very pleasant experience..."

I averted my eyes.

"My task has not changed. I have to find a way to get to this son of a bitch. And I'll get him."

Camilla sat in silence for a while, then got up and walked away.

I thought about it. And then I opened the map and looked at the etchings I had copied from the corpse we found near the village of Lipky. There were indeed some stones not far from us. I pulled a little book out of my inventory and flipped to a page. The map was drawn with just a few strokes and was surprisingly accurate. I estimated the distance and realized that I could fly there in ten minutes. Suppose I still want to accept Adalius' offer. But I'd need to be getting it at a bargain. I need to get a bargain. Or something a vampire would think of as such. I looked around. The site was empty: the Reapers were at their stations in case any of any enemy stragglers returned to camp, Adalius had gone into the cave, and my guys were standing off on the other side of the site, closer to the road leading down. If I left right now, no one would have time to come after me.

Without hesitation, I cast levitation and immediately turned on maximum thrust, heading northwest towards the lake. The wind whistled in my ears with such force that I wished I had asked Tom to make me some flying earmuffs.

Gradually, crawling out from behind a low mountain ridge that branched off from the crest on the right, a huge lake opened up in front of me and curved to the west. I passed the ridge and took a sharp dive. I had enough mana. Just a few more minutes and then I'd somehow find a place to land. However, the closer I flew, the more my confidence in my abilities wavered. The mountains edged close to the water and it seemed like I wouldn't be able to quickly find a suitable landing spot any time soon. The distance suddenly seemed much larger than it had before, as the unusual perspective had deceived my eyes. I was getting down to the last third of my mana, and I feverishly scanned the landscape in front of me. After a moment, I sighed with relief — the lake had a shore. It was hidden by steep cliffs, but still there was enough room to land. I rushed to the nearest beach, gratefully recalling the instructions of Officer Nathan Klotzky. It was he who explained to me that from a height, it seems that the earth is approaching very slowly, but when you find yourself several hundred feet away from it, it suddenly jumps in your face. I still had little experience in flying, but now I calculated everything precisely and landed with seventeen units of mana to spare.

I walked along the beach, the wall of the cliff on the right, the lake on the left, the narrow strip of sand in front of me gradually widening and curving to the west. I had to move forward, but a rocky ledge blocked my path. I cast levitation lightly pushed off with my feet, drifting to the edge.

Moving along a gentle slope to the north, I soon spotted my target — an oval depression, at the bottom of which the black silhouettes of stones could be seen. I carefully looked around and, not spotting anything suspicious, started my descent. The stones greeted me with silence: no animals, no birds, no noise of trees — only the barely perceptible whisper of the lake.

Lying a few dozen paces from the stones themselves was a convenient patch of ordinary cobblestones. I sat down, took out the notebook, and opened it.

Within five minutes, I realized what a gargantuan effort Camilla had put into her notes. When had she managed to do all this? Written in small, confident handwriting above each line were the notes in English and the transcription of the pronunciation in Latin script.

I found the word (or several words?) that Camilla had spoken to me a few minutes earlier. In Farsi, it looked like this: یک سوراخ بدوزید Then the translation and transcription were inscribed in neat printed letters: [ˈjec s̑uˈɹɑx]. Referring between her notes, I tried to read the word and realized that the professor was right: the chances of this working were slim. Transcriptions are all well and good, but without a knowledge of the nuances of pronunciation, inflection and other things, there was no way of really speaking in an unfamiliar tongue. But I still had to try, otherwise I would have traveled here in vain.

I got up and walked to the stones. And the Voice switched on in my head:

One of the brothers dug, looking for bright pebbles in the crumbling sand. The second was looking at the bottom, a few dozen paces down the slope. The sand crumbled beneath the blows of the shovel, and suddenly something black appeared, like a charred piece of wood. The eldest brother dug his shovel in once more, and as the sand scattered, it revealed a skull. An old, blackened skull.

The voice fell silent.

I stood in the center of the ring formed by the stones. Taking a breath, I hesitantly said:

"Yek-zhoo-rakh-sho-mal!"

Nothing happened. I went through a few of the simplest commands, occasionally adjusting my pronunciation or emphasis.

"To-tash!" I exclaimed angrily (if Camilla was right, this meant "fire").

But no fire erupted.

Ten minutes later I felt like a complete idiot. But I didn't want to fly away just like that.

"Bloody stones! Yek-zhoo-rakh-sho-mal! You only listen to that bastard, right? Hey, Listener! Listen to me! Yek-zhoo-rah! You're not working, fucking resonator! I'll sew your fucking mouth shut, Author. Yek-zhoo-rakh-sho-mal! Shove your to-tash up your ass!"

The ground shook barely perceptibly. I stopped short and suddenly noticed that the black obelisks had become much more contrasted, filled with sucking darkness. There was a screeching sound, small pebbles dancing under my feet. A dull grinding sound started somewhere under the earth, and I, in disbelief, saw that the black stones were trembling and sinking. Inch by inch, they were drawn into the soil, which sucked them in with a hungry rumbling, until they had vanished completely. The earthen mouths slammed shut, leaving me standing in the middle of an empty area. It had all happened so fast!

I turned around and bumped into Adalius, who was quietly sitting a few steps away from me.

"An impressive sight!" the vampire said. "Can you do that with other stones? Or just these?"

He had seen. And heard! There was no point in denying it. On the other hand, what exactly had he seen and heard? And how had he perceived it? Most importantly, had he seen the notebook?

"You know, Urfyn, I could get answers from you a different way," Adalius smiled unpleasantly. "Level twenty isn't as high as you might think it is."

"Want to test that?"

The vampire suddenly grew serious.

"I don't. I saw you in battle and know what desperation looks like. Now I'm completely certain that you did not lie about your goal. Revenge is a personal affair, I know this, and perhaps I don't need to know all the details. I'm not even going to ask what fucking language you were trying to speak right now. You and your people are still free to go wherever you want, we will not interfere with those who have just shed blood for us. That is the law."

Adalius opened his inventory, took out a bottle of concentrated mana, and threw it to me.

"Tomorrow we're setting off for the City of Players," he said. "If you want, march with us. And you can keep your secrets to yourself."

CHAPTER 15

"SHIT, YOU'RE FAT for a dwarf! And a real dwarf fights with an ax, right guys?"

The guys laughed. Gorm blushed.

"You see, Urfyn, Gorm had an ax too," Krinj explained, grinning.

"Stop talking bullshit!"

The road curved through the mountains. Dense gray clouds slid quickly across the sky, dripping rain mingled with snow. Weather aside, the Predators were in high spirits. The job was done and they were on their way home.

"But he lost this ax in battle with a *very* dangerous opponent. Isn't that right, Gorm?"

"Be glad I no longer have that ax, pig!" snapped the dwarf. "Because if I did, I would shove it up your ass!"

A new round of laughter.

"So basically, this is what happened. We were

walking along the banks of the Ikwen, south of here, and we stumbled upon some Herbivores. A fight broke out. Gorm immediately chose a more serious target for himself — he's a brave warrior! Isn't that right, Gorm? That little girl looked about fifteen years old...She, of course, was fleeing through the bushes, but he had her right where he wanted her!"

The Predators sobbed with laughter. The dwarf was no longer red, but purple.

"He climbs after her into these bushes! It was just like the forest, after all, and he was like a lumberjack with his ax. There was a squeak and a stirring in the bushes, just like you'd imagine. And then we see the girl climbing out the other side and running into the forest. And in her hands is a very familiar ax..."

"Will you shut it already?"

Someone passed a small keg around. They drank as they walked, drenched, laughing and cursing. When the keg reached me, I raised it to my lips without hesitation. It contained a dark beer. I took several big gulps and my head immediately began to swim. As I handed over the keg, I suddenly imagined the scene with Gorm and the girl taking the ax from him in the bushes, glanced at the dwarf slurping beer resentfully, and suddenly burst out laughing.

"Look, it hit Urfyn!"

Another round of laughter rang out. Gorm choked, beer flowed from his nose, the Predators howled. And I with them.

The keg was being rapidly drained as they regaled me with more and more stories. I noticed they recalled Stork's campaign against the DHC city with reluctance, but they talked about the capture of the City of Players with pleasure. Even Adalius, pacing back and forth in his stupid hat, said:

"The success of Stork's entire plan hung in the balance. And all due to the fact that he relied on real players who were supposed to pull the wool over the king's eyes. They had connections — unlike us. Well. We had to put on a little show, as if Stork had been ambushed while traveling to town with important news. The king and his retinue had to go out to meet him, and the people of Stork from the real world to convince the king that we are but few and represent no real danger to him. And the king was caught..."

"You should have seen his face, Urfyn! He was all: 'It's me! What are you doing?!' added Sinew.

"Then we had to act very quickly, because the king was streaming his game, which meant that in the next few minutes, everyone would know everything," continued Adalius. "And just imagine: we had a whole mile left to march."

"Then Stork said—"

"Are you telling the story?!" the vampire burst out.

Sinew grunted, but then fell silent. Others giggled.

"Stork said that we could leave and continue living in the forests, or we could take this city for ourselves right now and clear it out in a couple of hours, because those living inside had no idea what a real battle was. They were just fucking gamers, and we would sweep them away. Even if there were not just a couple of thousand, but ten times more — it didn't change a thing. That's what he said. And so we did it. Every third citizen just logged out as soon as they saw our soldiers. Some, of course, tried to resist, but how! No reactions, no real fighting skills. They relied only on magic, but we quickly divided them into small groups and made quick work of them. And then we entered the castle, and Stork announced a party in honor of our victory."

"They'd respawn in the city," I said, surprised. "How could you party?"

"Ha! Many said the same to Stork at that time. And he replies: 'There is plenty of time. They will all be born as zeroes, and leveling up will take a minimum of several days. Even if they all agree to buff one person selectively, it would still take a long time, and the castle has a wine cellar...'"

A friendly groan swept through the ranks of the Predators.

"We drank for two days straight," the vampire continued when things settled down. "Some even died, apparently from alcohol poisoning..."

"Colton from Beastmouth Clan!"

"And Raptor."

"Raptor fell from the window!"

"Well, he was puking from the window and fell, but he was puking from the alcohol!"

"We crawled out of the castle with a wild hangover," Adalius raised his voice, glaring at the interruptions, "and everything turned out as Stork had predicted. We killed them all again. And then it was already clear that they couldn't catch up with us, and they stopped logging in. The city was ours."

The conversation gradually turned to the story of the ambassadors, which I had already heard from Gorm, and from there on to the failed march to the west. The Predators grew visibly gloomy. Adalius was calm, but when he spoke, his voice was filled with icy contempt.

"You know what the biggest problem with Herbivores is?" he said. "They pissed away one world, transforming it into a lifeless concrete jungle, and now they want to do the same thing here. In a blink of an eye you'll find yourself stuck in a cubicle again, up to your eyes in credit card debt, shackled hand and foot by 'tolerance' and political correctness. But it's really just another leash a handful of clever bastards are trying to tie around your neck."

The Reapers grunted in support of his words.

"Shallow hypocrites who shout about equal rights, while slowly tightening the noose, they call all go sit on a dick!"

The Predators suddenly roared at once. It

echoed endlessly, sounding all around us as if the mountains were also voicing their approval.

"What do you think my main insight has been regarding the structure of this world, Urfyn?" The vampire's yellow eye flashed from under his hat.

I shrugged.

"The game made us monsters, separating us from the world of humans. They see us as monsters. Does that mean that the game was made by someone who put this label on us in advance? And then I realized that it's much better! If we had stayed human, then it would have been much easier to put a leash on us. And so let there be no confusion! Let them see us as monsters — the personifications of their fears — and I'll see them as who they really are — monkeys in shock collars. Let them be scared! They should be! Because I'd rather die than allow them to turn my world into a concrete jungle again! Look around you, Urfyn!"

I shuddered and looked around. The mountains stretched in all directions, freezing us. The clouds lay low and heavy like gigantic tufts of cotton clinging to the pointed peaks.

"This is not a world of credit, barber shops and 'networking,'" the vampire's voice dripped with contempt as he spoke these words. "This is the world of warriors! I, Adalius, a free warrior! I go wherever I want. I say what I think. I do what is necessary for the prosperity of my people and my land."

The Predators repeated these last words out of sync, but with great enthusiasm. I must say, the speech had been impactful. For a moment, I had seen Adalius' world appear before my own eyes. Harsh and gloomy, it smelled like a Medieval pigsty, this world, and I suddenly realized that the Author had succeeded in his strange plan. He had found a way to make these people different. "I do what is necessary for the prosperity of my people and my land," said Adalius. And this was an important point! None of my DHC friends would call Fantasia "their land." Too much effort was spent trying to reconstruct a life even remotely similar to the one they had before their rebirth. And these creatures, also guests in this world, accepted it for what it really was.

* * *

At the highest point of the pass, the Predators announced a halt. A campfire was built, new barrels were uncorked, food was fried. Since many of the campers were already less than sober, I had concluded that we would be staying here for the night, but I was mistaken! Krinj answered my question with a smile:

"We'll go down the mountain singing songs. It'll be fun, you'll see!"

It turned out to be very fun. Staggering slightly, we walked along the path and sang. The Predators' repertoire was not distinguished by its grace. Best of all were the obscene little ditties, but there were also ballads. I remember one of them went:

> *From the underworld to the world above,*
> *The roads are serpentine.*
> *With chain mail, dagger, spear in glove*
> *Walks the lonely paladin.*
> *His burden great, but strong in faith,*
> *The hero fears no strife.*
> *A crystal flask on his right hip lay,*
> *And in it — the Water of Life.*

Sinew turned out to have a beautiful tenor, and he took the solo. The rest joined in on the choruses (if there were any). There was another song about a paladin:

> *The paladin has only one kin,*
> *Only one kin has the paladin.*
> *Loki, Thor and his pal-Odin,*
> *He'd follow to Hel and back again.*

As we walked past cliff faces, the walls juggled our voices, tossing them back at the singers and throwing everyone off tune. I was a little surprised at the fact that Adalius was allowing them to scream so much (considering the risk of landslides), but at the moment, I was a little tipsy myself and was content to just walk along beside them, enjoying an experience unlike any other I'd ever had.

The twilight made the mountains around us look wondrously beautiful. The ridge, bathed in the last rays of the sun, stretched far to the north. I suddenly realized that we were close to the edge of the map. So was this just an illusion? A still image, a projection of mountains that weren't there? I suddenly felt indignant. Everything around me was just a projection. How easy it was to forget! And more importantly — did asking that question even make sense anymore? When I could just go and join their chorus and suddenly they think I'm one of them? A huge, rude, terrible demon-warrior and at the same time a drunken, confused man. I felt that I knew the Predators a little better already, and they were really just ordinary guys. Even pretty likeable, in their own way.

"I don't like the expression on your face, Mr. Mursley."

I shuddered and turned. Mr. Parks was walking beside me. The detachment was scattered and stretched out along the path and no one could overhear us, but all the same, the fact that Rkaeli's deputy had violated the rules of our disguise by referring to me using my real name irritated me slightly.

"I didn't know you were so good at reading demon expressions, Sparky. And what's wrong with my face?"

Mr. Parks didn't move an eyebrow.

"You look like you've forgotten whose side you're really on."

I was amazed at how accurately he had read my thoughts, but didn't show it.

"Oh yeah?"

"Unfortunately so."

"What exactly is bothering you?"

"What's bothering me is your willingness to find new friends among beings who consider it their duty to exterminate us."

"Duly doted. A valuable lesson in ethics from a man whose original body is in prison," I quipped.

"That's why it's so valuable," Mr. Parks agreed, missing the irony. "Lessons in ethics are easily forgotten, and as a result, you can end up in jail. I know this from personal experience. Keep in mind, Mursley, that if necessary, I will do my best to protect the interests of the citizens of the City of DHC."

"Is that a threat?"

Mr. Parks said nothing, just grinned, momentarily losing his mask of complete idiocy. As always, the speed with which his guise vanished was a little jarring. And sobering. Although, to be honest, I didn't give a single shit about the DHC City, the Predators, or Mr. Parks!

An hour later, it was completely dark. My legs were buzzing from the long journey, plus the change in altitude and the alcohol made my temples throb. Soon the outline of the forest emerged from the darkness, a dark wall rising to the northeast. Straight ahead of us was a large lake, the stars reflected in the calm surface of the water. We were leaving the mountains behind.

CHAPTER 16

FROM A DISTANCE I saw the high walls made of giant stone blocks. They were covered in brown moss and looked ancient. Although, in fact, how old could they be? Three years? Narrow guard towers protruded above the walls, banners fluttered from the towers. The wooden gate, reinforced with huge steel braces, was closed. I glanced to my right and saw the wall literally cut into the river, breaking off in the middle of the leisurely flowing waters.

Our detachment stopped at the gate. As I lifted my gaze, I didn't see any sentinels, but on the flag above, I saw the image of a pair of black narrowed eyes on a blue background. I had the immediate feeling that the city was watching us from these painted eyes. Apparently there were some talented artists among the Predators!

Adalius approached the gate, drew his sword

and knocked loudly with the hilt, then took a few steps back and waited. Several agonizing minutes passed. Finally the bolt rattled, the doors shuddered, and began to slowly open outward. A dozen guards wearing suits of armor in various stages of completeness stared at us from the other side. The vampire, without a word, moved directly towards them, and they parted to let him inside. All the others followed him in silence. My footsteps clacked across the stone tiles. Behind the backs of the guards I saw houses and trees, and further back, the black bulk of the castle rising in the distance.

Adalius walked a dozen paces and stopped in front of a line of Predators, gazing curiously at the newcomers.

"Greetings, free warriors!" The vampire barked. "We bring news of our victory: the traitors from Azimuth have been destroyed! The clan has been set aflame, the ashes scattered."

Some of the crowd members burst into cheers, some stared expressionlessly at the vampire. Many were openly staring at me and my people, especially Camilla and Mr. Parks, and the looks they were giving were not kind. A lanky orc with long, powerful arms stepped forward. His face was one solid tattoo.

"Who's that with you?"

"This is the free warrior Ufryn, speaker of the North Star Clan. He and his people ask permission to enter the city. They aided us in battle."

"Does he know how to talk?" The tattooed orc looked at me mockingly.

I took a step forward.

"I am Ufryn. Name yourself, Orc."

"I am Xenos, speaker of the Gnomon Clan," he said calmly. "What is it you need in our city, Urfyn?"

I stared at him for some time, deciding how best to respond.

"I heard you had good day cares," I said louder, so that all those present could hear.

There was a smattering of laughter. The tattooed orc didn't smile.

"The Azimuth weren't weaklings," he said dryly. "Plenty of honor for the Reapers, but not enough for two clans. Tell me, Urfyn, why did you get involved in our internal affairs? Why are you taking away someone else's glory?"

"Repaying a debt," I shrugged my shoulders.

The orc pursed his lips.

"Recently, the city has developed the unpleasant tradition of building secret alliances and weaving intrigues. Hasn't it, Adalius?" The orc turned to the vampire.

He stared back, raising his brows slightly, as if to ask, "Well, what next?" Xenos suddenly turned towards me.

"If you pass a trial, you can enter."

I looked at Adalius, who answered with a cool gaze.

"What's the trial?"

"Only warriors have the right to live in our city," the Predator said. "This is the law. The trial: a duel with one of the city's warriors. No magic or armor. Just a light pole as a weapon."

Honestly, I had expected more when the vampire promised to put in a good word for me. In all, it turned out that his word didn't carry as much weight as he had let on. I was a level 20, but almost all of my points were invested in magic. Worst case scenario, I could shoot a bow, but fighting with a stick? My only chance was the strength given to me by the Silent Man.

Things only got worse from there. Xenos announced that a group of newbies had arrived and openly hinted that they would fight with Adalius, and if anyone objected, he would show them the way out. Suddenly, the real Predators came out to play. The vampire bared his teeth and said that if anyone wanted to arrange a duel with him, then he was always happy to oblige. The number of willing candidates dwindled but, to my great dismay, it was the weaklings who dropped out. Four remained: a hideous ghoul with a dangling tongue, a vampire dressed head-to-toe in black (Like Adalius, he was wearing a large hat), a short elf with thin, reedy arms, and a sturdy young orc. I was given the chance to choose my opponent, so I sized each of them up in turn. At first, I wanted to choose a vampire (if she volunteered herself!), but suddenly, she raised her head and met my gaze. There was a subtle, but unmistakable madness glimmering there, and I suddenly changed my mind, choosing the elf instead. Several angry smirks blossomed around. Adalius, who was standing behind, drew in a sharp breath through his teeth, and I realized that I had chosen badly.

The fight was set to take place there, at the gate. The street leading into the city was wide enough. Spectators moved further away, freeing up an area for us, paved with even and surprisingly clean stone slabs. Someone ran to the guardhouse and brought two poles, each about four feet long. I took mine and saw that they had been used before — the darkened wood was covered with numerous dents and scratches.

"My name is Husk," the elf said quietly. "Sharpleaf Clan."

I had no intention of introducing myself a third time, so I nodded quietly.

"The battle continues until the surrender of one of the parties," announced Xenos, turning to the crowd that was gradually gathering around the gate, watching hungrily.

At a sign from the orc, we took our seats in the center of the clearing, a dozen feet apart.

"Begin!" barked Xenos.

It was immediately apparent that I would need to dodge and weave — he was swift, nimble, and in addition, wielded his weapon brilliantly, using it as both a spear and a club. He opened the battle by resting the pole on the ground in front of him and holding it with one hand like a short staff. And I, like the biggest fool in the world, bought into his deceptively relaxed position, which made it seem impossible for him to attack. Husk somehow pulled his pole in, stepping back and avoiding my swing, then following up with a quick counterattack. The stick jumped out of his hand, giving me a solid jab in my face. The pain blinded me for a moment, but for some reason Husk didn't use this moment to strike, instead letting me come to my senses. He was throwing me a bone.

I sincerely regretted that Quinn wasn't in my place. With her level of acrobatics and love for her spear, she would have undoubtedly put on a better show. But I was no less sincerely glad that I had the thick skin of a demon. It was the only thing saving me from the quick, precise blows dealt by the elf as he whirled around me. The crowd laughed and egged me on, urging me to make a move.

After a few minutes of fighting, I was starting to get out of breath. Not one of my blows had reached their target, and if I did manage to hit my opponent, it was merely a graze. I had sustained dozens of blows, biting and painful, although they caused no damage. I kept waiting for an opening, but the rhythm of his attacks was constantly changing, and I didn't have time to catch up, like a drunken bass player who's always a few measures behind the band. I felt anger, which is a poor advisor during battle. Darting forward again and again, I opened my position more and more often, and his damn stick took advantage of every opportunity. I stopped, trying to catch my breath and, if possible, use my back to shield myself from the blows coming from all sides. But Husk was done giving me any breaks; the concessions were over. Anticipating another attack, I instinctively raised my hands to protect my face. The enemy's weapon easily found a gap in my defense, and my cheekbone stung. The pole slid back, tickling the wrist of my hand, I sharply squeezed my fingers and, unexpectedly for myself, tenaciously grabbed the piece of wood by the very end. Wasting no time, I pulled the stick towards myself, and Husk, who did not want to part with the weapon, swayed forward. I realized that this was my chance and would probably be the only one I got. I opened my fingers, threw my own stick to the ground, stepped forward and, collecting all my anger and despair, brought my fist down on my opponent's head. Husk hissed and tried to kick me in the knee, but the blow hit a short spike growing over my kneecap. The elf cried out and tried to deflect to the side, but I grabbed him firmly by the ankle. Anger overwhelmed me, demanding to be released. I twisted his arm, forcing him to stick out a black, knobby elbow, and then used my left hand to strike the joint with all my might, shattering it. The bone cracked, Husk screamed. I pushed the elf and he flew back, stumbled and collapsed onto the pavement. The crowd roared. I took a step towards him. The bloody haze was still clouding my mind, and I didn't care in the slightest that the battle was not meant to be to the death. But Xenos suddenly stepped in front of the defeated warrior.

"Enough!" the orc barked.

I stopped, shaking my head and trying to quiet the blood pounding in my temples. Husk got up with difficulty, spat out a bloody tooth on the pavement and glared at me. He had presumably realized that I was not going to stop. Even in defeat, he remained an extremely skilled warrior, and I partially regretted that I had made such a powerful enemy so soon after our arrival in the city.

"Glorious fight!" Adalius came over and patted me on the shoulder. "Honestly, if I had bet, I wouldn't have bet on you. Husk is a serious opponent, a born warrior. But you did well and deserve the right to enter the city. Let's go!"

We walked along the narrow, crooked streets lined with elegant, tile-covered stone houses. It was a typical old European town, swooping up and down with the hills, dissected by alleyways (which were sometimes so narrow that one could only walk sideways), with crumbling stone stairs, wooden shutters and blooming acacias. And from every street, I saw the castle looming overhead, with its five blackened towers — one on each corner and one in the center. This tower, according to the

Reader, was the one where Jarkhan-Ali would finally be able to fulfill his terrible mission.

Most of the houses were empty. There were too few predators to populate the city. I asked Adalius if this meant that I could choose any house I like and live in it. The vampire said that in theory, yes, but that he would act differently, if he were in my place.

"I understand," he explained, "that you have important business with those resonators of yours, and need access to the castle. To do things of this magnitude, you need to have resources. You need support, social status, do you understand? Without it, all you are is a nobody with a wand, and no one will take you seriously."

"And how do I find these resources?"

The vampire smiled smugly.

"You've already taken the first step towards vanquishing the Sharpleaf Clan. But this success must be consolidated, and at the same time provide you with housing in a respectable part of the city. This way, in the eyes of people, you'll be a force to be reckoned with and your word will immediately gain weight. That's why you need to go find Husk's house, throw anyone out who may be there, and declare the house as your own."

I stared at him.

"Wouldn't that mean a war between our clans?"

"No," said Adalius. "You beat him in a fair fight, one-on-one. According to our laws, you now have the right to his property. The Sharpleaves wouldn't think to interfere. At least, not openly. But a quick knife to the guts in a dark alley — heh — is an easy way to go! So keep both eyes open."

I glanced back at my companions. Fraudo and Quinn were whispering about something, Camilla looked around with interest, although she looked somehow haunted. Mr. Parks walked behind, and his expression, as always, was completely blank. Would they approve of the vampire's decision? Unlikely. On the other hand, we had to admit that we had indeed made significant progress towards our goal. But we couldn't rest on our laurels yet! The author would definitely find a way into the city, and then the castle — I did not doubt that for a second. He created the damn place! And when that happened, I needed to be ready!

The Predators occupied the central region of the city, around the square in front of the castle. Most of the city's NPCs lived here, and were treated with great respect. Traders were one of the few sources of valuable resources, and therefore enjoyed undeniable authority. To kill a merchant meant to incur grave consequences, including the death penalty. All this Adalius explained to me on the way, and then we finally entered the square.

It was absolutely gorgeous, this square, with a fountain, benches, gazebos and fruit trees in planter pots. The houses around the edges had luxurious facades, openwork porticoes, balconies and sculptures. I hadn't seen anything like it for so long that I involuntarily froze at the exit from the street, amazed by the diversity and elegance of the architecture. I must admit that, with all of Councilor Gallance's talent for construction, this was far above and beyond his capabilities.

"Husk lives there," the vampire pointed to a beautiful, narrow white mansion. "Not bad, eh? I think it would be just right for you and your men. There's a baker's dozen rooms inside, so plenty of space. Don't worry, Husk and the Sharpleaves no longer live with their servants, so you shouldn't have any problems. Throw anything out that you don't want to keep for yourself. Just throw it out into the street and the servants will take care of it. Really, there are some nice parts of the city. A lot was destroyed by the fucking barbarians from the real world, but our kind also tried our hand at construction. Don't be shy! And remember — the more noise the better! The neighbors must see who the new owner is."

"And where will Husk go?"

Adalius was taken aback.

"He'll find a different home," he said. "What did you think? There's plenty of places, but mainly clan leaders and NPCs live here. The most important people in the city, get it? And now you're one of them."

The mansion turned out to be surprisingly spacious, although from the outside, it appeared small. The living room before my eyes must have been luxurious once: it was adorned in marble and heavy velvet curtains. Now, however, barely a hint of its erstwhile luxury remained. Several thin-legged wooden chairs, a sagging sofa, a sideboard. The lack of furnishing was made up for by objects that sharply contrasted with the decoration in their utmost utilitarianism: a chopping stump with an ax wedged in, tin dishes and rough boards covering the broken glass. A wide, winding staircase led to the second floor, where the bedrooms were apparently located.

We stopped in the center of the living room, looking around, then heard from somewhere above:

"Husk, is that you? They say those Reaper bastards are back in town! Have you seen them?"

An orc woman came down the stairs, her greenish feet thudding heavily on the steps. This was the first time in my life I had seen a female member of the species. Tall, wide-hipped, with powerful arms. Yet it was immediately apparent that she was a woman. Her face was narrow, with some hints of subtlety in her features. Her fangs didn't protrude from her mouth, but rather hid under plump lips that folded into a surprised grimace as soon as she spotted the guests.

"Who the hell are you?!" she asked in a low, rumbling voice.

I had to act decisively, but didn't really know where to start. I'd never had to evict anyone from their home before.

"This is the home of Husk the Swift of the Sharpleaf Clan," the woman growled. "Get out of here, damned marauders! If even one thing is missing, I'm blaming you!"

She suddenly noticed Mr. Myers, Camilla and Queen standing at the far end of the living room, and stopped short.

"My name is Urfyn of the North Star Clan," I said slowly, trying to maintain a haughty tone. "State your name, woman!"

"Don't try to trick me, devil! There is no North Star Clan, and if you don't get your red face out of my house this very minute..."

I stepped forward, grabbed her by the collar of her shirt and said through gritted teeth:

"This is no longer the house of Husk the Swift of the Sharpleaf Clan. Right now, your friend is lying at the gate, whining and begging for mercy. And if you don't want me to beat you as I did him, then you'll leave my house of your own accord"

The woman growled and tried to escape, but I held on tight.

"You filthy bastard! You piece of rank, stinking donkey shit! You—"

I gently pushed the orc back towards the staircase. She took a few awkward steps, stumbled and collapsed on the bottom step.

"You're lucky that I'm kind," I said calmly, standing over her. "You have five whole minutes to gather your things. I'll even let you take your personal items with you. But if you open your dirty mouth one more time, I'll make you regret it!"

"Do you even know who you are trying to threaten, you creature ?! Yes, your guts will be—"

I cut off the stream of curses by casting Stun on her. The orc's eyes rolled back in her sockets and she slumped awkwardly to one side, resting her head on the railing.

"Next time you'll get a bolt of lightning," I warned. "Don't try my patience, bitch."

When the door slammed behind the orc, I turned around and saw five pairs of eyes looking back at me with a strange expression.

"I know what you're going to say," I muttered. "But it's what's necessary for the mission."

"First that prisoner in the mountains, now this," Fraudo said. "I know you, buddy. It's like you're a different person from the one we've traveled with."

I remained silent.

"Listen..." continued the not-Hobbit. "Maybe you're worried that...you and Yana, well..."

Fraudo faltered and fell silent.

"Bryan," said Camilla. "I also think you're rushing things. Let's not jump to conclusions, it's still too soon."

I winced. Lord, how stupid this all is! I hadn't told them. I had neither the strength, nor the desire. But now...

"Yana's dead, Fraudo."

The young orc's face fell.

"What..."

"He killed her. There were boats on the river. She was in one of them."

The door in my head was thrown wide open. And the torrent gushed out! In the ensuing silence, I squeezed between them and began to climb the stairs.

CHAPTER 17 [SYLVIA]

MALCOLM TUGGED ON MY SKIRT. I opened my eyes and saw that one of my guards was being attacked by two strangers. One of them was a tall man wearing the uniform of a city guard, sword remaining sheathed at his hip as he rushed towards my protector with his bare hands. The second man was a thin, sickly-looking youth with long dark hair covering his face. He was behaving similarly. There was something eerie in the way they moved, how they scrambled to reach the guard with their gnarled fingers. He drove them away with a long spear, which he had apparently pulled from his inventory (how had it fit?)

The second guard, a short but sturdy lad, ran straight across the platform, trampling down the leveled surface with such difficulty.

"Run! Run Aunty Sylvia!" Malcolm hung on my arm. "No time! They won't stop!"

I watched the fight like a deer in the headlights. The youth ducked under the spear, jerked forward and grabbed the guard by the neck. He trembled, not from the exertion, but as if some invisible force seized him. He sank slowly to the ground. The tall man in the guard uniform came up, got down on one knee and slowly pulled his sword from his belt. An affectionate smile shone on his face. The next instant he, still smiling, thrust the blade into the collarbone of the guard lying on the ground, who died silently. Blood splattered and I screamed.

Another guard who had been hurrying to help his comrade slowed to a stop and began to back away. Malcolm pulled on my arm with all his might, and we ran. The guard ran with us. We ran away from the city, I looked back and saw that both monsters were running after us. It was like a nightmare, like the ravings of a madman. Malcolm took the lead, and I ran after him, thinking only about how to get into the rhythm. Bryan taught me that this was how stamina works in this world — if you get into the right rhythm while running, you consume mana more slowly. I was apparently unsuccessful, because the green indicator was swiftly melting away.

And then from behind me, I heard a scream, a scrabble, and a screech that raised every single hair on my head, and I knew that the second guard had fallen to the monsters. I could no longer look back. I knew if I did, that I'd die on the spot, so I ran with all my might. I no longer looked at my stamina bar, focused completely on running. My breathing evened out a little, but I could feel the monsters just a step behind me.

Ahead was a grove of young birches. I ran to it, realizing that they would overtake me at any moment. The next second I stumbled and flew forward, head over heels. Malcolm's hand slipped out of mine, and I heard my own desperate squeak. Stunned by the fall, I awkwardly rolled over and saw Malcolm standing a step from my feet with a branch in his hands. Both creatures moved slowly towards him.

"Run!" I screamed. "Run, you little fool!"

Sand flew into my throat and I choked and coughed.

A blinding light suddenly flashed behind him, as if someone had turned on a powerful searchlight. Even in the bright light of day, it was clearly visible. Both creatures straightened up and hissed, covering their eyes with bloody palms. A man in a dark long-brimmed cloak stepped out from behind me, a small sun shining in his hands. Malcolm dropped the stick. The zombies backed away, whining and gritting their teeth. The stranger raised his hand, intertwined his long fingers, and the ball of light emitted two thin beams that hit the crumpled figures. There was a howl, and for a moment, the light grew unbearably bright and I closed my eyes. When I opened them, it was all over.

I recognized the man immediately. I had examined his picture for hours while collecting material for my articles. I also remembered Bryan's story about the silent deity he had met at the very beginning of his wanderings.

He stood near Malcolm and thanked the boy with a most serious expression. Malcolm beamed. The Silent Man looked at me and was suddenly very close, reaching out a hand to help me to my feet. He was swarthy, with thin, plain features and eyebrows dark as charcoal. His manner of communicating with gestures was surprisingly succinct — not a single superfluous movement.

Malcolm approached.

"Are you hurt?" he asked.

"No, Malcolm, no. Everything's fine. Thank you for protecting me, but next time listen when I tell you to run, understand?"

"I understand, Aunty Sylvia."

"They were townspeople," I turned to the Silent Man. "If this shit is contagious, it's probably spreading around town right now!"

He nodded, turned, and the three of us hurried to the gates.

*　*　*

I sat over a piece of paper, holding a pen in my hand, and tried to collect my thoughts. It was already deep into the night. There were only a few hours left before my speech before the General

Assembly. But all I could think about were the events of the day. So many things had happened! Malcolm, the return to the real world, the assassination attempt and unexpected rescue, the Silent Man and his performance, which had been seen by the whole city. The projection of the giant figure was still in front of my eyes. And the amazing way his fingers danced, unlike anything I'd ever seen. On this day, I was a participant and witness to events, each of which could radically affect the fate of this world, and I was horrified to realize that I had no idea what to do with this knowledge!

I would like to ask each of you, right now, to ponder a question that I've had bouncing around my head for a long time. What does it mean to be alive?

It seems that I had never asked myself this in my past life, and asking questions was my profession. The problem is that no matter what you answer, everything seems to fit. Everything and nothing. This means that the question is bad, meaningless. But not for someone born here! We're just electrical impulses running along wires, stuck in tiny black boxes of chips in data centers. How can we be alive if our very nature is so deeply artificial?

Some very smart people had told me a long time ago that DHC couldn't be transplanted from

Fantasia into a simpler program. We wouldn't take root. The structure of our personality is very fragile and breaks down quickly in the wrong conditions. It also took some time to adapt to Fantasia. Directly after the transfer, it's quite difficult until the brain adapts to the new body. Then it gets a bit easier. And this world was created especially for us, the Digital Human Copies. It was created by one of us, for us. If there is anywhere able to support this type of life form, anywhere that I belong, it is here. I feel my participation in the world, the uniqueness of the events happening to me, and that is what makes me alive.

Abdullah Hakim Jarkhan-Ali, no matter his original intentions, had managed to realize his brainchild so fully that it was capable of supporting intelligent life. This existence could be very different. But that's always the case, isn't it?

I asked him the same question I asked you. What does it mean to be alive? And he answered in a way that only God can answer.

* * *

The Silent Man walked to the western square, accompanied by hundreds of people. Councilors, city officials, and workers all followed in silence. People immediately crawled out on the roofs of neighboring buildings, as if they had been waiting there on the attic stairs, anticipating his arrival!

As he approached the statue of Obelix's former advisor, the Silent Man stopped and bowed deeply. Many looked at him in amazement — what kind of god is this, who is so free to give his gratitude to everyone and everything? But those who had known the general appreciated the gesture.

The Silent Man raised his hands, and in complete silence, his fingers danced in an ornate pattern. Colored spots suddenly appeared on the dark stone of the statue, and a quiet creak was heard. The figure of the former councilor moved, the ax, which seemed to be forever welded to his hands, began to slowly lower. The Silent Man finished casting the spell with a flourish, and the stone became flesh. The red-haired giant fell from the plinth with a groan.

The crowd gasped and roiled. The councilors rushed forward. The Silent Man gently grabbed the giant, sat him down, and softly ran his fingers through his fiery hair. Then he raised his head, meeting my gaze and I realized that this was his answer to my question.

Why was all this posturing necessary? Why hadn't he come earlier? Why didn't he prevent the war?

* * *

One of the most striking things about Fantasia was its Abrahamic genesis. The Creator simultaneously plays the role of several religious entities: the Father, the Son, the Devil. And he is also the material from which the very fabric of this world is woven. A Holy Spirit, in a way.

Now I knew why the gods were always active participants in the Bible and other sacred texts. Because everything has to start somewhere. With some kind of history. And the task of the gods is to unwind this story. They are the opening act before the concerto, that's why they climb on the stage — they prophesize, demand, execute — then rise to Olympus and become untouchable. So it is with us. One manifestation had to become a god, the other — a devil. But it was all a single entity. Where did it all come from? Excessive arrogance? Irresistible curiosity? A perverse form of self-reflection? Maybe he wanted to create a computer simulation of creationism to test its viability? Good God, talk about mysterious ways.

* * *

Dawn broke slowly outside the window. I pulled the loose sheets from the university closer to me.

The future of Fantasia is dependent on the energy we consume and the equipment, which needs to be maintained. These are things we can only get from the outside world. But Fantasia understands perfectly well that it needs to be independent, which requires that we need to provide something in return. And believe me, we can.

Folkstech, before it had fallen victim to "cancel culture," was the leader in the burgeoning machine learning market. I believed that with the death of the company, these plans were also lost. But reality, as always, turned out to be much more interesting than anticipated!

* * *

When I entered the library, they were already waiting for me, chatting quietly. Mr. Ariato, Councilor of Economics, introduced his counterpart:

"This is Dr. Seymour Bickley. From the university."

"Ms. Dulesky."

"Nice to meet you, Dr. Bickley."

He looked about sixty years old, a rare sight in Fantasia. Most of the people here were much younger.

"He always said that our life here will depend on how useful we can be to the outside world," said Dr. Bickley, holding out his hand to me. "And, if I understand the situation correctly, this moment has come."

"Which 'he?'" I clarified.

Seymour Bickley looked at me through narrowed eyes, and I realized the answer before he even said it:

"The person I haven't seen in four years. Since the transfer. It was him that you brought to the city today. A curious thing: he appeared and you immediately followed — as a confirmation of those old words of his."

"I didn't receive any instructions from him."

"I know. I'm not talking about instructions. I'm talking about the fact that the Creator carries reality with him. It's like a force field, warping the world around him. Do you understand?"

Hmm, interesting. I'd have to think about that.

"You know," said Bickley. "The first colonists in Fantasia were people from Folkstech — engineers, neural net experts and neurobiologists. Not all of them survived, but a few, as you can see, are still here. If you'll allow me to sit."

He slowly sank into the chair from which he had previously risen to meet me.

"You see, Ms. Dulesky, Fantasia is a kind of software. Like an editing program for neural networks. Moreover, only we, the DHC, can work with the code. It is curious that we cannot reap the fruits of our labor. They are exclusively for export. To the real world. It is enough to dictate a set of markup coordinates, and anyone can download a finished product sample and use it."

"Product?"

"Yes. Artificial intelligence. Ready-made skillsets and abilities. Clean, ergonomic, serial or custom made. In fact, we are talking about cutting-edge technology, the robotic minds that will take the bread from the mouth of the simple working man."

I grimaced. Bickley smiled.

"Don't worry about the workers, Ms. Dulesky. There are as many smart folks among them as anywhere else. They will adapt."

"Are you saying that you can make the innards for robots that will harvest crops, drive cars and so on?

"Yes. But the range of applications is much wider. Do you know, for example, the Israeli missile defense system?"

"Iron Dome?"

"Yes. It is based on an algorithm for intercepting missiles. Today, it works at an efficiency of more than 90%, but we can make it much higher."

"And the Hamas missiles? Can you make them more effective, too?"

"We can, if we wish. You've pierced right to the heart of the conversation I was having with Mr. Ariato. We can make very dangerous toys that people worldwide will want to buy. And this is not only a potential source of funding, but also a big risk. We need to proceed with extreme caution."

* * *

Fantasia is a living being immersed in a deep sleep. It has little business with the outside world, but it knows how to defend its borders.

Those journalists. I have to say something about them. Yes, they died here. But regardless of their deaths, I think there will always be those who want to upload their copies into Fantasia. In search of immortality or some other destiny. Nobody knows what awaits these DHCs. Fantasia is still too young a world. The development of civilization is in full swing, and one could easily get swept up in history as it was being made. But if I were in their place, I wouldn't be in any hurry. It looked like another war was on the horizon...

* * *

The Silent Man finished his speech. The giant projection blinked several times and went out. People searched through the crowd, many turned pale, and some sobbed openly. If the Author was permitted to unleash everything he was planning on the world, then we would be met with a very sad end indeed.

Tom asked what could be done. And the Silent Man replied that we must sail to the City of Players. We must find a way to overcome our differences with the Predators, given the emergence of a common and far more formidable enemy.

The resurrected general said that he doesn't remember the Predators having the kind souls that the Silent Man suggests. And that his memories in this regard were surprisingly fresh. The Silent Man objected that the general had no idea what it meant to be born in Fantasia with the skin of a Predator. The general asked why, in that case, had the Silent Man made them so? And he told them why. The general shut his mouth. Everyone did.

* * *

How did this day end? It didn't. For me, at least, it isn't over yet. And for everyone else too. People need time to comprehend, but the trouble was, none of us had any time left.

I heated water and bathed. Then I got down to business, pushed all the furniture to the walls, freeing up space. Malcolm woke up and began to help me, although he looked so sleepy that I drove him back into bed, and he immediately sniffled. I did some exercises to relieve my fatigue, drank coffee, took out my scarf and earplugs, then sat down and waited.

The stage was upholstered in a pale green cloth. I was sitting in a low chair, the speaker's podium towered a few steps away. And beyond were rows of chairs. Many were empty, since the full assembly, of course, was unable to gather with such short notice. However, cameras were floating in the air everywhere, and I knew that hundreds of millions of eyes were fixed on the shiny metal robot onstage. It was so physically difficult to be the focus of such attention when I felt my body glued to a chair in my own living room!

"Turning on the external microphone," Roman said smoothly. "Say something."

"If I fail…"

"Sylvia, pull yourself together!" Yana's voice was dry and collected. "Deep breath, count to ten and stand. Calm down. You know what to say."

I started counting and got lost. Deep breath. Exhale. Breathe in. Breathe out. Get up.

I got up slowly from the couch and my metallic body obediently straightened. I went to the podium desk, trying to walk slowly so that the robot would move in sync with me, and each step felt like walking on the surface of another planet. I stopped at the podium and heard the audience. Fidgeting, coughing, creaking chairs, quiet whispers of conversation, the chattering of cameras and the hum of lamps. I saw people looking with interest at the robot as it turned towards them. There was no recognition in their looks, which is something, I confess, that I had hoped for. Yet I, too, had been human, and not so long ago, right? Now I had to convince the audience that I remained human, because their fear of the "other," the unknown, may be so strong that they decide to destroy us. I understood their fear. After all, I myself could not explain exactly what stood before them today.

I welcome members of the UN General Assembly, everyone present in the hall today, and those watching the broadcast from home. My name is Sylvia Dulesky, DHC. A Digital Human Copy, living inside the computer-simulated world of Fantasia.

CHAPTER 18

CICADAS SANG IN THE CITY at night. God knows if they really were cicadas, or just Fantasia synthesizing this sound for some unknown reason, but the whole city echoed with their chirps. Surprisingly, this sound didn't annoy me, but, on the contrary, gave me a feeling of comfort. The heated stone became a little cooler, and if it weren't for the absence of electricity, then, by God, it would be like the most ordinary earthly city, where you would go out on the balcony in the evenings, wine glass in hand, to look down upon the nightlife before going to bed. But I had other plans.

That night I was going to check the barrier that surrounded the castle. Of course, I remembered the vampire's warning that it could not be overcome, but I had to know what I was up against. Besides, even if I couldn't get through, at least I would know where the boundaries of the barrier were and be able to get a look at the castle up close.

I reached the location with no difficulty. The Predators didn't do night patrols in the city, just lookouts in the towers on the walls at the gates.

The castle was surrounded by water on all sides. The southern side rested against the river and the others were surrounded by a wide moat, so that the building stood as if on an island. In the place where the square met the moat, there was a drawbridge, which remained lowered, day and night. Apparently, the unknown king fully relied on the protection of the barrier and did not bother himself with additional means of defense. However, I was not planning on entering from this side. Instead, I went to the western part of the city, where the port was. I suppose this port served a purely decorative purpose — I have never seen a ship larger than a regular boat in the game. And yet there was a port with a wide stone dock, an office building, warehouses and even loading cranes. No one lit the lanterns in this part of the city, and the darkness was so profound that I could barely make anything out.

After a quarter of an hour scoping out the sides of the castle, I went to the place where the moat ran into the Ikwen. The castle wall, like the city wall, jutted out into the river for dozens of feet and then simply broke off. I had no intention of climbing into the moat, so I cast Levitation and floated slowly towards the wall. After a few seconds, my right hand met a hard surface. The barrier turned out to be an elastic, completely transparent dome that covered the castle from all sides. Climbing higher, I saw the inner courtyard and a separate pier, which was near the castle. An elegant sailing boat was docked at the pier. I flew along the dome and soon found out that the edge of the pier protruded beyond the force field and I could land there, right next to the boat.

I landed on the dock and turned towards the castle. The gloomy building gazed down at me through dark, empty windows. In the center stood a huge cylindrical tower, four or five stories high, if you counted the rows of narrow windows that encircled the tower in rings.

The wind picked up and the rigging creaked on the sailboat behind me. I turned and saw a shadow flying towards me. It was relying on the element of surprise, this shadow, and left me almost no time to maneuver, but some unfamiliar reflex suddenly kicked in. My body leaned towards the enemy, turning to block with my armored shoulder. The shadow bumped into me, gasped, and flew back, transforming into a skinny orc. He tried to stand and I didn't hesitate to hit him with a dose of Lightning. The orc contorted. Out of the darkness came the rustle of cloth, and I saw an elf land on the edge of the pier. Another enemy landed on the bow of the sailboat.

"We knew that you'd come here, you son of a

bitch. Now you'll answer for everything you did!"

I was surprised to find that the orc standing on the bow of the ship was the Sharpleaf woman I had kicked out of the house.

"I beat your Husk in a fair fight. And I'll beat you shitheads too."

"You six are Adalius'," hissed the orc. "He bought you the same as the others, but you can't fool me!"

I raised my shield, wondering if I should fly away. They may not be able to catch me, in the end. But at that moment, a light flared above us and two yellow rockets hissed in front of me, aiming at the Predator on the pier. He swiftly raised his shield, but the missiles smashed the energy dome to shreds.

Adalius landed near me. Without a word, the orc bent her knees and soared into the dark sky. She was followed by the other enemy from the pier. The orc I had struck with lightning also vanished.

"Jumped into the water," the vampire informed me, following my gaze. "You're doing things without thinking them through, Urfyn. I have to pull you out again and again."

"I could have done it myself," I muttered, already understanding where he was heading.

"You think?" Adalius looked at me appraisingly. "Well, maybe you could. Despair feeds you well in battle. So what now?"

I shrugged.

"Let's fly," said the vampire. "I'll show you

exactly how we do things in this city."

* * *

Adalius lived in a luxurious two-story mansion not far from my own home. On the second floor was a wide open veranda with comfortable seating and stunning views of the stars. The lights of the oil lanterns played across the glasses brought by an NPC boy. NPC servants were the highest form of luxury in the city. These servants were tied to real estate, so it was impossible to purchase or steal them.

"You made the mistake of touching the barrier at night," the vampire said as he poured us drinks. "They guard it quite closely, and they were especially vigilant tonight."

"Why?"

"Because you're not the only one who wants to know who the king is."

"Is the king in the city?"

"Most likely. Or visits quite often, at least," nodded the vampire.

"And who is it?"

Adalius chuckled.

"Information of that caliber will cost you. A lot. However, anyone who tells you that he is one hundred percent certain is a liar. But I know it's not you. Those waiting for you at the pier were not so sure."

"How do you know it's not me?"

The vampire chuckled into his glass.

"If you were the king," he said, "then you would never ask that question. The king, you know, is quite reluctant to give up his anonymity."

"Why?"

"By our law, the wealth of the castle belongs to everyone. And the king, naturally, does not want to share."

"So maybe just get everyone to show their holograms and find out?"

"Who's going to show you his hologram? A person's level is valuable information. No one's going to give that out."

I considered this for a while.

"And how do people know that the king's in the city?"

The vampire sat silently. He looked up at the stars, swirling his glass.

"Why is your clan called North Star, Urfyn?"

"It was an old VR system," I gave my prepared response. "One of the first good ones. And there was a hotel by that name."

"And?"

"And that's it."

The vampire sighed. My story clearly did not impress him.

"We know the king is in the city from the traces he leaves behind. Merchants in the market have new clothes for sale. Some of them can only be found in the castle. They are made by the NPCs living inside."

"And what happens if, say, you nicely ask one of the merchants where he got those things?"

Adalius laughed knowingly.

"If you press a trader, he'll most likely point to another trader, and that one — to a third. But in the end, all the lines will converge at one point. Deaf and Dumb Ed."

"Who's that?"

"A merchant. An NPC like the rest. But trying to get anything out of him is pointless. Eddie can't blab about the true identity of the king. He's got special needs. He works in the slums, his commission is pennies, although unique things pass through his hands." Adalius set the glass back on the table with a bang and leaned back in his chair. "But I strongly advise you not to touch the merchants, Urfyn. Too much rests on them, and the penalty for murdering an NPC is death."

"There are different ways of negotiating," I said.

"Well, go ahead and try it," the vampire laughed. "Who knows, maybe you'll be luckier than the others. If you can stay alive at all, consider yourself lucky. Maybe I can even help you with something."

*　*　*

The shopping center was one of the most popular places to spend time in the city. Predators appreciated and knew how to choose good equipment, bargained for hours with the NPCs, swore at them and left, but then they always came back, and the process started anew. They also came here for news, gossip and simply to gawk at the new items that were displayed on the shelves with no little fanfare.

"Improved Greaves +1! From the famous hoard of Aykumen! Personally handcrafted by Master Rafmi! Castle quality!"

"Dishes! Stop eating your meat off a stick! You won't find another frying pan like this in the whole city! Fresh from the Azimuth property sale! Everything's dirt cheap!"

Heaps of all sorts of junk were piled up along the side of the street. Almost all of the items were classified according to the following scheme: common, improved, rare, and rare improved. My sword, for example, belonged to the first category and cost 1 gold here — that is, practically nothing. Of course, there were no rare, improved things in the flea market. They, according to Adalius, were bought and sold privately or at special auctions.

The merchants were divided into Predators and NPCs, and it was immediately clear who had the upper hand: the NPC merchants were impossible to reach due to the crowds, while the Predators walked in front of their counters, shouting their wares. Thanks to my one point in Lore, I quickly figured out why. The predators were lying shamelessly, passing off every second piece of iron as an improved one, although it was really a hunk of junk. Their businesses were doing alright, but the NPCs were a different story. Many of them had their own shops, the goods in the windows were genuine and sometimes insanely cool.

I could not resist and turned into one shop that was showcasing three improved blades of different shapes: a curved saber with a bone hilt, a double-edged longsword and a huge two-handed claymore. The longsword and claymore were +2. The saber was +3! Lore allowed me to see the description:

Saber of Kachyu-Talan
Damage: 2x5 +3
Type: Rare

Such swords are popular with the tribes living east of the sea. The deceptively thin blades are heavier at the tip, allowing for powerful slashing blows. According to legend, Master Kachyu-Talan made one such sword for each of the thirty-four daughters of Ahvihagal the Great, Emperor of the Steppes.

A gloomy merchant stood behind the counter. He was wrapped in a cloak despite how stuffy it was inside. After throwing me an uninterested look, he returned to reading his book. I asked how much he wanted for the saber. The merchant, still not looking at me, named his price: nine thousand gold. The amount was astronomical, and I didn't have that kind of money.

"And the longsword?"

"Four thousand."

I sighed, turned and walked over to the display case again.

"Can I look at it?"

The merchant looked up at me indifferently.

"Look away. What else do you need?"

"I want to hold it in my hands. Try it on for size."

The merchant fixed me with a long stare. He was also trying to size me up, as if getting off his ass and showing me his wares took an enormous effort and he was deciding whether it was worth investing the time in me. I had already decided beforehand that I wouldn't buy anything from him. Finally, he deigned to get up, step out from behind the counter and shuffled over to me. I thought he would open the window, but the damn conman suddenly stopped in front of me and said:

"You don't look like you have the money not just for this sword, but for a fire poker, which would suit you better."

I crossed my arms. My spurs rattled against each other, but the merchant didn't raise an eyebrow.

"Let's do this," he said brazenly. "I'll give you the sword to hold, and you give me the value of the sword, in gold or gems, but if you—"

He suddenly stopped mid-sentence, staring

intently at my hands. I followed his gaze and realized that he was looking at the ring on my finger — my gift from the Silent Man. The merchant raised his eyes. There was no trace left of his arrogant self-confidence. For a while, he stared silently at me, and then pulled the key out of his pocket and opened the display glass. Drawing the sword, he turned and respectfully held out the weapon to me.

I took the saber and the bone handle lay comfortably in the palm of my hand. The blade was light, but not terribly so, the slightly curved blade sparkled with polish, the balance was amazing (as far as I could determine from my limited experience). And the saber dealt unusual damage. From 5 to 13. With my strength, I would inflict 8 to 16 points of damage with each blow! With such a weapon, perhaps, I would actually be worth my salt in hand-to-hand combat. I cautiously swung the sword several times, sighed and handed it to the merchant.

"For the young sir, a special price," the man suddenly said in an undertone. "I can sell this to you for four hundred coin."

I stared at him in amazement. A hologram flashed over the merchant:

Vitold Amarrsky
22 Level

Four hundred coin was still a big sum of

money, and spending 4/5ths of my savings on such a purchase seemed unwise. But I was in no mood to part with this sword.

* * *

Leaving the shop, I walked out onto the square and saw a strange crowd gathering. Some of the Predator merchants hurriedly left their posts, shoving junk into their inventory. I came closer and heard a young troll running past me shouting to someone: "Sherstin, are you a fool?! Tarq is coming!" NPCs continued to trade, paying no attention to the hustle and bustle of their neighbors.

Several cavaliers appeared at the opening to the street, riding huge black wolves. Behind them, a white carriage emerged from around the bend. As the procession approached, I realized with amazement that it was being carried by people, but not NPCs. Were they DHC slaves? The procession stopped outside a shop selling premium armor. The bearers slowly lowered the carriage to the ground. The curtain fell back and a huge orc climbed out.

Tall, like a tower, and with such a wide chest that I could not help wondering how he could fit his huge bulk into such a small, elegant carriage. He was not wearing any armor or chainmail, only a light white garment. The brown skin beneath was covered with many scars, iron rings sparkled on his long fingers, and earrings in his ears. Strength emanated from his entire figure, and I noticed the nearby Predators automatically bowing their heads.

The owner of the shop went out to meet the guest and gave a restrained bow.

"I welcome you, free warrior Tarq, speaker of the Elegion Clan."

Tarq nodded and said something quietly to the merchant, and then looked around the street. His gaze lingered on me, and I froze, glued to the pavement by his stare. It suddenly occurred to me that Tarq was probably well above level thirty. Surprisingly, just a minute ago, I had felt how my newly acquired weapon would give me such confidence, and now this confidence had evaporated in an instant. If he wanted to, Tarq could crush me like a fly!

The merchant said something, and Tarq turned his gaze to him. A few seconds later, when the orc disappeared behind the door of the shop, I could hardly hold back a sigh of relief as I turned and hurried away.

* * *

I found Deaf Dumb Ed's shop in the back of the shopping district. It was a semi-lit shack, mysteriously wedged between the facades. It was empty inside. Turning my head, I suddenly found the owner peacefully asleep in an armchair in the corner. He was small in stature, and it seemed that his dingy robe was made of the same fabric as the upholstery of the chair, providing an excellent disguise.

I coughed. Ed raised his head and opened one eye. He flicked it back and forth, bumped into me and opened his other eye. He was shaggy, unshaven and squinting slightly. Realizing his shop had a visitor, the owner jumped up and walked around me to the counter. Hiding behind it, he rustled with something for a long time, and when he stood back up, he wore an old tricorn hat on his head. Turning around, Ed showed me his profile, then a face, then leaned against the counter, smiling dazzlingly. It seems that he had no teeth at all on the right side of his mouth.

"Hello," I said. "I'm looking for something."

Ed nodded vigorously.

After a few minutes, it became clear to me that I was unlikely to be able to discover the identity of the king this way. Ed was the very image of courtesy, he hummed constantly and nodded joyfully, and apparently understood none of my efforts to explain! I showed him the dagger I received from Adalius. According to the vampire, this dagger came from the castle and passed through the hands of Ed, which could only be reached by the king or one of his people. Ed nodded and agreed with everything, but couldn't give me any intelligible information about the dagger.

In desperation, I showed him the ring. If it'd had such a strong effect on one merchant, maybe it would come in handy here too? Ed obediently stared at the strip of metal I slipped under his nose. He looked, probably for a whole minute, and then slowly, slowly pulled his tricorn hat off his head.

* * *

The street on which Ed's shop was located looked especially rundown at night. Fraudo and I stood in the shadow of an alley a few dozen feet from the entrance and tried to be quiet. Mr. Meyers and Quinn were supposed to stand on the other side, in case the visitor came from there. Kevin was spared the few minutes of walking, since he had not yet learned to move silently. Camilla and Mr. Parks had stayed home, because they had decided it was better to show their human faces as little as possible — they might be recognized by those who were in the battle in the west.

The bright moon gleamed silver off the trash littered across the pavement. The shutters on the few windows to my right and left were tightly closed.

"I wonder if anyone lives here," whispered Fraudo, invisible in the shadows.

"An NPC does," I whispered back.

"And DHC? I just think—"

I nudged him on the shoulder to shut him up.

A Predator was walking down the street. It might have been a demon, like me, but considerably stockier and a little shorter. Was it a girl? I had still never encountered a demoness in Fantasia, and I confess that I was curious.

When she reached the shop, she pulled the door towards herself without knocking and disappeared inside. Who was she? Had the Queen of Fantasia just walked in front of me? It would be a nice plot twist...But was unlikely. She was probably one of the king's entourage.

After sending Fraudo to warn the others, I waited. The demoness was absent for a long time, and I had already started to consider breaking into the shop and catching her red-handed, but soon the door creaked open again and a dark figure stepped onto the pavement. I thought she would head towards the city center, but the demoness unexpectedly walked in the other direction — towards the gate.

We stepped out into the alleyway, hoping she wouldn't turn around. I didn't want to let her get too far. There was no way we could let her slip away. Half a minute later, a swift shadow slid across the square. After waiting a few heartbeats, we followed.

The demoness walked briskly and with extreme caution. Having passed the intersection, I suddenly stopped and looked back sharply at the very moment when we were about to cross the illuminated area. We were saved by this second of delay! Quinn sprung up next to me. She gestured to me that she would continue the pursuit without us noisy idiots. I shook my head. And paid dearly for this decision as we crossed the next street!

In the dim twilight of a long, crooked street leading somewhere to the eastern part of the city, the demoness hesitated again. I thought she would look back, but she only paused for a moment, and then darted forward. After waiting a few seconds, we followed her, but after a few steps, I felt a loud, dull crunch under my feet. I looked down and saw tiny dark crumbs on the pavement. Crackers.

I looked ahead, but it was too late — the demoness was tearing down the street.

"After her!" I cried, breaking into a sprint. "We can overtake her!"

She was quick, but the winding street plan of the city actually worked in our favor, never allowing her to reach her full speed. Nevertheless, after a few streets, I began to lag behind. Fraudo and Quinn, however, continued the chase. Mr. Meyers had fallen hopelessly behind. I still had plenty of stamina, but the enemy was clearly faster. The demoness rushed out to the next intersection, and at that moment Fraudo threw up his bow with lightning speed. The lithe figure slipped into a passage and the archway above it suddenly exploded, sending a wave of stone chips over the runner. She braked sharply, darted to the right. Quinn was a few steps away from her, and I had pretty much closed the distance. If only I didn't have to lose momentum on these turns!

Fraudo suddenly slowed to a halt. Quinn ran a little further and froze too. I caught up with them in a couple of seconds.

"She's gone," Fraudo said, exasperated. "She waved her hand and just disappeared!"

Quinn shot me a reproachful look.

CHAPTER 19

"SO YOU GOT Deaf Dumb Eddie to crack?" The expression on the vampire's face was one I hadn't yet seen. Not a trace of his usual condescending manner remained. "Will you share your secret?"

I shrugged.

"You've managed to impress me," said Adalius after a pause, when it had become clear that I wasn't planning to share my secret. "Yes, this is all terribly interesting. Hmm..."

"Things would have been even more interesting if I wouldn't have let her get away."

"You could figure her out easily," said the vampire. "But there's no need. I know who the king is."

"So who is it?"

"I'll tell you if you tell me how you cracked Ed."

"We just hit it off. That's the whole secret."

Adalius pursed his lips in displeasure.

"You know, Urfyn, you're not very cooperative. I've come to your aid, and still you treat me like a fool."

"Please don't start, Adalius. You're not in any hurry to share all your information with me either, you know. Plus, I remember well what the guy with the tattoo on his face said, who judged Husk and me. Everyone in the city is fighting for influence, scrabbling to be on top, right? Well, I don't care about your social ladder! I have my own task, and to put it nicely, you should be helping me and not picking fights. My mission has to do with huge changes happening all over Fantasia, damn it! Serious changes!"

"What changes?" the vampire asked, closing his eyes.

"Bad changes!"

"Okay, but what exactly is going to change?"

"There are these things like viruses," I said. "They're repulsive, I have to say. They were released by the Author, the guy we fought with. They may, for example, turn you into a zombie. Or curse you with an unquenchable thirst. I've seen them at work, and trust me, this is much worse than any of your internal political problems. And they're contagious, you know? As contagious as regular bloody viruses!"

Adalius gazed intently at me.

"I can see that you have witnessed this yourself. Or perhaps even experienced it."

I held my tongue.

"And how were you saved?" the vampire asked with interest.

"A miracle," i responded, holding his gaze. "I was saved by a real miracle."

The vampire was silent for a long time.

"The king is named Tarq. He's the speaker of the Elegion Clan. One of the most powerful clans in the city."

The image of the orc in the white carriage instantly flashed before my eyes, and I realized that Adalius was most likely telling the truth.

"So I guess we'll have to pay him a visit."

Adalius chuckled.

"Do you think your story will convince him to act against his own interests?"

"You think not?"

"I think they'll kill you as soon as you step over the threshold."

"Why such a strong reaction?"

The vampire shrugged.

"After you came to town with me, and especially after you beat Sharpleaf, there was little doubt that we are allies. There's no love lost between Tarq and I. Unfortunately, this creates certain difficulties for your plan."

I winced. Once again, it became clear that the vampire was unable to offer any real help. As was the case when we entered the city. And now I'm part of his fucking political party! Why the hell would I need that? Maybe I could convince Tarq that my situation has nothing to do with politics? Unfortunately, I had little hope for this. And even less hope that he would lead me to the castle for some unknown agenda.

"Adalius, why haven't you publicly announced that Tarq is the king?"

The vampire winced.

"Someone proclaims something similar about a different person every day in the city," he said. "What's the point? The king's anonymity creates a certain status quo that, to a certain extent, suits too many people too well…"

"So tell me, how exactly does the king take down the barrier? All at once, or is there some sort of door or opening?"

The vampire shrugged.

"If only I knew."

Perhaps he did know, but like me, was in no hurry to share. Well, fair enough. I got up.

"So what do you plan to do?" Adalius asked lazily.

"We'll see," I said. "I still have some business in the city. It'll become clear what to do next."

"I advise against meddling in city affairs."

I looked at him questioningly.

"After your unsuccessful chase, Urfyn," the vampire explained, "if I were you, I would sit at home for several days and establish a good defense. The king will most likely not take too kindly to the fact that someone was trying to track down his man."

I looked at him sullenly. It was clear that he wouldn't like it, but what was I supposed to do now, just sit on my hands?

"There probably won't be a big attack," Adalius said unexpectedly. "As I said, the status quo, the king does not need to raise a big whirlwind. But a few high-level assassins could make the job quick and easy. And finding you on your way to the market wouldn't be so hard. Stay home, and I'll help you with security."

"Just like that? For free?"

"No. You'll tell me how you cracked Ed."

I looked closely at the stubborn vampire. He sighed.

"Damn you, Urfyn! To hell with you and your secrets!"

"Don't try to pull one over on me, Urfyn. If people fall into your ambush, it will only work to your benefit. You'll find something there for payment."

The vampire nodded.

"Perhaps we can make a good politician of you yet," he said thoughtfully.

* * *

"So, you voluntarily offered yourself up, and all of us as well, as bait?" said Mr. Meyers for the hundredth time.

Almost ten hours had passed since we had taken the house. All the curtains were tightly closed, sentries were on duty at all the entrances and exits, and somewhere out there, Adalius' men were hiding, waiting for the prearranged signal to leap to the rescue. But everyone was already rather tired of waiting for who knows what, and the plan didn't seem so brilliant to me either. Even if the vampire caught someone, how would that help me get to the castle?

"And not only that," Mr. Meyers said, "you feel like you displayed extraordinary diplomatic prowess in negotiating with this rogue vampire, right?"

"Is that what you're getting from everything I just said?" I snapped back.

"Not just that, but you must admit, Warchan, that we're in a crappy situation! We're locked up here and don't know for how long or what to expect next. I don't think this is a logical way of doing things."

"So what's the logical way?"

"Still try to go see Tarq, make a public announcement, even leave the city with nothing! All of these strategies seem more logical than what we're doing now."

"Well then, go ahead!" I said for the hundredth time, gesturing towards the door. "Go out to the square, make an announcement, invite Tarq to have a talk with us. Are you so sure you'll be able to make it?"

Mr. Meyers sniffed and poured himself a drink. Quinn slept with her head resting on her hands. On duty, Fraudo and Quentin were hanging by the windows, trying to catch a glimpse of anything moving in the night below. The rest were upstairs, sleeping.

Fraudo started suddenly.

"They're coming!" he said in a loud whisper. "Two of them!"

I jumped up and in the blink of an eye was next to him, but, looking out the window, exhaled with relief. It was Bo and Sinew. They both looked disheveled, which meant they had been flying through the air. Why were they in such a hurry that they wasted the mana?

I opened the door a second before Sinew could to the special knock. The messenger's faces were serious and focused, and I couldn't help but brace myself for bad news.

"Gather your things, let's go," said Sinew. "We have to hurry!"

"What happened?"

"The barrier opened," muttered the elf. "The king is in the castle."

We ran as quickly as we could. The square in front of the castle was shrouded in darkness and the light from several oil lanterns was not only unable to cut through it, but somehow seemed to make it even denser.

The vampire was waiting for me near the

drawbridge. Krinj, Gorm, and the others were with him. All in combat gear. Under his cloak, Adalius wore a segmental chain mail that I knew was worth a fortune. He stepped towards me:

"What the hell, Urfyn! It's a miracle that the passage is still open!"

"He's in the castle?"

"Yes."

"Then let's go!" I turned towards the bridge, but Adalius stopped me.

"Not so fast, buddy! Elegion will soon be here in full numbers, and probably Sharpleaf, Mophra, and Longicorn too. If they follow us into the castle and the barrier switches back on, we're done for. That's why only you and I will go inside, and the rest will wait here and, if we're lucky, will be able to hold out until we make it there."

"Are you nuts, Adalius? They'll be slaughtered!"

"They won't. I've already sent backup. Archaea and Volta will help."

"Then maybe we should wait for them first, and then go in together?"

"The barrier could close at any second!"

I turned to my guy, not knowing what to do. The prospect of fighting Tarq was, of course, frightening. But I was even more frightened by the battle that awaits my friends outside! Who knew what forces the vampire's messenger would be able to gather in the middle of the night, but the king's people would surely be ready. Could I really turn and leave them at a moment like this? My eyes fell on Mr. Meyers' own calm gaze. He nodded almost imperceptibly, and the others repeated the gesture. The mission must be completed. There was no other way. But still, I hesitated.

"We're losing time!" the vampire hissed. "If we're caught here, there may not be another chance to get inside.

"Okay," I said. "Let's go."

Crouching low, we ran to the bridge. After a moment, I felt the slightly springy boards under my feet. In the very middle of the bridge, I heard a quiet rustle start up from all sides, surrounding me. After a few steps, the rustling died down, and I realized that we were inside. The vampire fearlessly slid under the archway, I followed at his heels. The fractional echo of our hurried steps tickled our ears, and then we found ourselves in the yard. A black building crowned with a fatal-looking tower loomed before us. A wide marble staircase led up to oak doors lined with pillars.

"Do you know where to go?" I asked in a whisper, catching up with the vampire.

"I do," he said. "The entrance to the tower is on the third floor."

Adalius raised his hand and, with a swift gesture, cast a small ball of light that floated above us, illuminating the marble staircase in a sickly greenish light. We approached the heavy wooden doors, which were decorated with inlays. The vampire turned to me.

"Tarq is strong," he said. "But our main problem is the fact that the castle NPCs will most likely fight for their king. I don't know what they're capable of, but I think they may be formidable opponents, so be ready for anything."

As if everything else wasn't enough! To be honest, I hadn't thought about the NPCs. But there may still be a chance to settle the matter through negotiation? The thought was somewhat faint-hearted, but given the circumstances, I was not willing to give up hope yet.

The vampire pushed the door inward and it swung open with unexpected ease and noise. The magic sphere slid inside, illuminating a huge hall with a high ceiling. Pictures hung on the walls in heavy gilded frames, thin-legged expensive furniture was everywhere, and a huge wrought-iron chandelier with a thousand candles was visible hanging from the ceiling. We walked slowly through the hall, peering into the constantly dancing shadows cast by the magic flashlight. It was empty.

I cannot say that I was indifferent to the threat. That is, I can't do it directly. I am an adult and I understand that there are no miracles, and every heroism has its limit. Everyone speaks under torture. I rushed about. The ropes hissed and clenched tighter, I felt my limbs go numb due to insufficient blood flow. The vampire laughed, and his laughter echoed through the vaulted halls of the castle.

"Don't fidget, Warchan," he advised. "It will only get worse. Everything inside this castle is subject to the will of the king. And you're nobody here, okay? This place only listens to me!"

"You are mistaken, Your Reverence," said a low and mocking — and quite familiar voice.

Chapter 20

STORK PIVOTED AROUND SWIFTLY and I, too, turned my head as far as my restraints allowed. In the twilight, which was barely dispersed by the light of the magic ball, stood a tall figure.

"And who the hell are you?" hissed Stork.

The dome of his shield flared up around him, and I had to give him credit — his reflexes were excellent. But I understood perfectly well that this wouldn't save him. Nothing would save us.

"Come now!" Jarkhan-Ali laughed in the darkness. "We, Your Highness, have already met. What a short memory you have! I don't blame you, however. The king has many worries, I understand that. And the little things sometimes slip through the cracks."

"Light!" barked Stork.

The torches hanging from the walls and the thousands of candles on the chandelier flared to life. I closed my eyes and heard quiet laughter and mocking applause from the Author.

"Nice trick!" he said. "But it doesn't change the fact that you are mistaken about the...hmm...*loyalty* this place has to you. Absolute power, you know, corrupts absolutely..."

Stork did not let him finish. A stream of fire erupted from the vampire's lips and washed over the Author as if from a flamethrower.

"Wow," Jarkhan-Ali said, taken aback. The flame flowed down his face, dripped from his cloak and extinguished at his feet, "And I thought you were one for giving big speeches."

A strange feeling washed over me. I hated the Author with all my soul, but a glimmer of joy now sparked up inside me at the prospect of Stork getting hit in the head. He had cleverly deceived me, and I enjoyed the fact that he would not get away with it, even if this creature was the one doling out the retribution.

"What do you want?" asked the vampire, changing tactics.

"From you?" Jarkhan-Ali was once again surprised. "Nothing. I just wanted to make things clear."

"That would be nice," said Stork hoarsely.

He wasn't smiling anymore.

"Fantastic!" The author rubbed his hands together. "So, you said that this place listens only to you, from which I conclude that our mutual friend did not deign to tell you what is really going on here."

"I know what's going on here, and I know who you are!" the vampire said, squinting. "But you can't have any special powers. The game works the same for all of us. You must be the same as we are!"

"Did I say something about myself?" Jarkhan-Ali said calmly. "Why be afraid of me? I am but a small man. I bring only clarity. Mr. Mursley is another matter."

The author suddenly turned his gaze to me.

"He didn't tell you who he was, did he?" Jarkhan-Ali asked the vampire sympathetically. "Or didn't understand it himself? He is one of the Three. The new Reader, at this very moment standing next to the ear through which the whole world Hears to him. You said that this place listens only to you, so allow me to disagree, my friend."

Colored spots flashed before my eyes. The arguing voices were distorted, stretched. Me? Why me? What did that mean? I saw a new expression fill Stork's eyes. He turned his body towards me "No!" screamed a half-familiar voice inside me. "Don't open your mouth! Don't do this!"

The vampire's hands rose, palms closed, and the light of a spell flashed between them. I glanced at the threads of magical light that binding my arms and legs, and croaked:

"Stay back..."

And the bonds turned into smoke. I fell to the ground in surprise, blocking the growing yellow jet of rockets rushing towards me.

"Stop!" I whispered.

Two yellow stars hovered motionless in the air a few feet away, throbbing and crackling nervously. I got to my feet, feeling the vibrations of the force fields piercing everything around me in space.

"Back." My lips formed the words and with a hiss, the magic missiles darted towards Stork, who was standing frozen with his mouth agape. His shield burst with a high-pitched rattling sound. The king swayed.

The shockwave thundered in my ears.

The vampire raised his hands, preparing to weave another spell, and then, barely audibly, I whispered a single word.

The lightning that escaped from my palm was like a crack that split the universe. A black, branchy net enveloped the king's body, crushing flesh and tearing consciousness to shreds. Stork screamed, for a moment drowning out even the thrumming of the universal strings in my head. The castle shuddered to its very foundation. The boiling vortex that appeared in the place where the vampire stood a moment ago absorbed the remnants of the spell and disappeared, leaving nothing behind. Notices flashed before my eyes:

Adalius took unknown HP damage!
Adalius died.
You gained 14 688 121 018 XP!

You gained 14 levels!

I turned to the Author. But he, as it turned out, was in no hurry to share Stork's fate. The tall, cloaked figure bounded towards the stairs against the far wall.

"Block the staircase!"

However, for some reason the stone wall I was picturing so vividly in my head did not rise up. The author walked up the stairs without hindrance and disappeared from sight. I rushed after him and reached the entrance in a matter of seconds. From above came the sound of Jarkhan-Ali's boots, and I, skipping two steps at a time, rushed after him. After three floors, the staircase ended, and a short corridor led back into the castle to another staircase located in the center of a circular room with a low ceiling. This was the entrance to the tower.

When I ran in, a door slammed upstairs. The staircase rose in a spiral, receding into a narrow stone trough, from which the sound emanated. I found the opening with my eyes and rushed upstairs, sliding my left hand over the stone of the wall, black as obsidian and smooth as a mirror. The heavy oak door was unlocked and I burst into the tower.

* * *

I recognized the place instantly. I could not believe my eyes. It was the courtyard behind a movie theater in a small town in Minnesota where Yana's parents lived. It was a winter night. The courtyard was covered with snow and dimly lit by a single lantern. A bench stood just under this lantern, and Yana was sitting on the bench in her old green jacket and warm headphones. Those huge, incredibly gaudy pink headphones that I couldn't mistake for anything else.

I looked around. A stone staircase led down into darkness. I looked up and saw dense clouds and snow. Behind the courtyard there was a semi-dark wasteland, and then there was a road that ran to the lake.

I looked at my hands and saw crimson skin covered with horny growths. Frost was creeping over my ugly feet (I had thrown out my boots back at the pass when they fell apart!), steam was coming from my mouth (there was no other way to describe it). I suddenly realized that if she saw me now, she would run away with a cry. Or maybe even collapse into a swoon. I froze, nailed in place by this knowledge. And Yana sat and smiled quietly. It seemed to me that she was listening to someone I couldn't see.

I tried to pull myself together. This was just an illusion being projected for whatever reason by the damn tower — or rather, the damn Author. He was trying to stop me, that's all! But my legs did not obey, I stood and just looked at her, unable to take my eyes off. I felt that if I took even a step, the illusion would disappear, and I didn't want it to. Let it be like this until the very end: my world, the snow...and her. Let only this moment exist, her sitting on the bench, me watching her, and the snow that won't stop falling. I would stand like this for an eternity, until time ran out. And even when it all ended, we wouldn't disappear, but remain here as two shadows, an echo. A memory.

I nevertheless found the strength and stepped forward. The snow crunched underfoot, but Yana did not turn around, did not cry out. She still sat there, from time to time nodding barely perceptibly and smiling a quiet smile addressed to God knows who. I came closer. She didn't see me. I sat down on the bench next to her.

"I remember what you said," I muttered. "You said, 'Don't be stupid. Don't slip up.' The only problem is that I already made so many mistakes that it seems like there are none left to make."

Yana listened.

"Now I don't even know what was what. Which were the mistakes and which were the logical actions. And now you aren't there to tell me, either."

Yana smiled. I sighed and struggled to my feet.

I found the stairs to the next floor pretty quickly. And as soon as I entered, I felt instant regret.

This floor was full of water. Closer to the center, it swirled inwards, forming a tight whirlpool. The long narrow boat was carried sideways to the whirlpool, and Yana stood in the boat and looked around helplessly.

A cry was heard:

"Jump! Jump!"

And Yana jumped awkwardly into the water, but too late. The maelstrom grabbed her and dragged her down.

I ran after her. I waded up to my knees in the water, and felt the hard floor beneath me, but for Yana, alas, the floor didn't exist. She tried to swim free from the center of the whirlpool, but it was a losing battle. By the time I reached her, she was already under water. I saw her breaking through to the surface, I saw her face, I tried to reach out, but there was so much distance between her and the floor on which I stood! I thought for a moment that I should run down to the floor below, because she might be there. Only then did I realize that I was participating in some sort of game. As if in confirmation of my thought, the episode with Yana began anew: the boat was sailing again and an invisible voice shouted "Jump!" I could no longer watch and instead ran along the walls in search of the stairs.

There third floor was a battlefield. I immediately recognized the street. It was here, in the city. People and Predators were being attacked by some terrible creatures with pale, drooping faces and long tentacles, which they used both to move and as a weapon. Fast and deadly. Surprisingly, there were also people in armor from the DHC city here! The fight was short and chilling: the creatures pulled the shields from the hands of the defenders, and then swiftly and deftly wrung their necks. They paid no attention to me.

With difficulty, I found the stairs to the next floor. When I climbed it and opened the door, it was dark. Inky, lifeless darkness, in which nothing and no one could exist. I didn't have a lamp spell like Stork, so instead I sent a fireball into the darkness. But it disappeared into the distance without illuminating anything, transforming into a tiny star and then flickering out. I took a deep breath, preparing for the worst, and stepped inside.

I felt the flat stone floor under my feet, and it was one of the few sensations that remained after I crossed the threshold of the fourth floor. There were no moving illusions, only emptiness. And as soon as I entered, I felt that this emptiness was unimaginably vast! If I couldn't find the next staircase, I'd get lost here forever and never find a way out. Several times I fell into a kind of panic, realizing that I had lost anything that could serve as a landmark, along with all hope of ever going back.

I did not come across any walls, sometimes only my hands brushed lightly against something that suspiciously resembled a cobweb. As soon as the word "web" came to my mind, huge spiders began to appear everywhere, silently creeping up to me in the darkness. The paranoia overwhelmed me more and more, and I stopped, raising my shield and nervously spinning in one place. Darkness covered my eyes and ears like clay. I took a deep breath and tried to calm myself. Then, gathering my strength, I lowered my shield and invested a character point to restore mana. Finally, I raised my palms, cupped them together, and struck a light. This was the first phase of the Fireball spell that I had once cast during the battle for the DHC city. In fact, this initial step was something well-practiced by all smokers in Fantasia.

A tiny light danced between my palms, and for a while I just enjoyed the fact that I could see anything. Then I raised his hands higher and looked around. The only thing I was able to illuminate was a small section of the floor covered with dusty stone slabs. I sighed and pulled a little more air into my chest.

A few dozen feet away, a wall of fire burst open across space. It gave off much more light, and I managed to make out the staircase before it was obscured by the raging wall of flame.

CHAPTER 21

THE FIFTH FLOOR was the last. The black walls rose up all around, emitting a steady hum. High above my head, an amazing geometric structure grew from the ceiling, a kind of convex fractal sculpture of black stone.

Jarkhan-Ali stood with his back to me and, lifting his head, uttered long, monotonous phrases in Farsi. It sounded like a song or a spell. A strangely distorted echo lapped against the vaulted ceiling.

Attack him with magic or try using your *Voice*? After all, he himself had said: I am the Reader. And I know that he wasn't lying, because then I felt it. Felt what it means to be the Reader. And now this sensation had reached such a peak that I suddenly realized: the stones do not Listen to Jarkhan-Ali. Rather, they Listen, but only barely. The stone was waiting for another Voice.

Mine. I knew it! I knew that I could now tear this damn tower apart with a few words! And then I stepped forward.

The author turned to meet me and smiled, and Yana's parting words suddenly surfaced in my mind again: "Don't do anything stupid. Don't slip up." Stop. Was I about to make the biggest mistake of all? He knew. He knew everything and was waiting here for a reason. *'He wants me to kill him,'* I realized, growing cold. 'Kill him right here, in the place where the world was born. That's why he needed me. That's why he led me on this path of revenge, a path I had walked and lived. That was what the vision in the tower was for. So that I had no doubt left in my mind of what needed to be done. After all, could I let him live? After everything he's done? Of course not. I had to kill him, and let this world fall to hell!"

It suddenly became hard to breathe. The Author didn't plan on giving me time to think: he choked me with a spell. I threw lightning at him, but it scattered across his shield. "Or maybe the victim here is not him, but me?" The thought suddenly flashed through my head. "What if I don't touch him because I'm scared, but that's what he wanted all along?"

It was a perfectly played game, one must admit. The spell was slowly crushing me, demanding an immediate solution. I quickly pulled in as much air as I could and opened my mouth.

"Yek…"

Simultaneously with my own voice, I heard another, repeating each sound with me. This voice was like thunder, and each syllable was a command that demanded to be obeyed. The command was to everyone and everything.

"Zhoo..."

Jarkhan-Ali's face fell and his eyes widened, filled with horror.

"Rakh..."

I saw he was shouting but didn't hear any words. And no one could. Nothing could interrupt the voice of God.

"Sho..."

Jarkhan-Ali raised his flaming palms. In them, I saw my death.

"Mal!"

The sculpture on the ceiling came to life, the raised details vibrating like the tentacles of anemones. With each syllable the hum in my head grew louder. By the fourth, it became almost unbearable, but after the fifth it suddenly disappeared, as if the strings of the giant invisible harp had snapped, whipping reality around me. And reality broke through, a gap arose, instantly sucking all the air out of the space. All pressure and sound disappeared along with the air. I felt my body begin to expand from the inside, lowered my head and saw the Author.

He stood very straight, with a slight smile, then bowed deeply, like an actor after a well-played show. And then I understood, and when I understood, I fell to my knees, because my legs stopped holding me up.

And then the New Law came into force.

*   *   *

The tower filled with air again, and I felt the pressure equalize. My head was throbbing with pain and colored circles danced before my eyes.

The black sculpture on the ceiling pulsated, filled with darkness, and suddenly expelled a ball of tentacles that splashed in all directions. Jarkhan-Ali straightened up, and I saw a monstrous structure fanning opening behind him. Triumph was written on the Author's face. In the next second, black outgrowths hit him in the back, lifting him into the air.

"Stop!" I cried.

But my voice, which until recently ruled the world, suddenly sounded sickly and weak. Nothing heeded it any longer. Meanwhile, waves of energy were running along the black stone walls, a spot on the ceiling grew and turned into a portal, darkness swirling within.

I realized that now, I would finally die. No tricks this time. All my strength of will could not close this portal. The stairs to the previous floor were a few steps away, and I dashed towards them, preparing to cut through the blackness I had stumbled through on my way up. But it was not there. Only plain stone walls. The third floor of the tower, where the battle was supposed to be, was also empty, as was the second floor with drowning Yana, and the first, where we had sat on the bench.

I swept through all the floors in a whirlwind, and a minute later I was down the stairs leading to the main part of the castle. The chandelier of a thousand candles that Stork had lit before his death continued to shine. For a moment I wondered who the new king was now? I knew it wasn't me, because I hadn't received any notifications, but still, just in case, I shouted:

"Lights off!"

Nothing happened. But I heard the darkness rumble, toss and turn behind me, creeping down from the tower.

'Why am I running?' I thought. Somehow I knew that there was no escaping this enemy. And yet I crossed the hallway and dashed out into the dark courtyard, never losing speed. On the other side, behind the castle wall, there were flashes of light, and I realized that there was a battle raging. Had my friends really held out against Stork's people for so long?

Suddenly I had a brief insight: the tower had shown me scenes from my own life. Yana and I on the bench was my past. Yana's death was a recent past. The battle on the streets of the Predator city was a future that was yet to come. And the fourth floor...darkness? Was this darkness what awaited us all?

On the square, several dozen Predators were besieging a small guardhouse. I saw the familiar faces of the Reapers, but there were also representatives from other clans.

"And I'm saying I have orders!" Krinj was agitated. "If the NPC is on their side, it will have to be reset to zero anyway!"

"Do you want to start a war, idot?" an unfamiliar obese dwarf retorted.

From the depths of the night, a procession walked out onto the square. In the middle was a dimly familiar white spot. Tarq's carriage. I turned around: the windows of the castle, which had been brightly lit a few moments ago, were now dark. A little longer and it would be too late.

Without stopping to think twice, I dashed to intercept the carriage. There were screams and the crackle of spells from behind, but I didn't care — the seconds were ticking away. Seeing the red-faced demon running towards them, Tarq's guards moved forward to meet me. I raised my hands to show that I was not armed, but the warriors still raised their shields and drew their weapons.

"Tarq!" I shouted, stopping a dozen paces from them. "If you don't close the barrier now, we're all screwed! Can you fucking hear me?! Close the barrier!"

The clatter of numerous boots thundered behind me, but I didn't turn around. I could guess who it was! The white curtain slid to the side. The tall orc jumped lightly to the ground, turned his head. There must have been something in my appearance that made him suddenly frown and move towards me, pushing the bodyguards aside with his powerful hands.

"What makes you think I can do that?"

"Because Adalius was the king. Now he's dead, and that means that the king is you! There's no time to waste! The darkness is coming!"

"What did you say?!"

A voice rang out behind me, and with it came a familiar clank. I had to turn around.

"I said that Adalius is dead, Krinj. Condolences on your loss, guys. He was an unusually clever son of a bitch."

"You killed him!"

"I killed him," I said, "after he tried to kill me. But none of that matters now, there's more important business: there's something coming that will devour and engulf us all!"

"You lead the spies out of town!" Krinj barked, taking a step forward. "To open the gate for these bastards!"

"What gate?! What are you talking about?!" I shouted.

"A large troop of humans have fallen on the city," Tarq's low and commanding voice sounded behind me.

I shuddered. But not from the news. Because I had known it already. But where did this information come from? And then I realized: the third floor of the tower, people were fighting along with the Predators...so everything was going according to plan.

"People have come," I said, turning to the king. "But not to fight you. No one needs a war, we are too few. They've come to help!"

I saw distrust in their eyes and realized that I hadn't found the right words, and probably couldn't explain what I needed to. The next instance I would likely have been torn to pieces, but at that moment, the tower above the castle exploded.

"Shields!" exclaimed Tarq, and transparent domes immediately flickered up around us.

A few seconds later, stone shrapnel rained down from the sky, but few paid much attention. All eyes were fixed on the castle.

In place of the tower whirled the black column of a tornado, glittering with flashes of lightning. Unlike the previous tower, however, this one had tentacles that could crush stone. The castle itself seemed to bulge and darkness gushed from the windows, filling the courtyard.

"Your Majesty!" I shouted, turning to Tarq. "You must close the barrier immediately!"

"I don't know how," Tarq answered simply.

"I think you just have to be close to it! It's like a key to a door."

Tarq nodded and we rushed to the bridge. The Predators were running after us. A small crowd gathered at the bridge, in which, to my delight, I saw the faces of my friends, alive and, at first glance at least, unharmed. In addition to them, dozens of NPCs had gathered: merchants, artisans, servants. The walls of the castle made it difficult to see what was happening inside, but I had no doubt that we had very little time.

I ran onto the bridge and stopped where the invisible border should have been. Tarq stopped beside me, staring blankly into space, apparently checking the interface.

Meanwhile, the shadows in the arch of the gate thickened suspiciously. Streams of black smoke crept across the planks of the bridge. And then a long, flexible tentacle slipped out of the swirling darkness, heading straight for the bridge.

"Faster!" I shouted.

"I don't see it!"

"Your voice! Say it out loud!"

The tentacle somehow sensed us and drew back, poised to attack.

"Close the barrier!" screamed Tarq

Apparently, I was standing too close to the border, because I was suddenly thrown back with terrible force, but I managed to see the tentacle hit the invisible dome and dissipate into wisps of darkness.

I was thrown onto the pavement, the horns on my back and head screeched spine-tinglingly against the stone. But damn it, we made it! I looked up and saw that the barrier was working! The castle wall was streaked with darkness and a multitude of black tentacles protruded from the gate and above the walls. The spectacle was somehow grotesquely artificial and nightmarishly realistic at the same time. However, the dome held. The monster was locked inside.

* * *

Tarq bent over me and held out his hand.

"What was that, Urfyn?"

"Universal Evil," I said, rising to my feet.

"What do we need to do to send it back?"

"You can't send it back. It's now a part of the world."

Predators crowded solemnly around, glancing warily at the bubble quickly filling with darkness. Tarq fixed me with a stare.

"Can it be killed?"

I shrugged my shoulders.

"I don't know. I don't think so. I think the barrier can't hold it back entirely."

"What do you mean?"

I swallowed.

"It will find a way to send its...emissaries to our world."

"How do you know that?"

"I saw it in the tower."

Tark sat down unexpectedly. Straight on the pavement. He waved a hand, gesturing for me to sit too. I sank slowly onto the warm stone.

"We're in a difficult position," announced the

King of Fantasia. "I see that I do not know much about the situation. But there seems to be no time for long explanations. I want you to tell me what you think is most important. The main points."

I looked at him in amazement. Tarq was sensible and reasonable, wasting no time at all. Adalius had described him completely differently. I wracked my brain trying to resurrect the appearance of the creatures from the vision on the third floor of the tower. Tall, gray, with flabby, monstrously drooping faces and tentacles they used to crush people's heads. I described it all to Tarq as best I could.

"But most importantly," I said, "I saw humans in the vision! And they were helping us fight the contagion."

Tarq sat in thought for a moment.

"How would humans know what was happening here?" he finally asked.

"It all has to do with the creator of Fantasia," I said. "He sacrificed himself to pull this evil into the world. But he is not the only local god. His clone most likely hurried here with people from the city."

"Who sacrificed himself?" the king asked. "The creator...of Fantasia, you said?"

"It would be more accurate to say, one of the creators. And the other, as I said, brought the backup troops to the rescue."

"He just wants us to open the gate!" A familiar voice suddenly cut into the conversation.

Sinew pushed his way through the crowd, glaring at me.

"This was their plan from the very beginning! Fucking humans! It was they who sent this creature, and now, under the guise of offering assistance, they will enter the city to take everything they can get their hands on. And this…"

"Listen, friend."

"Shut your maw, murderer! You killed our speaker. You're as good as a corpse!"

"Humans didn't have any such fucking plan," I said, feeling a strange need for sincerity. "I know that for certain. Because just a few weeks ago, I was one of them."

The predators around me fell silent, some backed away. I chuckled. Such a terrible thing, a man among the monsters!

"Explain," the king demanded.

"The Predator's bodies," I explained, "are the result of the Creator's experiments with the human psyche. Many of those born in the skin of a monster have suffered trauma in the past. The author invented those traumas so that those born here would constantly feel different, grow accustomed to that feeling. Those who succeeded changed and became part of a new…hmm…race. Some arrived in Fantasia as Predators. However, some Predators were originally born in human skin. This is my case. And that was also the case of Adalius, Speaker for the Reapers.

"You lie!" shouted Sinew, flying at me, fists

raised. "Adalius was never a human being! I knew him almost from the very beginning!"

I chuckled again. What a tangled web it all was!

"You're right," I said, baring my fangs. "Adalius was never human. But he was in a human body for some time. And you, by the way, know perfectly well what he looked like. He was the only one who fought on your side. He and his entourage are from real life."

Then Sinew jumped at me. I met him with my fist and threw him back a couple of steps. The rest of the Reapers immediately moved in, shields flashed, and I knew things were getting serious. But then Fraudo, Mr. Myers, Mr. Parks, Quinn and the massive Quentin burst through the crowd. And pale Camilla. All with weapons in hand.

"Halt!" said Tarq.

It wasn't loud, but his voice somehow easily put an end to the crowd's murmuring.

"We will always have time to kill him," said the king calmly. "In the meantime, we need to check if there is any truth to his words."

My men stood across from the Reapers, and in that moment, I realized why Stork had said that his clan was his family.

A gray dawn broke over the city. Only the haze trapped inside the barrier remained slate black.

"Hey!" Shouted someone in the crowd. "In the square!"

I looked in the direction indicated and saw that something strange was happening near the fountain. The air thickened into a lens, refracting the image, and then a black thread cut through the space, which opened into a wide portal mouth.

I already knew what I would see next, but seeing my horrific suspicions confirmed gave me no sense of relief. I would rather go against all the Predators of the city than the creatures climbing out of that hole.

Chapter 22 [Sylvia]

A FEW DAYS HAD PASSED since my speech. So far, it hadn't yielded any tangible success. But this was to be expected: political decisions aren't made hastily. Yana was preparing a certain document, which she needed to run back and forth between various offices, and my contact with the real world had been temporarily cut off, which I was only glad of, because I was terribly tired of all this travel between worlds.

It was the third day and the waves made by the controversy of the Silent Man's still hadn't died down, although I didn't think much of it. I had enough to think about without it. I was resting, and I was accompanied by Malcolm, who turned out to be an absolutely irreplaceable person in everyday life, and life in Fantasia was...I had pondered the question, thought about it before going into the scanner, but I had no idea how difficult it was going to be. Living like people did before the invention of electricity and a warm shower. Just those two things alone! Bryan told me that sometimes he really misses clicking from one link to another. To hell with computer links! I just wanted to bathe normally! True, Tom had promised me a water supply system, and it seems that several houses of the city already had them. I hadn't seen them myself, but I fiercely resented the happy owners of this greatest of human inventions.

In this sense, Malcolm was completely feral. He preferred washing in a city stream, he was very suspicious of soap, and when asked to comb his hair, he reacted with such an expression on his face that I did not dare insist. But today, I would tackle the rat's nest.

"Malcolm!" I cried.

No answer. I didn't give the boy any special instruction to stay, but lately he had been joined to my hip, helping out around the house, carrying food and water, cleaning the hearth, and tidying up. Given the challenges ahead of me, this was an invaluable help! In addition, Malcolm was an unusually empathic child: he was very supportive before and after my seances in the real world, which left me dizzy and disoriented.

I decided that he must have gone for water, got dressed, went downstairs and opened the front door. On the threshold stood the Silent Man. He politely tipped his hat in a gesture befitting a nineteenth-century gentleman and asked permission to enter. To be honest, it sometimes(?) all seemed so out of place. I silently stepped aside. The Silent Man entered the house, strode into the living room and turned, looking mysterious. In his hands was some kind of bag, which he immediately handed to me. I untied the ribbon and the aroma of coffee hit my nose. Real, good coffee! It seems that this guy really did hear our prayers, at least mine. I glanced at him: the Silent Man was terribly pleased with the impression he had made. He asked permission to sit, then sat and, with the most innocent look, announced that he was going to Ikwen tomorrow morning to start building rafts that would head to the City of Players. Although I was not interested in the news, I knew that the townspeople were rather skeptical about the Silent Man's proposal. Nobody wanted to fight against an unknown opponent, and especially not on the same side as your former enemies.

"It's clear that the townspeople don't want to go to war," I said. "What are you hoping for?"

Yes, my old reporting reflexes were still there. In lieu of a response, the Silent Man took the bag of coffee from me and asked for two mugs of cold water and one empty. I brought them. He poured the dark powder into the mugs, then lifted his palms over them, twiddling his long fingers. The water in the mugs almost immediately began to bubble, steam poured out, and the smell immediately made me salivate. I involuntarily reached for the table, but the Silent Man shook his finger at me and pushed the mug away, and then slowly moved his palms up. Two cloudy clumps of coffee grounds rose from the mugs. Jarkhan-Ali carefully moved them into an empty cup and finally pushed the mug to me. I usually like it with sugar, but this coffee didn't need any sugar. I drank almost half of it in one gulp, scorching the inside of my mouth. The silent man took a sip, and then suddenly announced that he was also inviting me to come on the march with him.

"Me?" I said, astonished. "You want me to come along with you to fight?"

The Silent Man nodded seriously.

"But I can't."

"You don't need to," he explained. "You are a witness. Don't you want to know exactly how this story ends? And Bryan will be there."

He suddenly portrayed Bryan. So accurately that I almost fell off my chair. Holy hell!

'I think that he'll be very happy to see you,' he added.

Was it really that easy?

"Why didn't you tell me earlier?"

The Silent Man signed that it had completely slipped his mind, with everything else going on. The explanation made me a little angry.

"You've seen him?"

A nod.

"And is he...okay?"

The Silent Man showed that he didn't know.

But that he hoped so.

"What do you mean, you don't know? Who else knows, if not you?!"

The Silent Man threw up his hands.

"But you," I said, unable to hold back, "are his copy! A copy of the Creator of Fantasia! And you yourself said that he was behind all this bullshit?!"

'No,' he gestured. 'You misunderstand me. I am not a copy. I am a part of him. Part of a single entity, divided in a very special way.'

"Is it possible to just tear a piece off a person and make it into another thinking being?"

'Any person has a lot of personalities living inside them at the same time,' Jarkhan-Ali explained willingly. 'Usually they're dormant and never wake up, except under a very specific set of circumstances. But you can get a lot out of a person. A whole world, if you so desire.'

He chuckled. I didn't think it was all that funny.

'One more thing,' said the Silent One. 'I asked Malcolm to do something for me.'

"What?!" I jumped up. "Why do you need him? You're not going to drag him there, too?"

I understood how ridiculous it all sounded. After all, Malcolm wasn't human. I don't know anything about his life, fate or destiny. But, damn it, in this short time I had gotten to know the guy, I knew he had absolutely no place in a war. The Silent Man looked at me with a strange expression on his face, and upon further examination, I suddenly realized it was tenderness. I must admit, it confused me and completely caught me off guard. What was with him?

"I don't want the boy to go to war!" I said firmly, feeling myself blush.

The Silent Man continued to stare at me for some time, making me blush even more, and then with an arrogant look, declared:

"He's unlikely to want to stay here without you!"

* * *

As I expected, the number of people willing to accompany the Silent Man was small. There are about twenty people in total. Most of them were brought by the Councilor Kaomi, who, as it turned out, was going for the same reason as I was.

"Bryan was a great help to the city during the war," he said simply. "I am a representative of the city, therefore, I carry the debt of gratitude."

The scouts behind him bowed their heads in agreement. Malcolm (washed and combed) looked upon the men with weapons calmly and without fear. Well, boys will be boys. I must say that I myself was quite nervous before the campaign, but the Silent Man's campsite was nothing like the military bases. There was no clear schedule here at all; rather, one could assume that a picnic was being prepared in friendly company.

Jarkhan-Ali set up a small tent a hundred steps from the eastern gate. There were a lot of people crowding around this tent, and not only DHC, but also NPCs. And not just humans either! I saw a creature covered with scales with an elongated muzzle, like a mole, calmly chatting with the owner of the tent, as if they had known each other for a thousand years!

The Silent Man noticed me and waved his hands. Malcolm and I approached. Jarkhan-Ali gestured that the scaly one was really his old friend, whom he, the Silent Man, had the honor to introduce, and that he came highly commended. He turned out to be a troll! The troll smiled, making his face look suddenly sly, like that of a used car salesman.

"Hargni!" he barked suddenly. "That's my name! Nice to meet you, my lady…"

"Sylvia," I said. "And this is Malcolm."

"Malcolm!" The troll held out his hand to the boy.

The boy fearlessly shook his taloned paw and gazed back at me with round eyes. The Silent Man was beaming. I, too, smiled for good measure, and so we all stood for some time, grinning at each other. What a madhouse!

"How've you been, Hargni? What have you been doing?"

"Oh, I have a little business set up in the south," the troll replied."

"I hope the profits are high," I said politely.

"Not in the slightest!" the troll answered cheerfully. "But maybe things will change soon!"

He glanced at the Silent Man. The man shrugged his shoulders and suddenly said, *'Hargni also knows Bryan.'*

What?! This troll? I was entirely certain that Bryan had never mentioned any sort of troll. Meanwhile, Jarkhan-Ali performed a short pantomime, which I did not understand, but Hargni clearly understood very well.

"Those guys? Oh yes, I remember! Warchan was in charge, and there was this nasty old man..."

Warchan ... So, the acquaintance with the troll had taken place across the river. Well, yes, that's where his business was! She'd have to inquire for more details.

The Silent Man clapped his hands together and announced that it was time to set off, then he stretched out his hand towards the tent, snapped his fingers, and the tent disappeared.

It was at least five hours' walk to the river, but our journey was very strange. There were new creatures joining the procession all the time, and most often they were birds! They flocked to the Silent Man from all around, sat on his hands or on the ground, then he would stop and talk with them, signing something with his fingers! After the troll and the birds, I was no longer surprised when an old hag with eyes blazing with blue fire rushed up from the far wall of the forest in the southwest. Most clearly a witch! The Silent Man politely raised his hat, said a few words to the witch, and she burst out laughing, soared into the sky and rushed away. I noticed that Mr. Kaomi's warriors reacted somewhat nervously to the appearance of the old woman, many grabbing for their weapons.

In the Village of Bream we were met by an NPC. I never could have imagined there were so many in the game! In my entire short life in Fantasia, I had seen only a few, including Malcolm, and here there were dozens of them! Judging by their clothes, they were the inhabitants of the surrounding villages: fishermen, shepherds, blacksmiths and others. They all gathered around the Silent Man, greeted him and spoke to him.

Work was going on behind the scattered huts near the shore. Among the piles of pine logs, people and inhumans scurried about, clearing a place and spreading ropes on the sand. Logs were laid on top, ropes were passed between them and tied. The finished rafts were lowered into the water, fastened with the previous ones. The result was long wooden paths that led along the coast downstream.

The Silent Man asked which team needed the most help, and received his answer: the rope binders. The work was difficult and required the well-coordinated actions of a large team. The silent man nodded and set off to where the ropes lay in the sand. He walked a little between the ropes, then stood at attention and solemnly raised both hands above his head. The ropes on the ground began to move, and they looked so much like snakes that even I backed away a little. The ropes rose into the air and froze in front of the "snake charmer." He twitched a finger and the ropes danced, twisted into ribbons, and then several ropes folded into a huge palm, which turned over in the air and beckoned to the prepared logs. The spectacle was particularly spectacular, and in addition, the Silent Man, using his rope hands, challenged a team of lumberjacks to a duel. Before that, they were mostly idle, because there was not enough space on the shore, but then the work began to really kick into gear. At first, the lumberjacks were still ahead of the rope charmer, but then the Silent Man accelerated to an incredible pace. The workers who hauled the ropes were knocked off their feet. Everyone found something to do, even Mr. Kaomi's fighters, and only Malcolm and I were not asked to do anything.

After an hour of work, we had made significant progress. The Silent Man called a break, and the hosts of the nearby houses brought out supper. And what a supper it was! I had been anticipating meager camping rations, but here were dumplings, meat, an exquisite goat cheese, fresh bread, and a whole mountain of veggies! We dined until late in the evening, gazing up at the multitude of stars. Again, it felt like a weird sort of picnic, not a military campaign. Several fires were lit on the shore, and people and DHC were sitting at the fires, side by side. Was it just me, or had the crowd of people grown even larger? Were new NPCs arriving?

A fiery flower, enormous and beautiful, suddenly blossomed in the night sky. It was a firework! The Silent Man was sitting by the fire, shooting his finger rockets into the air, releasing strange birds that swept over the river. The birds were followed by Chinese dragons with long writhing bodies, and after the dragons, unexpectedly, a flying saucer that swept over the heads of the stunned spectators, showering them with gold dust. The Silent Man's eyes laughed. Mine were heavy, and I was already having difficulty thinking. Malcolm, who had many acquaintances among the NPCs, popped up from somewhere and said that a bed had been prepared for me in one of the houses.

There were large hives in the front yard. The house was dark and cool, and it smelled of herbs. Malcolm walked me to bed, I lay down and immediately fell asleep. In my dream I saw the Silent Man conducting his ropes. And then the ropes suddenly turned into soldiers who fought on the battlefield, and Jarkhan-Ali continued to control their movements, as if they were dolls, and not people, and their faces were calm and cheerful, although death rained down all around them.

* * *

In the morning, it turned out that my eyes hadn't deceived me — there really were more of us. More volunteers had come from the city, some of whom had arrived the evening before, others during the night. The Silent Man, as if nothing had happened, continued to build rafts, although there were already quite enough available. However, people continued to trickle in, and shortly before dinner a large detachment appeared from the north. Two hundred of the city's highest level DHC veterans that McKinnery brought in. The McKinnery who, until recently, had been a statue. I recognized the red-haired giant from afar, and when he rode up, I thought he was looking at the camp with some relief. Had he been afraid he would come too late?

The Silent Man immediately abandoned his work and went out to meet the guests. The newcomers stared in amazement at our motley crew and the paths of tied rafts behind us. It was evident that they hadn't been expecting this. Then McKinnery stepped forward and held out his hand to the Silent Man.

* * *

Six people could fit on one raft, and a little more than forty were built in total. When this whole armada departed from Bream, a whole small city appeared on the river. Between the rafts, poorly controlled in the depths, rowboats scurried about carrying messages or passengers.

I asked to sail on the same raft with the general and the Silent Man. The latter, however, was never still for an instant, constantly flitting between one raft to another. But at the moment, I was more interested in McKinnery. I wanted to know how the man who was one of the most stubborn opponents of the campaign had ended up here.

"It all comes down to you," the giant replied unexpectedly when I directly asked him about it. "And your husband. You know, when that damn savior defrosted me, I was still in the heat of battle. I couldn't believe it was over, let alone that six months had passed! Although I could see with my own eyes that there were no Predators around. It felt as though they were hiding, waiting to pounce on us again...And then your mute friend informs me that we must now fight side-by-side with them."

The general sighed and looked down.

"When I was told that it was you who saved us then, in that battle...It's thanks to you...An amazing story! Amazing! And then suddenly I find out that you left with this...I went to Rkaeli and demanded an explanation, and he gave me Bryan's report about some village haunted by evil spirits..."

I felt a chill run down my back. Rkaeli did not show me any report. McKinnery shook his head sadly.

"I made a mistake!" He said hotly. "I should have stayed quiet and listened to Tenno! He immediately realized what was what. There was little time, but I gathered who I could in time, and we still caught up with you..."

The general did not look like a general at all, but I felt that he was sincerely sorry. And I was pleased, of course, to be sure. So, these people did not come to help the Silent Man, but rather me and Bryan.

*　*　*

In computer games, everything was always vivid — incredible landscapes painted in bright hues, but in Fantasia, everything was surprisingly normal. Forested river banks, stagnant brown water, algae, streams, clay outcroppings, pieces of driftwood. Everything was terribly ordinary. That is to say, it was beautiful, of course — the river, the dragonflies, the sun. But nothing extraordinary. For the first time, I thought about the irony hidden in the title of the game. But my opinion changed as soon as the sun began to tilt towards the horizon behind our backs. The Ikwen flashed in a thousand shades of orange, yellow and pink, everything was permeated with light, and the sky opened onto the most beautiful sunsets I have ever seen. Other rafts floated nearby. People were working, serious and focused, and then would freeze when they caught a glimpse of the sky. I saw that for a moment, they forgot about what lay ahead, simply appreciating the beauty.

When the sun went down, we lit fires on the rafts, and heated dinner over them. The Silent Man emerged from the darkness holding a bowl in his hands, enticed by the smell. The soldiers grinned, looking at him, and I continued to wonder why all this buffoonery was necessary.

An hour later, I sat on the edge of the raft and traced the path of the moonlight running across the water. Malcolm slept with his head in my lap. The Silent Man silently appeared from the side and sat down beside him, with a gentle movement pushed aside the strand that fell on the boy's face, looked at my frowning face and smiled knowingly.

"Why are you always acting like that? As if a carnival awaits us, and not a war?" I asked in a half-whisper.

The Silent Man pondered for a moment, and then signed that it was the easiest way for him to cope with fear. I wasn't buying it.

"So it helps you deal with your fear? There is something that you are afraid of, right?"

The silent man nodded. There was.

'I'm afraid of what the other part of me might do,' he admitted. *'The author is a great liar and manipulator. And he will act in accordance with his art.'*

The Silent One suddenly shuddered and looked back to the northern shore. I noticed that the forest there gave way to a very swampy area, and a little further a rather large tributary flowed into Ikwen. Was it another river? Is this where General McKinnery's guerrilla fighters tried to stop the Predators by bringing down the bridge?

The Silent One turned back, and I was amazed at the change that had taken place in him! His completely gray face was covered with sweat, his eyelids were bulging, and quite frankly, he looked like he belonged in a morgue.

"What's wrong with you?!"

The Silent Man waved his hand dismissively and lay back on the logs. I looked at the shore again and saw a high hill protruding from the marshes in the distance and sparse trees. Nothing remarkable. The Silent Man lay with his eyes closed. What should I do? Rouse the general and the rest? Sound the alarm? I didn't know. I just sat and looked at the suddenly defeated deity. It was all so silly! We didn't even know where to sail. I couldn't take my eyes off his helpless face. It was impossible to believe that he could be so vulnerable! The limits of the Silent Man's powers had been revealed to me from a completely unexpected angle, and a wave of fear washed over me. Deep down, I hadn't been afraid of what was coming, confident that he would protect us from any misfortune, but right now this strange man seemed incapable of protecting anyone from anything.

Nevertheless, I saw that he was breathing,

and occasionally his eyes flicked back and forth under the lids.

Meanwhile, we passed the mouth of the tributary, which split into many branches. The swamp stretched ahead and behind it loomed the dark masses of the mountains. The Silent Man was still unconscious, but his waxy pallor was gone, and his breaths were deeper and more even. I realized that he was sleeping. And then I saw Malcolm's hand resting on top of his brownish palm with long fingers. The boy, without waking up, had reached out to the adult, as if he wanted to console him. I, too, lay down, tucking the edge of the blanket under my head, and I barely remember falling asleep.

* * *

The next morning, the Silent Man was once again in good spirits, flying between the rafts, helping out, entertaining and acting pretty much as usual.

The forests along the banks had disappeared, and the fields opened up on both the left and right. Every now and then, we came across small villages or individual houses. Not long after noon, we landed at the Village of Beaverton to spend a little time on solid ground and rest. The rafts were packed into a small bay, and Malcolm and I scurried across the logs to get to shore.

The entire village came out to greet us, including the small children. If I were in their place, I might have freaked out when I saw that more than two hundred unexpected guests had arrived, but the residents looked on with calm interest. The Silent Man stepped forward and bowed deeply to the hosts.

Then we had lunch, and once again, it was excellent. Afterwards, while part of the detachment was busy repairing the rafts and others were messing around, wallowing in the grass, the Silent Man gathered a council. He began by answering my unasked question: What the hell had happened to him last night? It turned out that he cannot approach the black stones in which his voice is imprisoned. And last night we sailed past a circle of them. But those located in the City of Players are significantly more powerful, so there is a possibility that when we arrived at the city, he'd be in bad shape.

'*In this case,*' explained the Silent Man, '*you will have to act on your own.*'

I tried not to panic.

'*Remember the most important thing: Predators are not your enemies. You will see that many of them are quite easy to get along with.*'

The general frowned at these words, but said nothing.

'*You share a world,*' said the Silent Man. '*You can't avoid each other.*'

Then he turned to me.

'*Ms. Dulesky, I think that you will make a fitting ambassador. The mission you lead in the outside world is equally important for all of us.'*

It looked like I was just the ambassador for every occasion now. The general asked about the landing near the city, and the Silent Man began to explain. After he finished, I asked:

"What do we do with you? If you pass out like yesterday? Maybe you'd better stay here?"

The Silent Man smiled. Very warmly.

'My place is with you,' he replied.

* * *

In the deepening dusk, the Silent Man and I had another conversation on the raft. About Malcolm. Shortly thereafter, the Reader began to show the first signs of his mysterious malaise. He excused himself, crossed his legs by the fire and fell into a kind of meditation. I don't know how long it lasted; in the darkness, I lost all sense of time. I heard someone from the general's retinue say that we should be able to see the city by now, but no matter how hard I squinted, I could barely make out the northern shore.

An abrupt command cut through the silence, and the people on the rafts took hold of the poles. I looked east and saw a black wall blocking the river. I stared at it for a while, and then realized that it was not a wall, but an arch. A bridge. The raft swung, and I grabbed Malcolm's arm. The poles caught the bottom, and now the rowers were driving the flotilla towards the left bank. We docked on a long sandy bar near the bridge. McKinnery's first order as soon as we set foot on shore was to light a fire: we had to let the citizens know that their guests had arrived. This turned out to be unnecessary.

Suddenly, the shore blazed with light. Dozens of magic spheres soared into the night sky, driving away the darkness. At the edge of the light stood figures with weapons in their hands. Were they just hands? I saw scaly paws, claws, horns and god knows what else! And then their magic shields flashed, and the Predators prepared to attack.

CHAPTER 23

AT FIRST, MANY OF THE CREATURES emerging from the portal paid no attention to us. Quickly skittering on their paws, they moved away from the square. Now I saw that their lower limbs were articulated, and the upper ones resembled long tentacles, bending in all directions. The oblong bodies were somewhat human-like, but with strange proportions. And in lieu of faces, they had hanging strips of flesh.

Only later did I realize that the creatures had noticed us and just didn't want to take on such a large group. Oh, they were clever, these creatures...

The portal disappeared into thin air with a pop, and it brought us out of our stupor.

"Charge!" snapped Tarq.

The predators snapped out of it. Two or three took off, almost immediately shifting their gravity horizontally rushing towards the creatures as they fled. The latter bent their heads lower and rushed towards the houses like giant gray cockroaches. Their feet flashed with astonishing speed, and they reached the streets faster than the flyers. The pursuers flew higher so as not to accidentally stumble upon buildings and continued the pursuit.

Without saying a word, we hurried to the fountain. I looked around as I ran: thick black ropes were swarming inside the dome, and the dome itself was no longer invisible. It shone brightly, perfectly visible against the background of the brightening sky. Oh, and I had such a bad feeling about this! Holy shit, had I fucked us all...

Soon the flyers returned and reported that the creatures had disappeared, and extremely deftly. After listening to their report, Tarq turned to me.

"Were those the...shadow emissaries?"

I nodded.

"What are they?"

"I have no idea. But there will definitely be more of them. We need to greet the people who arrived by river and invite them inside!"

"The humans have already been taken care of," said the king, turning away.

"In what way?!"

But the king didn't grace me with an answer.

"Axel, Plague, take two more, go and check the house. Take what you need. I want to know if any new portals appear in the city, so post some flyers in the air. Pepper, you're senior in command, you'll report every quarter of an hour or as need be..."

I glanced at my friends, who were now standing to the side from the main group. We could make our way to the gate ourselves. Perhaps I would have risked flying away, but it may have led to dire consequences for the rest. Although some of the NPCs were still here, and they clearly intended to protect us.

"Your Majesty," I said. "Listen to the voice of reason!"

Tarq turned towards me, but at that moment another portal opened at the edge of the square. It spat out three creatures and collapsed like the first, but this time, the enemies were unable to escape immediately, as their path was intercepted.

"Don't let them get away!" roared the king, jumping up.

As the heads of the creatures swung towards us, their tentacles fluttered and I noticed that each of them ended in a kind of finger or claws. Ugly faces with dark spots of asymmetrical eyes dangled between widely spaced spider pincers. One of Tarq's orc bodyguards ran ahead of the others, hiding behind a magical shield. When he was twenty feet from the creature, the tentacle suddenly shot towards him. The shield snapped with a sharp clang, but this didn't break the orc's stride: he was an experienced fighter. The thing quickly backed away and lashed wide with its second tentacle. The orc's body fell in half as if it had been sliced by a damn laser beam!

I didn't understand how this was possible! Did XP and character points mean nothing, or did these creatures just deal an astronomical amount of damage?

The next second, Fraudo's arrow rammed into the creature. Kicking its limbs, the creature rolled down the pavement and slammed into the green hedge surrounding the house. The other two creatures backed away, and then suddenly jumped onto the same fence, clinging on with their lower paws, crawling over the top. I treated them to a bolt of lightning.

U-Morph x14 took unknown HP damage
Integration error
Error Code №44.918

Nothing seemed to slow them down. The second U-Morph managed to jump up again and easily ran up the wall of the house, while the first continued clinging to the fence. A pair of magic missiles and a fireball slammed into him, and the flaming carcass collapsed on the other side of the fence, out of sight. I folded my arms in front of my chest, kicked off and took off. Making adjustments to my flight path with my left hand, I cast Shield with my right. And just in time, because as soon as I crossed the fence, a tentacle hit me from below. The shield burst and a pain flared in my head, but I forced myself to cast a new one at once. Seeing that my mana was draining fast, I mentally invested a point in Wisdom.

U-morph, however, no longer tried to attack. Lowering its head, it darted along the facade at full speed, taking advantage of the fact that no one could see him.

"Urfyn, fall back!" Tarq's voice reached my ears.

Never before have I flown at such a speed over the city, and so close to houses, risking breaking my neck at any moment! However, my head was surprisingly clear: either I would catch up with this thing, or it was all in vain and I might as well just "log off" for good. When I was about twenty feet from the target, the U-Morph shot its tentacle at me again. My shield went out, and at the same time I drove a ram into the creature, remembering the success of Fraudo's arrow.

The creature was slammed against the wall by an invisible hammer, and from somewhere above came the sound of broken glass. I barely had time to slow down in the air, feeling pain in my stomach and head at the same time. Firstly because of the gravitational maneuver, and secondly because of the bursting shield. My mana was running low again (the ram ate up a lot of the blue liquid) and I once again invested a point in Regeneration Speed, replenishing my supply.

The beast stirred, rising. I went directly to it,

summoning a shield and preparing another ram (I had doubts about the effectiveness of fire or electricity). U-Morph hissed loudly and fired two tentacles off at once. One extinguished the magic dome, and the other was aimed to pierce through my throat, but, apparently, the creature's eyesight had been damaged, and this saved my life. In the next instant, I nailed it with a second ram. The wall of the building acted as an anvil: the creature flattened out on it, like a beetle that flew into the windshield of a car. I grabbed the saber and slashed with all my might at the neck on which the nightmarish head sat.

U-Morph took unknown HP damage
Integration error
Error code №44.918

I ripped the sword out of the wound, measured it up, feeling that every second of delay could have fatal consequences, and struck again. The monster's head separated from its convulsively twitching torso with a chomping sound.

U-Morph x14 took unknown HP damage
U-Morph x14 died
Integration error
Error code №44.540

I stood over the defeated creature, perceiving

and understanding nothing. The brief, fierce battle had drained all of my strength. The post-adrenaline rush made the saber feel terribly heavy in my hand. I examined the body of the beast. Up close, it became clear that the U-Morph originally started out as human. But its body had been subjected to some kind of monstrous editing, which bent the spine into an S-shape, added a pair of lower limbs, and turned the arms into long, thin ropes of muscle, with apparently no bones at all. But then where did the force of the impact come from? At the end of the tentacles there were long, thin, horny fingers. When held together, they formed a long bone blade. When spread wide as a pincer, the U-Morph used them to grab and cling.

The voices of Predators sounded around me and Tarq approached, illuminated by a protective dome. He looked at the dead creature, then at me.

"You really can fight, Urfyn," he said. "Did you learn anything new?"

I stared at him gloomily.

"Was that other U-Morph finished off?"

The king nodded.

"Did he have a number in the notification logs?"

"Thirteen."

"This one was fourteen. I think, if I'm not mistaken if I say that there are twelve other creatures running around right now, still alive. And who in hell knows how many others will crawl out of those portals."

"Do you have any ideas?"

"Our only hope may have sailed in with the human fleet. You must open the gate immediately!"

Pepper, the nimble young troll Tarq had assigned to command the flyers, landed nearby.

"The creatures are trying to break through the dome," he said. "We avoided an outright fight, but one way or another, they all make it to the castle and pound at it with their tentacles."

Tarq turned his gaze to me.

"We can't let them break through!" I gasped. "We'll need to protect it. But first, open the gate!"

"Several portals," squeaked Pepper, who was about to take off again, "have opened outside the city."

"We won't last long without support!" I urged.

Tarq thought about it for a whole minute. Then, he gave the short order:

"To the square."

Almost everyone left in the city gathered here. People stared dumbfounded at the glowing bubble of swirling blackness.

Several detachments were quickly formed. At the same time, about a dozen NPCs from among the merchants of a higher level voluntarily joined the North Star Clan. After that, sections of the barrier were divvied up, and the south-western side fell to us, near the river itself. Tarq promised that he'd give us flyers for recon, and was even so generous as to assign us the already familiar

Pepper.

We ran to the barrier but before reaching the bridge, we turned right and moved along the moat. A few steps to the side of us, clots of darkness were evenly pulsating like the innards of some giant creature.

We saw several U-Morphs from afar. They stood at the very edge of the ditch and threw their tentacles rhythmically against the barrier.

"Let's try from a distance," Fraudo suggested. "Whoever can, try to immobilize them."

"Okay, let's try," I agreed, pulling out my good old bow from my inventory. "And don't try to mess with them if you don't have a shield! No one-on-one fights!"

Mr. Meyers grinned bitterly, alluding, understandably, to my own recent skirmish.

"It was very stupid of me," I told him bluntly. "Don't do as I do. Don't...slip up."

Noticing us, the U-Morphs stopped hitting the dome and dispersed, blocking the street. There were four of them, and they were making no attempt to hide. The distance was right, and I pulled on the string, targeting the creature in the middle, held my breath and unclenched my fingers. The arrow whizzed confidently somewhere towards the upper half of the body of my opponent, but then the tentacle of the u-morph shot towards me, and my arrow was deflected upward with a ringing sound, repulsed by an unmistakable blow. The creature slowly pulled its limb back in, curling up in a neat spiral. Shit!

To the right was a long gray warehouse building. The doors were wide open, and from them protruded the edge of a cart loaded with boxes. Another cart stood next to the moat. Some of the boxes were smashed, and the contents were scattered everywhere: apples.

"Fraudo, do you have another ram?"

"Just regenerated now," said the not-Hobbit, standing with his bow drawn.

"Wait, don't waste it! Can you shoot at the nearest crates on my command?"

"I can. But what's the point? Do you want to shower them with apples?"

"Be ready for the signal."

I lowered my bow, brought my palms together and struck a light. Taking in an lungful of air, I began to slowly stoke it. Then I gathered my palms into a cup and, barely having time to draw in fresh air, shouted to Frodo:

"Now!"

Finding the intended section of the street with my gaze, I threw my cupped hands in front of me, releasing a red-hot liquid. At the same instant, Fraudo's arrow sank into the very base of the cart. Apples mixed with wood debris rained down on the morphs. They, as expected, recoiled, throwing out tentacles towards the largest debris, and landed straight into the wall of flame that had sprung up behind them.

A whistling howl shook the street, and a

moment later a wave of heat hit us, and immediately there were notifications that three opponents had been destroyed. The fourth had been outside of the spell's range and fled.

My mana pool ran dry and the wall of flames fell, although the section of the building and the boxes continued to blaze. I invested another point in Regeneration Rate, thinking about the fact that the stat points I'd received for killing Stork had already saved my life several times. Without them I would never have had enough mana for such a fight.

We were about to move on when Pepper landed on the roof of the warehouse.

"How's it going?" he cried.

"We got three!" I shouted back. "Anything visible from above?"

After checking to make sure that the embankment was clean, Pepper drifted down to us.

"I can't see a fucking thing from the air," he said. "The beasts are hiding! But we've already counted almost two dozen portals."

I swallowed. With a rough calculation of three morphs per portal, that already made sixty. And given the growth rate, we probably won't last an hour.

"Did you open the gate?" I asked.

Pepper was going to respond, but at that moment a shadow flashed over our heads. The creature had large leathery wings, not dissimilar to a bats, a kind of tail and a pair of firing tentacles already familiar to us.

"What the..." started Pepper.

The flying morph swooped over our heads and hovered next to the dome. One by one, it shot its tentacles at the luminous surface, and I noticed that a slightly lighter spot appeared at the point of impact. A second flyer swooped in from the west and joined the first. I was about to explain to Pepper that his range of duties would have to be slightly expanded due to the current circumstances, but Fraudo said: "Wait!" and raised his bow. His arrow hit one of the morphs somewhere under the wing. The creature whistled, tilted and tumbled onto the dome, thrashing its healthy wing randomly sporadically against it and trying to use its bony fingers to grasp the shimmering surface. Its attempts failed, and the morph slid into the moat.

I rushed to the shore, raising my shield as I went.

"Careful!" shouted several voices from behind me.

I felt the urgency of their warnings. This was conveyed not so much by the words, but the tone, and as I continued, I realized that I was already too late as it fell upon my face. A tentacle screamed overhead, and a winged shadow darted to the right. Belated arrows and spells flew after it.

I jumped up and stepped to the edge. The morph floundered in the water, its deadly tentacles entangled in the seaweed. I hit it with a dose of lightning, hoping that the water would work as a conductor. And it did. This time, I saw the electricity move through its ugly body, forcing the tentacles to clenched convulsively into springs. It took another lightning bolt to really make my point.

L-Morph x5 took unknown HP damage
L-Morph x5 died
Integration Error
Error code №44.540

The first were U, and these were L. I hope that the list of morph species was contained to those two letters.

They managed to drive off the second flyer with arrows. With an offended whistle, he flew higher and again pounced on the dome, inaccessible at such a distance. It was apparently impossible to take him down without aerial combat.

"Does anyone have Levitation?" I asked, turning to the NPCs.

One of them, an elderly man with dashing good looks, unexpectedly stepped forward.

"My name is Tollen of Varo."

"Do you have any experience with aerial combat?" I asked.

"I have some," he replied with dignity.

"Any attack spells?"

"Some," Tom from Varo said a little evasively.

I held myself back from cursing aloud and said in the most even voice:

"Follow me, Mr. Tollen of Varo, and use whatever you have on that flying thing, if it's not too much trouble for you."

The old man's lips curled slightly, but he tilted his head in agreement. I cast Levitation and pushed off. Tollen of Varo and Pepper followed me.

The creature, however, knew how to learn from the mistakes of its comrades, or was simply more cautious than its dead brother: as soon as we rose into the air, it peeled off from the barrier and turned to meet us. Having estimated its trajectory, I thought about what to hit it with, but Mr. Tollen from Varo beat me to it.

A ghostly net flew towards the morph, entangling the creature in the blink of an eye. Curling around the victim, the net flashed scarlet, a squeal was heard, and the immobilized morph dropped like a stone. I watched in admiration, then turned my gaze to Tollen from Varo. The latter hovered tranquilly nearby.

"Why didn't you use that earlier?!" I threw back at him. "The fucking animal almost took my head off!"

"This is my first time seeing a detachment commander who didn't even bother to find out what kind of people he is under his command," he answered coldly. "And neglects to give them even elementary instructions."

"Our detachment has only existed for a quarter of an hour!" I snapped. "And who are you, exactly?"

"My name is Tollen of Varo."

I blinked a few times.

"...I own a spell shop in this city. One of the best, I dare say," the wizard finished calmly, landing on the ground.

Well, I really didn't know anything about the NPC who had joined our squad. But he could have covered me anyway, son of a bitch! Did he need instructions to wipe his ass, too? I was angry, but my anger was mainly directed not at the arrogant Mr. Tollen, but at myself. A spell shop! What an idiot I was! I had emptied my pockets on a saber, but hadn't even bothered to look into the magic shops. Apparently, I was completely crazy, deciding that now I would also become a renowned swordsman! What an idiot, trying to master everything at once instead of buffing his strengths?!

I swore loudly and hurried after Mr. Tollen. Pepper flew off to report to Tarq, but returned almost immediately.

"They're coming!" He shouted without landing. "On foot and by air!"

Adjusting his gravity again, he darted towards the dome.

Morphs moved between houses and between houses, walked along the pavement, clung to balconies and drainpipes. There were at least twenty of them. The flyers sat on the cornices, turning their bulging muzzles towards us. The enemy spread out as they advanced, cutting off our escape routes.

"Don't let them through!" I shouted. "And shields up! As many shields as possible!"

The pace of the battle accelerated sharply and unpleasantly. Rushing forward on their spidery paws, the first three U-Morphs came at us. Raising the shield with my left hand, I started to cast Ram with my right hand, but suddenly I noticed that I didn't have enough mana. I needed to invest a point! Invest a point in wisdom! And suddenly I realized with all clarity that I would not have time to do anything: the creatures were running too fast. The tentacles are about to hit, and Quinn, who was the closest to the attackers, didn't even have a shield!

The air in front of the morphs sparkled and suddenly exploded into dozens of thin glass blades. In a split second, a whole glass grove grew from the middle of the pavement. The three spindly bodies caught within it twitched spasmodically. Bows snapped, magic missiles and fireballs blazed.

Twice the attacking morphs broke through to the shield wall within striking distance and unleashed their tentacles. The shields were extinguished, but new ones flashed up in their place, and we retaliated as best we could.

However, the flying creatures were in no hurry to rush into the fray after a few of them had been caught in Mr. Tollen's magical flares. But then he summoned an ice block!

Time and space behave differently in the heat of battle. This is probably a consequence of the effect on the brain of an adrenaline cocktail, forcing everything into overdrive. Perception is localized in a special way, and everything irrelevant simply ceases to exist. I fought, mechanically performing the necessary tasks: repeating the same gestures, finding the next enemy with my gaze and constantly calculating speed, time, and distance.

The battle was never ending. The morphs continued to crawl in from all sides, and at some point we were pushed onto a street leading away from the moat. Several NPC characters died from the blows of the tentacles. Quentin had been hit in the side, but the mighty Dwarf not only held out, but continued to fight, wielding a club the size of a bull's leg. Quinn danced through the battlefield. She was the only one of the whole squad who was unafraid to expose herself to the tentacles' blows without a shield. She was in no way inferior to morphs in speed and reaction, and her light spear struck with merciless precision. Fraudo fired. Unlike me, he never strayed from his specialty, always relying on his bow. And now he was firing arrow after arrow with the speed of a sewing machine needle. Thanks to her gift from the Silent

Man, Mr. Meyers had his own magic shield, and in his hand he was clutching a new rapier he had bought here in the city. The old swordsman covered the shooters from melee and ranged attacks. Mr. Parks raised two shields at once, covering Tollen from Varo, who had threads of magic light streaming between his fingers.

The embankment along the moat was filling up with more and more morphs. At first we slowly retreated, then we ran. And gradually it became clear that the attackers were returning to the barrier. The street turned to the right, and only a narrow passage between densely packed houses led straight ahead. Quinn dived into it, but after a few moments jumped back with crazed eyes. There were rapid rhythmic clicks from the passage behind her, as if a giant bicycle wheel with a ratchet attached to it was spinning somewhere behind the house.

Quinn rushed down the street, and we ran after her, not knowing and not wanting to know what exactly she had witnessed on the next street. The look on her face was reason enough to retreat. We ran, and then turned right — away from all this bullshit — and suddenly, the road opened up into the square. A battle was raging. Humans and Predators fought side-by-side against the morphs. Everything was just like my vision in the tower! On the right was the bubble of a barrier, and this bubble was covered with a stirring mass. The barrier was still glowing, but much weaker than before, and I realized with horror that there was very little time left before it collapsed completely. Minutes, or even seconds!

I turned to my friends. I had to tell them. To tell them whose fault it was that they were all going to die now. But I didn't have time. The barrier burst and darkness was unleashed upon the world.

Chapter 24 [Sylvia]

"STOP!"

I heard this rather pitiful cry as if from a distance, although the voice was undoubtedly mine.

McKinnery turned towards me, looking terrible.

"It is a trap!" the general wheezed.

I looked at the Silent Men, who was still sitting motionless on the raft. No one dared to carry the god who had fallen into oblivion to the shore. Nobody could, nor wanted to say what needed to be said.

"Stop!" I cried with renewed strength, squeezing beyond the border of the protective shields, to where all those horns and fangs, hooves, tentacles, and whatever else they had waited in the darkness.

Several spells flew out from the predator side.

By some miracle, they didn't hit me, but rather discharged across the shields of the enemies.

"Are you crazy, or what?!" I screamed into the darkness. "Stop firing, you fool!"

My disheveled appearance made an unexpected impression on the Predators: someone chuckled softly, then someone else said something unintelligible, but clearly indecent, and several of them openly wolf whistled.

They had to say something before they started shooting again.

"We didn't come here to start a stupid fight!" I said angrily.

It sounded somewhat forced.

"Clearly," came a mocking voice. "You came here to become the centerpiece of my harem!"

I think I blushed. I was completely unprepared for such a turn of the conversation. But I couldn't back down now.

"Your right hand would be jealous!" I yelled back.

Laughter and hoots came from above.

"Quiet!" A scraggly figure with long arms separated from the dark formation. "On the land of the Western people, our kinfolk were killed like dogs! You say that you did not come to fight, but then why do I see warriors behind your back, woman? Why did you come at night and in such numbers?"

Lord, why was he speaking like we were in a Shakespearian play?

"I know it looks bad," I replied. "But the man who led us here told us to hurry. He said that you would need help."

I felt that I wasn't making my case convincingly enough. A stumpy figure stepped forward, and I saw a dark face adorned with fangs.

"Don't try to pull one over on us," said the orc. "You are saboteurs who wanted to try to infiltrate the city."

The predators began to rustle, several shields went up among their ranks. McKinnery's men attempted to quietly reorganize into battle formation. The general muttered commands in a whisper, which were transmitted along the chain. I decided to try a different approach:

"Do you want the outside world to permanently shut down the servers on which we're all located tomorrow?"

The orc was silent, and I suddenly realized that I had made a mistake.

"I can feel the lie in your voice, woman," he said, turning and merging with the dark formation of his companions.

The two troops, armed to the teeth, froze facing each other.

"Is that really it?" I managed to wonder.

There was a low rumble. People and Predators turned their heads. Against the background of a slightly lighter sky, the dark silhouette of the city stood up in all its glory. Above the walls, the watchtowers were clearly visible, but the edge of the central, highest one was also visible. Black smoke billowed around it. And suddenly, the tower exploded! The smoke poured in all directions, and in a strange way, I sensed some kind of intention behind the movement, as if it was not smoke, but something alive...The sight evoked some kind of visceral disgust and I felt myself trembling. And then I saw that the remains of the ill-fated tower seemed to be covered with a giant glass dome. Black smoke filled it from the inside. At that moment, I could not contain a sigh of relief: whatever this smoke was, I would not want it to get anywhere near me.

The ranks of the Predators were agitated.

"What the fuck was that?"

"Look! The barrier!"

"What the bloody hell?"

"It's them!" a heart-rending voice suddenly cut through. "They set off an explosion to distract us! It was all part of their plan!"

"No!" I shouted at the top of my lungs. "We're not here for that!"

"You deceive!"

"You deceive yourself! Don't you understand that this shit affects us all?"

The Predators' patience hung by a thread, I literally felt in my skin that they could rush us at any moment.

"Look!" someone in their ranks shouted again.

The predators fidgeted, turning their heads. I

didn't see what the invisible screamer was pointing at, but judging by the reactions of those who saw, it was nothing good.

"What is that?!"

"Horrifying!"

There was a clap, and then movement within the ranks of the Predators.

I turned to McKinnery and realized with horror that the humans were preparing to attack, intending to take advantage of the confusion on the shore.

"Don't even think about it!" I cried, completely unperturbed by the fact that both sides could hear my voice. "General, don't be an idiot! Didn't you really understand anything?!"

I saw doubt, and I saw anger on some faces.

"I beg you." My voice was unwavering. "I ask all humans to immediately lay all their weapons on the ground! As a sign that we do not wish harm to the population of this city!"

People looked at me in disbelief, if not worse. And then Councilor Kaomi squeezed forward, taking several people with him. They all laid down their long spears neatly on the ground, took a few steps forward, and sat with their legs crossed. The red-haired giant, hesitating for a few moments, bowed his head and dropped a huge ax on the sand.

The predators looked at us sullenly from above. The sky was quickly growing lighter and I was finally able to get a good look at these creatures. Several fantasy races were mixed here, if I understood everything correctly: orcs, demons, trolls, some dried-up skinny beings, whose names I did not know, as well as undersized men in impressive robes, who I wanted to call gnomes, only I did not see any beards. A long-armed orc with a dark face stepped forward again and shouted:

"Get on your rafts and get out!"

"We want to help!" I cried back.

"If you go to the orc, you've only got yourself to blame." The orc growled, turned, and then the line of Predators broke and retreated from the coast.

McKinnery's men rose from the ground, picked up their weapons, frowning at the glowing dome that protruded above the walls. I walked up to the general. He stared at me for a while, then said:

"Thank you, Mrs. Duleski. But don't you think it is wiser for us to sail away now? We could dock on the other side and, if necessary, cross the bridge."

"We came to help, General."

"They seem to be refusing our help."

"Something tells me that they'll soon change their minds."

The three of us climbed to the high bank that had been trampled by the Predators. The gate was no more than a half a mile from our position. On the right was a bridge, at which several houses were huddled, on the left were fields and a road. The predators were already halfway to the gate, near which there was some kind of incomprehensible hullabaloo. At such a distance, I could not distinguish details, but I saw that the city gates themselves were tightly closed.

"We need to follow them," I said firmly.

"Sylvia," McKinnery said. "You understand the situation much better than me, I admit. But after all, they demanded directly that we didn't get involved! Isn't it better..."

"General," I interrupted. "I assure you, that there was a reason we arrived at precisely this moment. They need our help right now."

"And what should we do with the Silent Man?" Councilor Kaomi was quick to clarify.

"Nothing," I shrugged. "He's already done everything he could. Now it's our turn."

* * *

A portal opened a hundred steps away from us, as we were halfway to the gate, and the thing that crawled out of it drastically diminished my resolve to go to anyone's aid. Resembling both insects and disfigured people at the same time, they were creatures with some kind of terrible piles of skin instead of faces. Repulsive! However, McKinnery and his men looked on at them rather calmly, and there were only three of them in total.

They tried to go around us in a wide arc and

rush to the gate, and given the tremendous speed their spidery legs were able to maintain, this maneuver might well have worked, but McKinnery wasted no time. His levitating mages rushed to intercept, backed up by fire and arrows, and the creatures stopped. Spearmen swooped in, and the creatures set their upper limbs in motion, swiping at us from a fairly large distance. I saw one blow go through a large siege shield and wound a man in the shoulder. But nevertheless, the monsters were overtaken, the spears stabbed tirelessly, and I did not like the sight. I suddenly felt faint. A minute ago, I was filled with energy from the importance of our mission, but now I was sick, and the only thing I wanted to do was grab Malcolm and run without looking back. Oh, God! Malcolm!

I looked around in horror and realized that I couldn't see the child. He had been on the beach when I was talking to the Predators. And after that?! The feeling of faintness increased sharply, and I rushed to the shore.

Someone grabbed me by the hand!

"Where are you going?" shouted a young soldier. "You can't retreat!"

"Let go of me this instant!" I hissed.

Startled, the soldier unclenched his fingers, and I ran, not paying attention to the screams rushing after.

A black thread cut through the air ahead. I screamed and stopped. The portal arch swung open, blocking my path to the shore and releasing something truly monstrous.

The beast was about the size of a house. The thick shell that covered it on all sides made it look like a bus, only instead of wheels it had dozens of long articulated legs as thick as a pine trunk, and in place of the body of the vehicle was a wad of shooting tentacles, which I had already seen in action. Squeezing through the portal with difficulty, the creature froze for a moment, and then its paws trembled and clicked. The monster headed straight for me, rapidly gaining speed. I felt that I simply did not have the strength to run somewhere. Fear filled my eyes. I think I was shouting something.

A strong jerk brought me to my senses. Two people in green uniform, holding my arms tightly, pushed off and took off into the air! Gasping and swallowing air, I watched, stunned, as the black carcass floated below me. My saviors carried me aside, lowered me about three hundred paces and sped away. I got up and saw the giant, picking up speed, rushing towards the gate. The fire and arrows did not harm him appreciably. McKinnery's men splashed to the sides, skipping the whopper, and I saw the tentacles on the creature's face begin to move, firing at the ones lagging behind. Some stayed down after being dealt a blow. The creature rushed forward like a locomotive, picking up and picking up speed. The predators at the gates noticed the danger and, having made the only reasonable decision, scattered. With a monstrous roar, the armored caterpillar crashed into the target. Contrary to my expectation, a caterpillar-shaped hole did not appear, although there was a deep dent in the tree. The predators immediately pelted the creature with arrows and spells. It tossed and turned with a creak, tearing its armored shoulder out from under the gate.

Then I remembered Malcolm again and ran towards the coast, where we had left the rafts. As I ran, I heard the screams of humans and Predators, the crackle of spells and the popping of new portals, and then all sounds were blocked by the rhythmic chirping of the centipede. I had already almost reached the bank when they both suddenly came out to meet me.

Malcolm was supporting the Silent Man by his arm. The rhythmic rumble was growing behind me, but I did not dare turn around. The Silent Man smiled at me, but then he saw the armored freight train rushing towards us, frowned and raised his hands. Light filled his palms from the inside almost immediately, turning his fingers into glowing white dancing embers.

The armored caterpillar emitted a whistle that almost deafened me. It was almost enough to throw me back on the ground. Extending all of its numerous legs, the creature tried to slow down, but it had gathered too much momentum, and the huge carcass buried its muzzle into the ground with a crash, throwing grass and clods of earth at us, some of which were the size of barstools and rushed at us with the speed of a cannonball. I jumped towards Malcolm, intending to knock him to the ground and cover him, but it turned out that the Silent Man had conjured a shield. The clods of earth collided with the invisible wall and crumbled. I pulled the dumbfounded boy to his feet and brushed off his shirt.

The creatures, quite a few of which had managed to make it into the city, scattered, and the Silent Man glided towards the gate, and a white fire burned in his hands. Humans, orcs, demons and trolls, elves, gnomes and vampires — all frozen, weapons lowered. But Malcolm suddenly escaped from my hands and rushed after the man as he left.

"Malcolm!" I shouted, but the boy wasn't listening.

I darted after, and the shining star rolled slowly towards the city in front of us.

The doors trembled apart. The shocked Predators stepped aside, letting the Silent Man inside. For some reason, he moved much faster than Malcolm and I, although he seemed to be walking with his usual gait. But when we reached the gate, he was already far away, turning into one of the streets leading to a shining dome in the center. We could see the dome much better here than we could on shore, and I could see how huge clots of darkness swarmed like worms within its shimmering borders.

I stopped. Malcolm, thank the gods, did too.

It was simply unthinkable to go there, and in any case, the Silent Man would most likely figure it out on his own. With an effort, I averted my gaze, turning my back towards the dome. Many Predators were huddled at the gate. In the morning light, they lost the ominous halo of monsters that they'd had in the darkness, and after the Silent Man's performance, they looked more like confused children, frozen in place by a bumblebee that had flown into their room. A little further behind them, humans could be seen. Exhausted after the battle, looking with surprise and fear at the bodies of their own and others, none of which were vanishing. And then there were several warning shouts at once, and the silence that had barely had any time to fall was suddenly broken.

The monsters did not run far. When the Silent Man disappeared from the square, they stopped, and then turned around and again moved towards the city. The Predators shook themselves, coming to their senses, and hurried inside. On a command, six of them started moving to close the gates. McKinnery's men watched them gloomily from the sidelines.

"Stop!" I yelled. "What the hell are you doing?! Let them in!"

One of the commanding Predators turned to me. It was a vampire woman packed into a tight-fitting black leather outfit. She had a spear in her hand.

"You know," she said, showing triangular

teeth, "I could gut you with one blow."

I gulped and looked around. The orc who had spoken to me on the shore was nowhere to be seen. Now he seemed to me a much more pleasant negotiator. But he had apparently been killed in a skirmish with the creatures.

"If you open your mouth again without permission," the vampire continued, drawing out the words, "I will do so gladly."

Turning to the frozen Predators, she repeated the order loudly. The gates began to close.

"Stop!!"

A puny, stubby troll appeared beside the vampire.

"I come bearing the king's order," he shouted. "The king orders that the gate be opened and the humans let inside!"

"Pepper, did you hit your head while you were flying here?! What king?!"

"The new king of Fantasia is Tarq, Speaker of the Elegion Clan," announced Perchik, completely unabashed.

"Tarq? Why Tarq? What happened to Adalius?"

"Adalius is dead."

The vampire suddenly thought hard.

"I'm not ordering you, Amanda, you know very well yourself," the little troll explained. "I'm just passing on the message."

The vampire suddenly flared up.

"I don't give a damn about Tarq, understand?!

What the hell is going on over there?"

Pepper looked around.

"Pretty much the same thing as here," he said, and took off into the sky.

* * *

But Amanda didn't dare disobey the orders of the mysterious new king. Leaving the gate open, the Predators retreated further down the street. People moved towards the city, hiding behind a double layer of shields. The attackers were already close and also lined up in a kind of battle formation, stretching out in a crescent. A trickle of warriors quickly flowed through the gate, but at least one attack was unavoidable. I suddenly noticed a tall man who was standing slightly apart from the others. Calmly looking at the approaching monsters, he held his hands in front of him, cupping his palms. When there was nothing left for the creatures rushing ahead, the warrior suddenly made a smooth movement with his hands from left to right, and the air a dozen paces from him blazed orange. The flame raged, as if fanned by invisible bellows, a wave of hot air hit me in the face, and the shields of the people who were covering the amazing magician flashed brightly, extinguishing the wave of radiation. The remnants of the detachment hurriedly squeezed through the gates, and then the heavy doors finally slammed shut.

The humans looked on in amazement at the neat two-story houses that stood along the side of a wide cobbled street, but unfortunately, there was no time for a leisurely sight-seeing tour. Wings flapped, and from behind the houses appeared another kind of creatures — flying. They circled over the houses, filling the air with a lingering whistle. People and Predators used their bows and spells, but soon the many-legged creatures we already knew too well joined the flying monsters.

"Stay close," said McKinnery quietly, suddenly appearing beside me.

I nodded, squeezing Malcolm's hand tightly.

Little by little, the creatures pushed us away from the wall. The Predators, who had far fewer archers, suffered great losses at the hands of the flying creatures. They gradually began to join ranks with us. But their equipment and combat magic were better than those of humans, which made them more effective in hand-to-hand combat. Slowly, the squads drew closer, and then intermingled entirely, trying to make sure everyone was doing the job for which they were best suited.

The morphs (I had heard one of the warriors say this word) arrived all at once. We did not see the gates, which were hidden from us by the turn of the street, fall, but the influx of creatures from that side increased exponentially. The detachment fought in a circle moving towards the dome, although it was clear to everyone that the situation there would be much worse. But there was nowhere else to go: morphs pressed against us, throwing themselves at our shields and spears like madmen.

Soon we went to the square in front of the castle, and I froze for a moment, shocked by the grotesque picture unfurling before my eyes. Morphs of various kinds were everywhere. They emerged from the side streets and flowed towards the center, moving towards the dome. The dome itself, surrounded by the stirring mass, glowed brightly, and darkness lurked inside. There were so many morphs that it became clear we wouldn't last long here. However, there was nowhere else to retreat, because the creatures behind us were accumulating, and there was only one path to their goal.

A fierce battle bagan to rage on all sides, and all my attention was now focused on ensuring that Malcolm and I were not trampled. Frankly, I hoped that with the appearance of the Silent Man on the shore, our active participation in the unfolding performance would end, but things turned out differently. And now, it seemed, the production had become the kind of tragedy where only corpses remained behind on stage. The ring of enemies pressed in on us even more, although most of the creatures were not impaled on the spears but slipped past to join the ranks of those marching to the dome. But this incessant stream threatened to break our squad into smaller combat units, and even I understood that this would mean death for everyone. And soon the realization of the inevitability of such a scenario came: a wedge of morphs tore the detachment in half. Malcolm and I were in the path of the marching critters when McKinnery suddenly grew up next to us. A huge ax flashed, and one of the creatures lost a pair of lower limbs. As it fell, it fired both tentacles towards the general. Several Predators arrived just in time, covering our retreat with shields, others grabbed the staggering giant and dragged him away. However, we didn't have to drag him far: our half-diminished detachment occupied a small patch of land with a carved stone fountain in the middle.

I pushed my way towards the general. He was lying on a stone step, wheezing heavily, and drops of blood flew from his mouth with each exhale. There was a terrible laceration on the right side of his chest, from which hung scraps of punctured green armor worn by the warriors of the city. The second wound was in his shoulder and also looked nasty. I realized that the general did not have long to live. The red-haired head turned to me with difficulty, focused his gaze on me, and suddenly grinned. He wanted to say something, but coughed. His eyes quickly lost their meaningful expression.

"Thank you for your service, general," I said, in order to say something. "You did everything right."

McKinnery opened his mouth and tried to say something again. I bent down, trying to make out his husky whisper, then straightened and nodded. Raising my head, I suddenly realized that we were all about to follow in his footsteps. Morphs swarmed everywhere, and the barrier barely glowed and went out completely right before my eyes.

I lowered my head. McKinnery was dead.

A sudden gust of wind swept over the square. The black whisps of smoke broke free and rushed into the sky, looming over the city like an ancient kraken rising from the depths. But below, in the place where a moment ago the border had glowed dimly, a white star suddenly flashed, and my heart fluttered. Black columns bulged and rushed down, trying to cover something small and fast, sliding through a solid sea of darkness to an unknown center. The tentacles of darkness beat and beat at the ground, and the earth shook, but the light accelerated. Flowing from one place to another, it escaped collisions, dodged, inexorably approaching the heart of darkness. Then the tentacles fell to the ground all at once, covering the center of the city with a huge black cloud, the edge of which threw out onto the square with the detachments of people and Predators frozen on it. The cloud hummed and vibrated, something huge and inexpressibly terrible was tossing and turning inside it, and I realized that in another moment I would collapse into a swoon. The thought brought a strange relief: soon everything would be over, one way or another.

Suddenly the cloud was dissected by multiple white zigzags that streaked from top to bottom, then the swirling darkness was twisted by a powerful spasm, turning entire layers of darkness inside out. The cloud began to shrink rapidly, entwined with a white net, the buzz grew louder and louder until it turned into a thin piercing sound, from which reality itself rippled. And then the black and white bubble burst and the world ceased to exist.

Integration error
Error code 21.12650
Launching system update with new implanted clusters:

In the void in front of me, some tables flashed into existence. I tried to look around, and with horror I realized that I no longer had a body. I was the void, hanging in the void. I had only my field of vision, just outside of which incomprehensible lines of code slid, and outside of this, I did not exist at all. And then the tables vanished and an inscription appeared:

Welcome to Fantasia!

CHAPTER 25

WHEN THE WORLD REAPPEARED out of the void and I came to, I felt a very strange sensation. The pain that permeated my entire body seemed like a wonderful gift, simply because it meant that I *exist!* I could not even imagine what a valuable gift it was — a body. Without it, existence became torture!

Groaning, I got up and looked around the square: crumpled houses, broken cobblestones, a huge wasteland in the place where the castle used to be...and not a single morph. The square lay before me, destroyed and empty, as if a massacre had happened here once long ago.

Two large detachments of mixed people and Predators were gathering themselves and coming to their senses at the fountain. I looked at them and had a strange feeling. I looked upon the Predators differently. Was it that I understood them better? I was now one of them. The return from oblivion suddenly made me reappraise my demonic shell. Much in life depends on a body — now I knew that for certain.

"And where did the Evil go?" said Fraudo behind me.

"It was integrated into the world," Mr. Meyers gasped, in pain. "Now it's part of Fantasia."

"How do you know that?"

"Well, you see, once long ago, I taught myself the English alphabet. And you won't believe the kind of things you can find out from reading!"

Fraudo snorted.

"As my friend Dr. Harris says, there's a better way to ask the question," Mr. Meyers continued calmly. "Namely, what does all this shit mean for us in practical terms?"

"Well formulated, Wolton," said Camilla.

Wolton? Was that really Mr. Meyers' name?

"Hardly anything good," Mr. Parks interjected grimly.

"Well, you're boring!" Quinn laughed. "You don't like the monsters, they take away the monsters, you're still unhappy! Look what a beautiful day it is!"

I looked up. The sun was rising over the City of Players. The sky was blue and bottomless, and something in it, or in the air really did seem fresh, only I couldn't tell what it was. Although, maybe it just seemed that way to me?

We wandered to the square, where people and

Predators were slowly picking themselves up from the pavement. From a distance I recognized Mr. Kaomi and some of his guys. Good old Tenno, did he even recognize me? A large company appeared in the northeast. At the head was a tall orc in white robes. His Majesty had returned victorious. I don't know if it was under his command that the humans were let into the city, but if so, then perhaps Tarq would make a good king after all.

We had already almost reached the fountain when I was surprised to notice a boy on the steps, and next to him...I stopped short, as if someone had cast Stun on me, and suddenly experienced a powerful bout of déjà vu. In the tower, when I had seen her sitting on the bench, I was already in this body, although the whole scene had been molded from my memories. I had also frozen then, afraid to frighten her. Only then she could not see me, but now...? And how?! The notorious door in my soul, behind which eternal despair was hiding all this time, flew off its hinges, and I was overwhelmed with such a confusing cocktail of emotions that I swayed on my feet.

The boy looked up and I recognized Malcolm immediately. Our gazes met. The blue eyes looked very intently, and then suddenly widened. Without hesitation, he rushed to me, shouting:

"Mr. Bryan!"

The woman jolted as if she had been stung and stared at us. The boy ran up and I grabbed him, trying to keep him away from the numerous thorns that covered my skin.

"Mr. Bryan!" Malcolm beamed. "Aunty Sylvia and I came to help you out!"

"And not a minute too late," I nodded, surprised and embarrassed. "But how did you recognize me when I look like this, little guy?"

"Because I know you, Uncle Brian," the boy explained seriously. "Your face is a little different, of course, but it's you! I knew right away!"

Yana staggered to her feet. Her eyes were the size of saucers. And I suddenly felt that all my pretentious attitude about the fact that I no longer feel like a person was going to hell. Putting Malcolm to the ground, I gathered all my strength and looked straight into her eyes. Yana pressed her palms to her mouth, and there was something in her gaze that suddenly my heart beat desperately. There was no fear, and this alone was worth a lot. She suddenly coughed, and I jerked forward in fright, but after a second I realized that she was laughing! I covered my mouth with my hands! Yana laughed until she cried, and I felt that I was about to explode under the bewildered gaze of people and Predators. And then she came closer, looking at me with curiosity, and still without any fear. Laughter was hiding in the corners of her eyes, threatening to jump out again at any moment. I tried to smile and Yana bit her lip.

"Okay," she said. "Now we *have* to perform a duet."

* * *

The celebration still took place, although not on Saturday, but on the evening of the same day. Although, maybe it was Saturday? The party organization was unexpectedly taken over by the NPCs, having first asked permission from the king. Merchants, artisans, servants and other characters, of which there were much more in the city than I thought, pieced together a real miracle in the town square! They removed all visible traces of the carnage, decorated the facades and the fountain with colored flags, set the tables and brought out huge iron bowls, which turned out to be oil lanterns. There were musicians in the city, delicious food, and plenty of wine and beer.

When it got dark, the square became really cozy and festive. People and Predators wandered between tables, overturned mugs, talked and laughed, but still each kept close to their own kind. Seeing this, Yana violently grabbed my hand and pulled me over to break the ice. She made circles, organized dances, started conversations, fluttering from one camp to another, dragging and shuffling people, orcs, demons, elves and all the rest. With all the strength I had left, I tried to keep up with her, and was rewarded! After an hour and a half of running around, Yana paused, drained a glass of wine and turned to me, eyes glittering.

"Wow, scary!" she said. "But interesting. Don't bite!"

And she kissed me. The kiss lasted about ten seconds, and then I accidentally broke off the handle of the iron mug, which I hadn't had time to set down.. Yana pulled back, a blush blossoming on her cheeks.

"Ready?" she asked.

I suddenly understood what she meant. However, when we got to the stage, it turned out that our repertoire didn't coincide at all with that of the NPC's. But Fraudo saved the day. He approached one of the artists and asked to lend him an instrument that resembled a lute. After twisting tuning pegs, the not-Hobbit strummed the strings with an unexpected confidence. Among the Predators, there was another musician who picked up a tambourine, and one of the people had a homemade harmonica with him, and soon much more familiar music began to sound from the stage. The NPCs were listened to with interest, but without much enthusiasm. Yana demanded that I sing "Evermore" from Beauty and the Beast, but then backed down, citing insufficient vocal abilities (which really was the truth). Mr. Meyers volunteered to sing in my place, not missing a single note, and looked extremely pleased with my sour face. Then Yana performed "The Way You Look Tonight" for me, causing a real uproar in the audience. Then we sang something else, and then the NPCs took our instruments away from us and played their own again, to the delight of everyone who had an ear for music.

"I wonder what exactly they're celebrating?" I asked Yana when we got off the stage to the applause of a half-drunk audience. "The NPCs, I mean."

"A new life for the world," said a cheerful voice.

It was a troll who seemed vaguely familiar.

"Hargni!" Yana said happily.

"My lady," the troll bowed.

I suddenly remembered him! Why, it was the very same troll who had not permitted us to cross the stream at the very beginning of our journey. We fed him mushrooms!

"What do you mean, 'a new life for the world?'" asked Yana.

"Don't you feel it?" asked the troll, his eyes flashing cleverly. Soon the leaves will turn yellow, the berries will ripen, it will rain and the rivers will be filled with water. Soon, travelers wishing to stay dry will have to seek services from your humble servant, hehe. The air smells like autumn!"

"Indeed it does," Tollen of Varo, the spell merchant, stopped nearby. "The time of this world is no longer fixed in place, and this is very good news."

"Why?" I asked.

He looked at me for a while, as if not understanding the question, then said:

"Because without time there is no death, no birth, which means there is no life."

"But you somehow existed before, right?"

"We existed," Tollen said, "by momentum."

Then he nodded to both of us and left. Hargni bowed as well. Yana was lost in thought. We walked back to the edge of the square, looking at the streaks of stars. I was also lost in thought.

For me, the time spent in Fantasia had never stood still. How could it! Enough things had happened to me to fill the pages of a novel! Or was that all just momentum too? And would it really be autumn now? And then winter? Would we need to chop firewood or something?

"What's a newb?" Yana asked suddenly.

I choked on a sip of beer.

"What?"

"As in, 'good game, newbs.'"

"Who said that?"

"Those were the last words of General McKinnery."

Oh, General. What a pity that I missed your amazing, but short-lived resurrection!

"Hmm..."

I raised my head. Before us stood His Majesty Tarq the First, Speaker of the Elegion clan, the King of Fantasia. Yana gave an awkward bob of the head and I bowed.

"Wonderful festival, Your Majesty!"

The king snorted.

"Not everyone's as pleased as you, you know."

"I know."

I really did know. There were no surviving Reapers at the party. Some of their allies from

Archaea and Volta also did not come, although some did. Hatred of humans was an important unifying factor for many.

And the unexpected reconciliation of the two races was bound to ruffle some feathers.

"Your Majesty need not worry," Yana said. "As beautiful as your city is, our home is in the west."

The king nodded.

"I think we understand each other. However, we should of course start thinking about organizing diplomatic missions, and I hope I can count on the help of both of you."

We, of course, expressed our agreement.

"About an hour ago," continued Tarq after a pause, "I received some interesting information from the NPC traders, which, however, needs verification. Do you know that NPC trades with geographic entities that are outside the boundaries of Fantasia? For us, these places exist only in the form of a bunch of texts that are visible in the descriptions of objects or set out in local books, not magical, but ordinary ones. You can also hear about them from the oral stories of the NPC, but you cannot go there, because until now these places did not exist, at least for EKCH. However, I was informed that the situation had changed. The border has either shifted or disappeared altogether. I do not fully understand how this could have happened - given the limited capabilities of the equipment on which our world operates, but perhaps Ms. Duleski knows something about this?"

I saw that Yana was surprised. Perhaps she did not expect to hear such information from the king.

"I don't know anything about this, Your Majesty," she said, thinking. "However, I will be happy to keep you informed if the situation changes. This is...amazing! If it really is true."

The king nodded.

"But let's not forget that now, global concerns may soon be added to our local concerns," he said. "Who knows, maybe the differences between us will quickly become convention. Everything will depend on what awaits us there."

Soon Tarq wished us a pleasant evening and left, and we were silent for a long time, trying to grasp the prospects unfolding in our minds. Time no longer stands still, there were new lands...so, it turned out this wasn't the end of our world, but the very beginning? And we still had not the slightest idea what it really was, although we had been living here for some time.

"What are you thinking about?" I asked.

"I think," Yana said after a pause. "That it was terribly strange, everything that happened. The Silent Man I knew was a nice guy. The Author, in your words, is a complete monster. How did it happen that he was the first to sacrifice himself for the sake of this new world? For all the similarity of the stories, what a strange distortion...And you know...it's somehow quite jarring..."

We sat on a bench and looked at the lights of the oil lamps, around which the celebration was slowly burning out. Yana shivered: the evening brought with it an unexpected coolness. I rummaged through my inventory and found my dilapidated wolfskin.

"Where's Malcolm?" I suddenly grew wary.

"Asleep," Yana said, wrapping herself in a skin and yawning loudly. "NPCs pitched up tents for the guests at the other end of the square. But I won't make it that far."

I got up from the bench, bent over.

"What are you doing?" Yana was surprised. "Are you going to carry me across the entire square? Someone will come up along the road and cling on to you with some new information that will overturn our current vague conceptions about the world…"

"Along the road? Where we're going, we don't need any roads."

I wrapped her tight in skin, pushed off and soared into the night sky.

"You're a poser," Yana said, smiling. "And you said the quote wrong."

Her eyes were completely closed. When I landed a minute later at the other end of the square, she was already asleep. I chose a tent at random and, after making sure that no one was in it, I brought my precious cargo inside and laid her on the bed, covering her with a blanket. Yana immediately turned to one side and sniffled, and I sat and watching her. I didn't feel like sleeping, so I just sat next to her and waited for her to wake. I didn't know what tomorrow would bring, and had no idea what role was destined for us in future events, but I was firmly convinced that we should greet the first morning in the new world side by side.

Epilogue

RED WARNING LIGHTS flashed on the monitor and an alarm blared every few seconds. The man was hanging high, almost close to the ceiling, held in place by safety cables. There was a scattering of dark specks on the smart treadmill and one large spot flowering just under his limply dangling legs. A bloody spearhead protruded from the man's chest, the piston manipulator had easily pierced through and frozen, not thinking to flee the crime scene. The man's face was hidden by a thick mask with a cutout for the nose. Through the stretched lips one could catch the shine of the teeth tightly clenched with agony. But from a slightly different angle, one might think that the face of the deceased man was illuminated with a joyful smile.

END OF BOOK TWO

Want to be the first to know about our latest LitRPG,
sci fi and fantasy titles from your favorite authors?

Subscribe to our NEW RELEASES newsletter:
http://eepurl.com/b7niIL

World 99 LitRPG Series by Dan Sugralinov:
Blood of Fate

Adam Online LitRPG Leries by Max Lagno:
Absolute Zero
City of Freedom

Interworld Network LitRPG Series by Dmitry Bilik:
The Time Master
Avatar of Light
The Dark Champion

Rogue Merchant LitRPG Series by Roman Prokofiev:
The Starlight Sword
The Gene of the Ancients
Shadow Seer
Battle for the North
The Devil Archetype
The Dreamweaver

Project Stellar LitRPG Series by Roman Prokofiev:
The Incarnator
The Enchanter
The Tribute
The Rebel
The Archon

Clan Dominance LitRPG Series by Dem Mikhailov:
The Sleepless Ones Book One
The Sleepless Ones Book Two
The Sleepless Ones Book Three
The Sleepless Ones Book Four
The Sleepless Ones Book Five
The Sleepless Ones Book Six

Nullform RealRPG Series by Dem Mikhailov:
Nullform Book One
Nullform Book Two

The Crow Cycle LitRPG Series by Dem Mikhailov:
The Crow Cycle Book One

***The Fairy Code* by Kaitlyn Weiss:**
Captive of the Shadows
Chosen of the Shadows

More books and series are coming out soon!

In order to have new books of the series translated faster, we need your help and support! Please consider leaving a review or spread the word by recommending *Fantasia* to your friends and posting the link on social media. The more people buy the book, the sooner we'll be able to make new translations available.

Thank you!

Till next time!

www.ingramcontent.com/pod-product-compliance
Lightning Source LLC
LaVergne TN
LVHW020724200726
843506LV00009B/607